T0278871

IF YOU CAN HEAR THIS

Also by FAITH GARDNER

IF YOU CAN HEAR THIS

FAITH GARDNER

HARPER

An Imprint of HarperCollinsPublishers

Library of Congress Control Number: 2023948579

ISBN 978-0-06-334710-6

Typography by Corina Lupp

24 25 26 27 28 LBC 5 4 3 2 1

First Edition

For all you young storytellers.

ONE

Friday, September 6

There was something sacred about being on campus when school wasn't in session. The desolate student parking lot, where a few hungry ravens pecked the asphalt for crumbs. The groundskeeper peacefully steering her mower in neat rows on the emerald front lawn. The hushed, dim halls that would soon be crowded and ringing with shouting and laughter. For now, it was only Posey Spade's footsteps on the gleaming linoleum, her Mary Janes clicking as she searched for room 12B.

There it was: the one lit-up room at the end of the hall and around the first corner. Through the window in the door, Posey caught a glimpse of a pale white woman with a shock of red hair—not ginger-red hair, but fire engine–red hair, lipstick-red hair. Posey knocked twice and waited, smoothing her bangs, rehearsing her introduction in her mind.

"Hello, Ms. Moses," Posey said when the door swung open. "My name is Posey Spade. We corresponded earlier this week?"

"Of course! Come on in."

Ms. Moses held the door open for Posey. She tried not to stare as she stepped inside the classroom, but it was hard not to—Ms. Moses was a sight to behold. The crow's-feet peeking from her smoky eyeliner suggested that she was more than twice Posey's age. But with her punky hair color, tight jeans with a studded belt, and a faded shirt with a skull on it, Ms. Moses didn't strike Posey as a grown-up. She was also short, at least an inch or two shorter than Posey, and she had a wild grin that was so wide, a silver molar shined back. She was a bit breathless, a bit sweaty.

The room itself was in an unfinished state. Desks were haphazardly pushed to the center of the room, a heap of rolled-up posters on one of them. The walls were blank except for letters pinned to the wall that spelled *Multimedia*.

"Have a seat, friend," Ms. Moses said, plopping behind her desk. "Sorry about the mess. I've got my work cut out for me." She kicked her boots up on the desk and leaned back in her chair as Posey took a seat across from her in a wooden chair. There was a warm tickle at that word, *friend*. Posey could already tell within a minute of meeting her that Ms. Moses was no ordinary teacher. "So you're new in town, huh? How are you liking Wild Pines?"

"It's very . . . rural," Posey answered, folding her hands on her lap.

"That it is. You said you were from San Francisco?"

Posey nodded. The open spaces and trees were a far cry from the crowded city of SF. It was still taking some getting used to.

"Quite the culture shock," Ms. Moses said, tying her hair into an explosive little topknot. "I'm from San Jose originally myself."

"Oh! What drew you out here?"

2

"The beauty, the quiet. It's pretty different from city life." She snickered. "I guess I wanted more nature, less human nature."

"There's definitely more of that. My dad almost hit a deer on the way over here. We swerved so hard we almost went off the road."

"Be careful driving on these roads in the mornings and at night. Even on sunny days, there can be ice."

"Okay," Posey said with a nod, grateful for this stranger's concern. She made a mental note to discuss the icy roads with her dad later. "Will do."

"So what was it you wanted to talk about?" Ms. Moses asked, fanning herself with her hand. "Sounds like you're interested in joining the AV Club?"

"I am! I do have some questions about what to expect, though." Posey glanced around the room, at the crates of equipment pushed against a far wall. Intimidating, those nests of tangled wires, the many black zipped-up cases that held mysterious devices she had no idea how to operate. "Honestly, I'm more of a writer. I've never done anything with multimedia."

"Right. You said you were at the school paper? Too bad for you we don't have one here for you to join." Ms. Moses opened a desk drawer and pulled out a tin. She shook it. "Mint?"

"No thank you."

"Well, anyway, the AV Club welcomes beginners." Ms. Moses popped the mint into her mouth. "I can tell you're a go-getter and we certainly need a little more of that when it comes to the club."

Posey let that statement settle in her mind before nodding and then pulling the folded paper out of her bag. It was the AV Club mission statement. She laid it on the table and smoothed it with her palm.

"Before joining the club, I just wanted some clarity on what you all do, to make sure it's a good fit."

Ms. Moses pointed to the paper, crunching the mint between her teeth. "May I?"

"Yeah, it's from the Wild Pines High website."

"Mmm." Ms. Moses squinted at the paper and then, with a nod of recognition, put it back down again. "Probably needs updating."

"I was hoping to discuss how some of the ideas I sent you— might fit in?"

When Posey had searched the school's website and learned there was no school paper, no journalism classes, nothing that aligned directly with her skills and interests, she had been disappointed. But with Posey, disappointment never lasted long. It became fuel for problem-solving. She conducted a solo brainstorming session to determine where she would put her extracurricular energy this year, and that's when she came across the AV Club—and set to work trying to come up with project ideas where she might be able to fit in. She had outlined some bullet points and sent them to Ms. Moses, and now, well, here they were.

"Yes, yes, thank you for your email." Ms. Moses picked up her coffee, which had countless red half-moons across the rim from her lipstick. "Very impressed by your accomplishments. You sound like you have a lot of ideas for content you'd like to produce. Profiles, interviews, news . . . which is great. But. I mean, you want the truth? Really?"

"Always."

Ms. Moses drank the last of her coffee and tucked the cup into her enormous purse. "It's . . . a bit beyond our capacity at the moment."

Posey nodded. She wasn't surprised to hear this. But she knew from years working on the school paper in SF that capacity was something you could find if you looked hard enough.

"And look, I get you were very active in your journalism department back at your old school, but you know, Wild Pines is not San Francisco. This school's small. Our resources are limited. We don't even have a journalism department."

"Yes, I noticed. But that's why I'm so excited to join the AV Club instead."

"This club was only formed in March," Ms. Moses said. "Six months ago. Three of those being summer. So we're still finding our footing. For now, it's been a lot of playing with equipment, watching documentaries for inspiration. I'm trying to get them out there more, but the school year ended before we could do much of anything. You have some wonderful ideas. It just, you know, might take a bit to get those ideas going is all I'm saying."

"Heard and understood," Posey said with a nod.

Ms. Moses took a tube of lipstick from her pocket and applied it, no mirror required. "If you're looking for something with more resources, more structure, I'd recommend trying out for the theater department. Our theater department is one of the best in the state of California."

"I appreciate the suggestion, but I'd like to be a journalist, not an actress."

"Well, there's a lot more to theater than acting, but okay." Ms. Moses gave her a wide scarlet smile, eyes twinkling. "Heard and understood." She sat back in her chair. "I consider the AV Club right now to be a bit more of a . . . a playground. You know? A place where some of my most creative students can hang out and tinker with their ideas. Sal—Salvatore Zamora, he's the director and founder, great kid—he's got an incredible eye, and I've been trying to steer him toward documentaries, since that's where his interest is. What do you think about documentaries?"

"I like them."

"These students in the club are amazing, I'm telling you. Artists. Each and every one of them."

Posey nodded and smiled and tried to ignore the flutter of insecurity she felt thinking about the students in the club. The ideas and journalism didn't frighten her, but there was one thing that did: her fellow students. If they were as amazing as Ms. Moses implied, would they like her? Would she fit in? Would they find her annoying like people in her old school did? Posey hoped not. That was what she was excited about: starting over. Getting to be new, getting to shed the reputation she had as a know-it-all.

There was a quiet knocking at the door.

"Speak of the devil," Ms. Moses said, smacking her desk. "Come in, Yash, come on in."

A boy walked into the room. He was so young-looking to Posey, she could have mistaken him for a sixth grader—she hoped it wasn't mean to think that, but it was true. He wore a bleached button-up shirt that matched his smile. His hair was gelled and styled and his skin was brown. There was a kindness in his round face that simply radiated, as if a human sun had just strolled into the room.

"Hi, Ms. Moses," he said, waving.

"Meet Yash Berman," Ms. Moses said. "Absolute genius. Can do anything. He's taught *me* skills with Final Cut Pro. Also the sweetest person you'll ever meet. Yash!" She beckoned him to her desk. "Meet Posey Spade. She's going to be your new buddy. She won the Junior Muckraker award at her previous school."

"The Junior Muckraker!" he said, eyes lighting up. "Wow. I—I hope to enter that one day."

"Yep, that's why I thought you'd get excited about this fabulous addition to the team," Ms. Moses said.

Posey's mouth dropped, stunned that Yash actually knew and was impressed about the Junior Muckraker award, since most people had never heard of it. She was also surprised that Ms. Moses was breezing forward as if Posey had already joined the club.

"Oh, okay," he said. "Really good to meet you, Posey. I was— well, I came to check the equipment?"

"Right, I know, sure," Ms. Moses said to him, then, to Posey, she added, "He's meticulous."

Posey loved meticulous. She got up and shook Yash's hand, unable to help but notice she stood a whole head taller than him. "Nice to meet you too."

"How about you take her down to the basement and show her the space—you can take inventory together?" Ms. Moses asked.

"Um, sure," Yash said.

Ms. Moses threw a set of keys at him, which Yash failed to catch. He picked them up off the floor.

Now? Posey hadn't come prepared to get straight to work—she was feeling the club out, discussing her ideas with Ms. Moses—but she was swept up in the moment and automatically answered, "Sure," and then followed Yash out of the room into the hallway.

"Are you a freshman?" Yash asked as they left the room together and Posey followed him into the dim hallway.

"Me?" Posey asked, a bit insulted. Didn't he notice how she towered over him? Her obvious maturity? But she let it slide. "No. Are you?"

"No, sophomore."

"Junior."

"But you're new?"

"Yes. Just moved here from San Francisco."

"Wow!" He said it like it was the most interesting thing in the world.

They reached the end of the hall, where Yash pointed down the stairs.

"We meet in here," he said. "Every day at lunch, in the basement."

She followed him down a short, dark set of stairs, where the air chilled like they'd entered a haunted house. It took a few tries and some mumbling, but Yash finally got the door open and soon there they were, in the basement. He flipped the light switch and they stepped inside.

It was a narrow, gray basement with no windows, carpet so stained its origin color was indeterminable, and eye-twitchingly fluorescent lights. She took mental inventory of the equipment against the far wall: tripods with spidery legs, cameras in cases either well-cared-for or barely used, a shelf with outdated laptops, a crate full of tangled headphones.

"I volunteered to take inventory today," Yash said. "I just wanted to make sure we'd be set up to actually *do* something this year."

"Right."

"Because last year it was, like, hard to get anything done," Yash said. "I mean, everyone's super nice and smart in the club, don't get me wrong. But most of our projects were left unfinished, you know? Everyone ended up just watching documentaries. It was boring."

The thought of unfinished business always made Posey's heart sink. "What are you hoping to do this year?"

"I don't know, make content for our YouTube channel?"

"What about news content?"

"I mean, sure, anything." He widened his brown eyes at her. "Is that what you want to do? News?"

"It's what I know how to do," she said, walking over to the crates and pulling cords out, surveying the contents.

Yash joined her, unzipping a case to examine the camera inside. "Oh. You, like, did a news show at your last school? That's how you won the award?"

"Newspaper."

Posey started writing for the paper as a freshman, mostly interviews and profiles. By her second year, she moved to features, including the story about the impact of underpaid teachers having to purchase their own school supplies. That story won the Junior Muckraker award for student journalism—one of her proudest achievements. After that, she filled in for the front-page editor when backup was needed. She'd had her sights set on editor in chief, but then her dad got his new job and they moved.

"Newspaper," Yash repeated. "I've heard it's a dying industry?"

"My dad works at a newspaper."

"Oh. I mean, not dying then. Just, um—" He zipped the case back up, his cheeks flushing. "Well, the idea of a news show—I think it's cool. I'd like to work on something like that."

Victory! She had someone on her side. Posey smiled as she studied the tripods and ring lights.

"But good luck getting everyone else in on it," he said, pulling a laptop out of a case and putting it back in. "It's like herding cats. They don't listen to anyone."

That statement fizzled in Posey's mind like bubbles in mineral water. A flicker of disappointment, followed by a stubborn determination. If there was one thing Posey loved, it was a challenge. She looked behind her, where the desks were, where she assumed she'd soon be sitting with these mysterious other students, these cats to be herded. She could imagine their ghosts in the chairs.

Yash finished looking at the equipment and announced, with

surprise, that everything was there. "We're ready to hit the ground running."

"I'm glad I met you, Yash," she said as they headed back upstairs.

"You too, Posey," he said. "Welcome to Wild Pines High."

The quiet, long hallway seemed to gleam with promise, with a little bit of magic. Posey couldn't wait to start the school year.

As they approached the classroom again, they could hear a low, hushed conversation. Posey and Yash hung uncertainly in the doorway. A short white woman in a pencil skirt and heels was talking in a dead-serious tone to Ms. Moses, who sat hunched at her desk looking like a student being reprimanded.

"That's Ms. Vance," Yash whispered. "The principal."

As if she could hear his whisper—surely she couldn't, unless she had supersonic hearing—Ms. Vance snapped her head to attention and stood back.

"Yes?" she said, turning to Posey and Yash.

"Um . . . I was just returning these," Yash said, jigging the keys in the air. "Basement keys? Checking inventory?"

"Why are there *students* here today?" Ms. Vance asked Ms. Moses.

"They're helping me get ready for Monday," Ms. Moses answered in a flat tone.

"Not a good look, especially for you," Ms. Vance said, then turned her laser-sharp attention to Posey. It wasn't the type of energy she'd like directed toward her ever again. "School is on Monday. Please vacate the premises."

"Bye, kids, thanks, see you Monday." Ms. Moses waved from the desk, but Posey could tell some of her fire had been snuffed out. The temperature of the room seemed to have dropped since Ms. Vance came in.

There was a story here, and when there was a story, Posey itched to know it.

"What was that about?" Posey whispered to Yash as they hurried away from the room and toward the front doors.

"I don't know the specifics. Ms. Moses is in some kind of trouble."

"How so?"

"There's an investigation—it's complicated."

"What kind of investigation?"

"I—I don't know enough to tell you." Yash pointed to a minivan. "I've got to go, my mom's here. You need a ride?"

To say the minivan was packed would be an understatement. It looked like it was not only bursting with yelling children, but the back was teeming with what looked like sports equipment, and two bikes were in a rack on top of the vehicle. Posey couldn't imagine fitting in there and didn't want to impose, so she shook her head.

"I'm going to take the city bus on a practice run," she said, waving. "Bye, Yash!"

He returned her smile brightly, so fixed on her he stumbled on a sprinkler head and then recovered. "Bye!"

The bus ride home was majestic: thick emerald curtains of trees, long dark hushes of shade, violet spills of wildflowers in meadows. It was so different here. Different was scary, but different could also be good. She closed her eyes and practiced positive thinking. She was not going to end up a loner here, she was going to be accepted, she was going to have friends. See how easy it was, how sweet Yash was to her, how Ms. Moses listened to her ideas? Everyone here was going to love her and she wasn't going to irritate everyone and she was going to get so many amazing things done. She pictured the trophies twinkling and audiences standing to give her an ovation as she accepted an imaginary award. But in the back of her mind, there was one word throbbing in her mind, invading those positive thoughts. A curious word, a word that made her brain prickle. She tried to ignore it. It didn't matter. It wasn't her business! She didn't want to be nosy. But—

Investigation.

Why on earth was Ms. Moses under investigation?

TWO

Monday, September 9

Despite all the positive thinking, despite how many times she rehearsed in her mind, sometimes life didn't turn out how Posey had expected, and this was one of those days. She showed up to the first AV Club meeting five minutes late with ketchup splattered on her turtleneck. Why was it always like this? She pictured it in her mind, she did her best to plan ahead, she worked to have a neat appearance, and somehow she still always felt like she came across as a freak.

"Hi!" She waved at everyone, hoping her giant smile would make up for the mess. "I'm Posey Spade. I know it looks like this is blood spatter, but it's not, it's ketchup. This morning I grabbed breakfast in the cafeteria and the bottle combusted all over me."

She watched as the students of the AV Club, each in mid-sentence or mid–sandwich bite at their tables, stopped speaking or eating. Yes, she was the new girl—ketchup-smeared and all—standing in the doorway, working up a cheerful smile, with her long brown hair tucked in a neat headband, wearing an outfit she knew would not be out of place in a Catholic boarding school. Her turtleneck was a Halloweenish disaster. Yash was the one person she recognized. She smiled his way, but even he seemed thrown off by her alarming appearance.

"And *that*," a white girl in a bandanna said to the group, "is how you make an entrance."

"The ketchup bottle was clogged," Posey continued explaining, walking into the room and sliding behind one of the empty desks in the club's haphazard circle. "And I tried to hit it from the bottom and then it was all over me."

"I'm sorry," said a boy with light brown skin and dark hair to his shoulders, who wore all black. "*Who* are you?"

"Posey Spade," she repeated. "I'm new here. And I want to join the AV Club."

Posey took out her reusable lunch bag and surveyed the room. It looked different than it had the other day—somehow smaller with all these new people inside it. Then she scanned the club members. Five of them. They were quite a random array at first glance, but all shared the same general misfit vibe. She waved at Yash, who waved back and gave her a nod. Posey was an expert at reading rooms and quick assessments. Hers? These people (Yash excluded) were judging her. It was as if she had interrupted a private conversation and her presence had silenced them. But that was okay. Like the long, dim room she sat in, the wall of silence only reminded her of potential.

"So what's on the agenda today?" Posey uncapped a purple ballpoint pen and opened an empty brand-new notebook. She took a moment to smell the fresh paper, closing her eyes to take in its splendid scent, then wrote the date at the top. The club members observed her, eyebrows scrunched.

"You are aware that it's only the first day of school and we've literally been sitting here for five minutes, right, Ketchup Girl?" the girl with the bandanna said.

"We're about to watch *Tiger King*," Yash told Posey.

"*Tiger King*," Posey repeated. She then noticed the large screen mounted on the wall, frozen and paused. "I'm sorry, why *Tiger King*?"

"It's a documentary," said the boy with the shoulder-length hair.

"I still can't get over that you look like you just stepped out of a horror movie," sneered a white girl with square glasses, a round face, and a CLIMATE CHANGE IS REAL T-shirt.

"I second that emotion," Bandanna Girl said.

Posey put her pen down. Clearly her entrance had made a shocking first impression. She couldn't blame them; she looked a mess and was trying hard to push through and ignore the embarrassment. By their wild, worried looks, she could tell that she was doing what she often did—she was moving too quickly. She wasn't listening enough.

She really didn't want to end up a loner again.

This was supposed to be a new beginning.

"I'm sorry, I feel we may have gotten off on the wrong foot," Posey said. "Would you all be open to an icebreaker?"

Boy in Black groaned and Bandanna Girl put her forehead to her desk and stayed like that.

"How about *no*?" the girl in the glasses offered.

16

Posey's heart broke just a little. There was truly no bond in life more sacred than the unexpected joy an icebreaker could bring to an awkward room full of strangers. But you had to be *receptive* to it. And these people were anything but.

"I feel like we're being punked right now," said a lanky boy with glittery eye shadow and an afro, speaking up for the first time. "Like Ms. Moses sent this girl in here to teach us something."

Bandanna Girl sat up. "Or . . . is it performance art?"

"Can we go back to the *movie*?" Boy in Black said, pointing to the screen where a blur of a tiger remained frozen.

"In the absence of a more formal icebreaker, may I at least learn your names?" Posey asked in a softer voice, picking up her pen again. "Names, what grade you're in? Again, I'm Posey Spade and I'm a junior." She settled her gaze on Yash, comforted by the familiar sight of him. "I know Yash already, but what about the rest of you?"

Posey moved her gaze counterclockwise to the girl in glasses who so far appeared to not be her biggest fan. Posey was not intimidated. By the glance over the girl's T-shirt slogan and the many pins that decorated her backpack on the floor, Posey was sure they were politically aligned and had plenty of common ground to explore. Posey looked her right in the eyes and coaxed her with a smile. "And you?"

"Lexy Kennedy, sophomore," the girl muttered, returning unflinching eye contact but not the smile.

Posey took notes and moved on to the boy with the afro and the glittery eye shadow. "And you?"

"Jeremiah Blum," he said, enunciating his own name with a level of theatrical gusto that indicated just how seriously he didn't take her, "B-L-U-M, senior."

The hush that followed as she wrote his name down assured Posey this simple exercise, stopping to learn the names of her club mates, was calming the room. She served an encouraging smile to the next candidate, Bandanna Girl, who wore a smoky-eyelinered gaze of amusement.

"Athena Dixon. Should have been a senior but I'm a junior."

Intrigued, Posey recorded all this information. Despite Athena's tone, which implied how foolish she found the exercise, Posey much appreciated the sprinkling of captivating details.

"And you?" Posey asked, addressing the Boy in Black with the shoulder-length hair, who was chewing the end of a pencil and exhibiting textbook horrible posture. He was a human storm cloud. He scowled without effort, hazel gaze fixed with suspicion. But he couldn't even meet her eyes, could he? And that made Posey feel powerful in her perpetual sunshine. "Name, grade?"

"Salvatore Zamora," he said.

When he finally met her stare, it was unflinching. Challenging, even. He sat up straighter in his chair and tucked the pencil behind his ear. He didn't look away. "Sal. Junior. And I'm the founder and director of this club."

"Oh," Posey said, a bit surprised. Right, now she recalled Ms. Moses saying something about him. But this boy didn't give off leader energy. "Excellent! May I ask what the club's official mission statement is?"

"The . . . what?" he asked.

"You know, the purpose," Posey answered. "Like at my old school, the AV Club was tasked specifically with recording live events put on by the theater department and sports teams."

"Yeah, it's not like that here," Athena said, shaking her head. "The theater department hires *professionals* for their productions. Fancy fucks."

"And sports, are you joking?" Lexy said. "Vomit. I hate sports."

"Then what's the purpose of this club exactly?" Posey asked.

The silence she was met with told her everything she needed to know.

"Because according to this web page I found online on the school website"—Posey said, plucking it from a folder in her backpack, so glad she brought her copy. *Thank you, past Posey*—"the stated purpose of the AV Club is 'to give students an opportunity to learn and practice video and audio production of live events such as presentations, assemblies, and awards ceremonies, as well as provide space for students to create independent multimedia projects.'" Posey showcased the paper to the group, who did not move to squint closer.

Jeremiah said, "Okay, now I *know* this is Ms. Moses. Her fingerprints are all over this ridiculousness."

"I'm still voting for an elaborate piece of performance art," Athena said.

"*I've* never seen this one before," Jeremiah said, gesturing toward Posey. "What if she's a hired actress?"

"I'm new here," Posey reminded them all.

"I mean, our website does have that statement on it," Yash said. "You all don't have to jump to conspiracies. I think it's good that we start the year off talking about the mission statement and figuring out what we, you know, what we want to accomplish this year."

Good old Yash. Already, he was her best friend. He gave her a half smile—a friendly promise. She returned the favor.

Posey was about to expand on Yash's excellent suggestion when the double doors swiveled open with a banshee croak and Ms. Moses blew in. She carried far too much: water bottle crooked in her arm, coffee cup in hand, another armful of paperwork and files, a pen between her teeth, a purse bloated enough to be an overnight bag. She was so striking! Lipstick so red. Hair so long, so wild, dyed red like an upside-down flame. A woman on fire. She was such an electrifying sight of overburden Posey stood up and asked if she needed assistance.

"I've got it, Posey," the woman said. "Thanks, I've got it. Carry on. How you all doing? Sal, did you reach out to the chess club yet?"

Sal didn't answer right away, because Ms. Moses disappeared around a corner with a few alarmingly loud *thunks*. When she returned without her load, she was taking her sweatshirt off over her head and catching her breath. Posey paid attention to the details of Ms. Moses: the peek of a tattoo on her wrist that disappeared when she pulled her sleeve down. The faded bright lipstick. The belt she wore with studs on it like a punk rocker.

"Um, it's the first day of school." Sal straightened his posture. "When I reached out last year they seemed . . . unenthused about being in the spotlight. And really, Moses, you expect anyone to watch videos about *chess*?"

"Yeah, Salvatore, I do," Ms. Moses answered, pulling her hair into a bun at the top of her head. "Do your homework. There have been multiple award-winning documentaries about chess."

Sal (or Salvatore, it wasn't clear yet what he preferred) gave an audible sigh.

"With the right approach, the video itself could serve as an explainer," Posey offered. "You could film the game of chess and use it as an opportunity to invite people in. Make it more accessible."

The room went silent. Ms. Moses crossed her arms, cocked her chin, and truly took in Posey for the first time today. "Hiya, Posey. Good to see you here." Her eyes fell to Posey's outfit, and she asked, "You okay, Posey?"

"No," Lexy answered for her. "She's a horror show."

"I had a ketchup mishap," Posey said. "It was an accident. Please excuse my appearance, I wasn't intending for it to be such a distraction."

"Actually, *you* are a distraction," Jeremiah said.

Ms. Moses held a hand up and said, "Come on, y'all."

"I was just trying to figure out what our goals are, as a club," Posey said. "Because I have some ideas—"

"What, you want to make horror movies?" Lexy asked.

"Lexy," Ms. Moses said sharply.

Lexy sat back and hid her mouth with her sweatshirt-covered hand.

Ms. Moses put her hands on her hips. "You want to take this one, Salvatore? How about you discuss goals, I like that idea."

"I mean, we'll feel out the chess club," Sal said.

Yash raised his hand before speaking. "I think we should be figuring out content for our YouTube channel." He turned to Posey. "Last year we posted an intro there."

"Nice!" said Posey. "What kind of videos did you make?"

The silence was long enough to hear a stomach gurgle.

"That's it," Lexy answered. "Just the intro video."

"Listen, we're a bunch of slackers. Speaking of which, can we please watch *Tiger King* now?" Athena asked.

"Seriously," Sal said.

Ms. Moses put her hand on Posey's arm and squeezed lightly. "How about you come back to my office?" She turned to the other students. "Go ahead, watch your video. We'll continue this conversation later."

"*Thank* you," Jeremiah said.

Posey followed Ms. Moses around the dark corner to a slate-gray room with a desk and two chairs that reminded Posey of an interrogation room. Which was exciting, actually. At seventeen, Posey had already dreamed up dozens of futures for herself, and one of her favorites involved an exciting career as a detective. Posey sat in a chair while Ms. Moses closed the door.

"Posey Spade," Ms. Moses said, with a half smile as she sank into the other chair. "You are something."

"I hope that's . . . a compliment?"

"Ketchup mishap, huh?"

Oh. Posey realized Ms. Moses was talking about her appearance. "Yes. Not the way I wanted to make a first impression."

"I should have warned you, they're a tough audience." She leaned in and shot Posey a tight, red smile. "Are you doing okay?"

"I'm fine," Posey said, sitting up straighter.

"I hope you'll stick with us," Ms. Moses said, leaning back. "I know it seems disorganized—and it is—but this group's got a ton of potential. Everyone's got drive, they just . . . need a direction to go in."

Posey lit up at this, the hope tingling through her like lovely goose bumps. "Maybe I can help with that?"

"I'm sure you will, Posey." Ms. Moses smiled. "I know it's hard to start somewhere new, somewhere so different. Listen, stick with the club. I'm here for you. We're here for you. Anything you need, anything bugging you, anything you're struggling with—email me anytime, day or night. I mean it. I'm here, okay?"

"Thank you," Posey said. "That means a lot to me."

Lingering a few extra seconds, Posey wondered if there was a tactful way to ask about what she overheard last week—the hint about an "investigation." Why would Ms. Moses, who seemed like such an enthusiastic, supportive teacher, be under investigation for anything? But sometimes, as much as it itched, there just wasn't a tactful way to satisfy one's curiosity, so Posey returned to the dark room where *Tiger King* played.

The other students were talking softly, and when she slipped back into her seat, she noticed they quieted. She took her quinoa salad out of her bag and ate it with her compostable fork, pretending to watch the documentary. But really she was watching them all out of the corner of her eyes. Studying them. Each member of the AV Club seemed so intriguing, she wished she could sit down for an in-depth interview and pick their brains. Who was Lexy texting the entire time with a sour look on her face? What was Yash drawing at his desk while the movie played? When did Jeremiah learn to play the guitar in the case he had stashed behind his desk? Where was Athena planning to post the selfie she was taking? And Sal, with his poor posture, his all-black clothes, and his backpack held together with safety pins, was the only person not eating lunch. Even when Jeremiah passed him some French fries, he just passed them right back.

Why?

Posey was overwhelmed sometimes with the questions inside her, with the untold stories that swirled around her. She ate her food, and though she wasn't welcomed today, she was grateful to be tolerated. It was a decent starting place. There was so much potential here in this room; how excited she was to realize it.

THREE

Posey's dad, Peter Spade, had been a freelance reporter before Posey was born. A roving national correspondent for the *Washington Post*, which was how he met Posey's mother—a waitress in a diner in a small Texas town near an oil spillage disaster in the Gulf that Peter was covering. After Posey came along (oops) and they got married (at a drive-through chapel), the new family relocated to San Francisco, where Peter settled down with a job as deputy editor at the *Chronicle*. Then one day when Posey was a toddler, her mother left to take a vacation with her girlfriends and enjoyed herself so much she never returned. She sent a few postcards over the years—palm trees, always palms—and made one awkward happy birthday call on Posey's tenth, but nothing else. This was the looming, ever-present mystery in Posey's life: What was it that made her mother go? To never return? And she loved her dad double, more than double, for the fact that he had always been there for her.

Now, nearly two decades later, her dad moved them again so

he could take a job as editor in chief for the *Sierra Tribune*. He was a wonderful dad when he was home. But he was rarely home. Posey learned to cook her own meals when she was eight. Rode Muni and BART by herself at the age of ten. She was used to tucking herself in at night. It wasn't a big deal.

It was harder in Wild Pines, though. It was so *dark* at night. The house creaked. They had a bear box for their garbage outside because, well, there were actual real-life bears that wandered around her neighborhood. It was harder to be alone here.

"The good thing about squirting ketchup all over yourself on the first day of school is the year can only get better from there," Posey told him when he called from his desk at the office while he finished laying out the upcoming paper.

She had the phone on speaker, on the sill of the kitchen window in front of her. The window itself was black with the night. She saw herself in the reflection and quickly returned her gaze back into the sink full of suds where she was washing their breakfast plates.

"That's one way to look at it," he answered. She could hear him typing during the pause. "You like your classes?"

"They were acceptable."

"'Acceptable.'"

They had been awkward at best—she'd had to explain the ketchup spatter way too many times. A group of girls in matching puffy jackets told her she was a biohazard. In addition to that, she'd mispronounced a teacher's name. Then there was the AV Club.

"I think it's too early to make a judgment." She pulled the stopper and watched the bubbles sink down and disappear. Then

26

she ran a cool stream of water, rinsing the two plates, two cups, two spoons from breakfast, the bowl and spoon from her cereal dinner. "The pluses? It's truly like summer camp. Cedars and damp earth everywhere. There are these trails that loop around campus and this medieval-looking staircase that winds down the hillside to the theater building. It smells amazing, fresh and dewy and herbal. And the bus ride home was long enough I got all my homework done."

"And did you end up going to that AV Club to talk about your show idea?"

"Well," she said, putting the last dish on the rack and drying her hands on a dish towel printed like a crossword puzzle, "I did attend a meeting. I sense I'm going to need to build more social capital before that group will be open to my ideas."

"And I'm sure they're busy with their own agenda."

Their very important agenda of watching a Netflix show that has nothing to do with audiovisual work, Posey didn't say. But she shouldn't judge. She really shouldn't.

"You doing okay?" her dad asked her.

"Doing great."

"I should be home in an hour or so."

An hour or so, in Peter Spade time, meant you'd be lucky to spot him before midnight. Even so, Posey said, "Love you, Daddy" before switching off the kitchen light.

"Love you too, Pose. Maybe take some time to relax in that hot tub."

"Maybe I will."

They hung up and Posey stood there, hand on the sliding glass door, peering out into the night. The night, filled with orchestral, insectile sounds, silhouettes of trees, and a shocking ceiling of jewels that were the stars. Five minutes later, when Posey returned in her one-piece black bathing suit, she gazed again out the sliding glass door. She paused.

She was thinking of bears.

It was embarrassing. *Embearassing*, Posey thought to herself. That she should live in this paradise, in this log-cabin dream house that felt more vacation than home, with a hot tub on a deck under an extravagantly starry sky, but she was too afraid to go outside because of bears.

Posey didn't like to be afraid of anything. She ground her teeth, unable to open the door. But the night was so dark. She could imagine beady eyes flashing back at her, the gleam of jagged teeth.

She circled the interior of the house, checking every lock.

Then she went upstairs, swapped her bathing suit for pajamas and her hot tub soak for a quick lukewarm shower, and returned to her half-unpacked room to dive into the sweet escape of research.

AV Club Promo

Wild Pines Buzz   13 subscribers

67 views   May 12
(A middle-aged woman with flame-red hair and red lips

addresses the camera. The caption flashes the words
MS. MOSES, MULTIMEDIA TEACHER.)

Transcript

MS. MOSES
AV Club is a brand-new club to help Wild Pines students
explore video as both an art form and historic record.
We're hoping to be able to help produce promos for Wild
Pines High and all the amazing work it does—everything
from filming projects for our award-winning theater arts
program to creative projects spearheaded by our students.

(The camera pans out. Ms. Moses sits on a stool
alongside a boy with shoulder-length hair covering most of his face. Soon the caption reads SAL
ZAMORA, AV CLUB DIRECTOR.)

MS. MOSES
This is our founder, Salvatore Zamora. You want to
share a little bit of your vision for the club?

(Sal shrugs)

SAL
Nothing I love more than a little escapism.

(Ms. Moses laughs)

SAL
But seriously, I'm here for the creative projects.
Hoping to make some documentaries to serve as,
I don't know, beautiful little time capsules for the
school.

(Footage of Athena, Jeremiah, Yash, and Lexy
waving as they play with camera equipment.
Cuts back to Ms. Moses sitting in on her stool,
smiling a red half smile next to Sal)

MS. MOSES
Stay tuned for all the beautiful little time capsules
to come.

Posey watched the video twice. The sound had an annoying buzz to it, background noise. The color was unsaturated. And she wasn't sure what story it was telling. She had learned nothing new about the AV Club, except that the club seemed as lacking in purpose in archived form as it had when she encountered it live and in person earlier that day.

So even though she was tired, Posey opened a Google Slides presentation, her heart swelling at the blank gleam of her screen. She loved that moment—the moment before she was about to dive into a new project. The contemplative pause before she had everything in the world to say and prove. She savored it, then chose her favorite template and feverishly typed. She typed until it was so late her father was home, kissing her head and rubbing her shoulders and saying, "Pose, you should be asleep by now."

But it was so hard to sleep with dreams this vivid in her head! Sleep, ugh. Sleep was the place where nothing ever happened.

FOUR

Tuesday, September 10

The energy in the AV Club was notably different today.

Perhaps it was the fact Posey arrived a few minutes earlier than she had the day before, or the fact she no longer resembled the victim in a horror film. But when she arrived at the basement today, there was laughter. Lexy was standing up with an open bag of popcorn and was throwing pieces of it into Jeremiah's mouth. Jeremiah was dashing in zigzags to catch them with the grace of a trained dancer. Yash paced in a corner with a phone to his ear. Athena was putting on black lipstick and using her phone as a mirror.

When Posey came in, the group members eyed her for a moment and went back to what they were doing—which felt much more accepting than Posey had expected.

She sat down at her desk with her backpack and observed the room. There were things today she hadn't noticed yesterday. For example, Jeremiah was much taller than she had initially estimated, because yesterday he had been seated. Lexy had a guffaw of a laugh, whereas yesterday Posey had been uncertain if Lexy was capable of laughing at all. Athena had a lot of makeup. A *lot*. Her entire desk was currently occupied with compacts, brushes, and tubes. Then there was Yash, saying loudly into his phone, "You have to put it on HDMI 2.0! How many times have I told you?!" Who knew Yash could sound so angry? And then there was the fact Sal was nowhere to be seen, his seat empty.

"Look," Lexy said to Jeremiah, holding her bag of popcorn upside down. "You ate it all."

Jeremiah breathlessly took his seat next to Posey. "Phew. That was a *workout*."

Posey wasn't sure if he was speaking to her, but she answered, "It did look intense. Do you dance?"

"Yes," he said, flattered. "Six years of ballet, eight of modern." He pointed a blue fingernail at the rainbow flag on her bag and raised an eyebrow. "Well then. Hello, rainbow flag."

Lexy had slid into her desk on the other side of Posey and unwrapped some kind of burger. Suddenly it was like the whole room went silent and a spotlight was on Posey.

Posey opened her bag and took out her lunch. "I identify as bisexual and/or pansexual."

"Yeah, you do," Jeremiah said in a congratulatory tone as if this raised his opinion of her.

Yash was coming back to the circle now, phone back in his pocket. "My mother is going to drive me to an early grave," he said as he took his seat, and then shot Posey a big, friendly smile. "Hey!"

"So what's on the agenda today?" Posey asked the group.

"What's on the what now?" Jeremiah said.

"Haven't you learned?" Lexy bit into her burger ferociously. "We don't have 'agendas.'"

"Well, I have an item to add," Posey said to her. "If that's okay?"

"To the nonexistent agenda?" Lexy said through a mouthful. "Be my guest."

Posey had been expecting more resistance to her hijacking the meeting today with her slide presentation, from Lexy in particular. She was pleasantly shocked at the reception. It was funny how people could be different one day to the next, like weather: yesterday brooding and cloudy, today sunny and breezy. Posey pulled her computer case from her bag and unzipped it.

"Does anyone have a cable that connects a laptop to the TV?" Posey asked.

"USB-C to HDMI," Yash said. "And no."

"Ms. Moses probably does in her office." Athena was putting all her makeup carefully into a glittery bag with a zipper. "Check with her. She's back there right now."

Such helpfulness! Posey's heart swelled at the prospect of this group being kind to her, a stranger—accepting her. The next step was to earn their trust and lead them in becoming a stronger, more defined, more productive club. The elements were here. They just needed a vision. Which was where her slide presentation came in.

Posey got up and walked down the hall lit with a single blinking bulb and poked her head into Ms. Moses's office. She took a step back, though, when she saw Ms. Moses standing close to someone with her hand on their shoulder, murmuring into their ear. Posey turned to return to the other room when Ms. Moses saw her. And Posey saw that the person she had been talking to so familiarly was Sal.

It was uncomfortable. The discomfort was palpable as the three of them—Posey, Ms. Moses, and Sal—exchanged looks. Posey wasn't sure what to think, but she did have the sense she had stumbled upon something she wasn't supposed to see.

"A USB-C cord," Posey said, breaking the silence. "I'm looking for a USB-C cord. To HDMI."

"Ah, yes, of course!" Ms. Moses said, turning around and rifling through a drawer.

Sal shoved his hands into his sweatshirt pocket and left the room, passing Posey without so much as a word. She wasn't sure if it was coldness toward her in general or if it was the fact she saw what she just saw.

"Here." Ms. Moses handed Posey the cord. Posey noted the smudged mascara under Ms. Moses's eyes, the way she seemed out of breath when she was standing still. Posey thanked her and went back to the main room.

Sal was up near the TV when Posey returned, cord in her hand.

"What are you doing?" he asked her when she joined him.

"I was going to give a short presentation," she said. "That okay with you?"

"On what?"

"Just an idea I wanted to share with the group."

"We're about to finish *Tiger King*," Sal said through his teeth.

"*Tiger King* will still be here when I'm done," Posey said, her gaze steady.

Sal returned her stare. The color of his eyes reminded her of the ocean, and not in the way most people think of the ocean. There was no blue to them. They were muddy and green, with a light that danced on their surface but a depth to them that held infinite unknowns. Finally, he scowled and relented, stepping back.

"It's all yours," he muttered, taking a seat.

Posey plugged in the cable and asked, "Yash? You mind dimming the lights?"

Yash, who Posey now regarded as her number one partner in crime, got up and flipped the lights off.

The presentation was called PIVOT TO NEWS and contained twenty slides. Not to toot her own horn, but Posey's presentation was well researched and was also *fun*. She had incorporated many cute pictures of hedgehogs to liven up the pitch visually. Hedgehogs were Posey's favorite animal.

"Awwww," Lexy said when they got to slide number four called BUILDING INTEGRITY. It had bullet points about how the AV Club could branch into journalism to become an award-winning entity. "He's wearing a little tuxedo!"

They were eating out of the palm of her hand.

"This is how I see it," Posey said excitedly once she got to the meat of her presentation. She had laid out a sample show structure—headlines, weather forecast, followed by the feature investigative report. Simple. Easy to complete. A template. "This format would be doable for us, easy to follow week after week."

"Awww, he's reading a newspaper," Lexy said about the hedgehog.

"Yes," Posey said.

"Is he smoking a *pipe*?" Athena asked. "Dude. Pack us a bowl, li'l guy."

"It was photoshopped," Posey said. "But let's get back to the show—"

"A stoner hedgehog," Sal said. "You really think that's appropriate? Bringing visuals of drugs into this meeting?"

Posey almost took the bait, arguing with him, but he was clearly trying to mess with her head. She had learned long ago the art of ignoring aggravators.

"The headlines would be easy." Posey pointed to the screen where it had some samples she had made up: *Sloppy Nos: The Juicy Truth Behind Your Cafeteria Lunch*; *Drama-Rama in the Theater Arts Department.* "Just quick tidbits of news we've heard around the halls—confirmed with proper sourcing, of course."

"What's the truth behind the cafeteria lunches?" Jeremiah asked, sounding a little worried. "I always eat those sloppy joes."

"And if you're talking about the drama in the theater department I *think* you're talking about, how about we *don't* go there?" asked Athena as she unwrapped a protein bar.

"These are fictional headlines," Posey said, taking note of the fact her theater headline had hit some mysterious nail on its mysterious head when it came to Athena. "Here to serve as examples of what kinds of headlines we *could* present."

Posey flipped to the next slide. Out of the corner of her eye, she watched for Yash's approval and was disappointed to see him engrossed in something in front of him. Drawing, it looked like. He wasn't even listening to her.

Lexy was texting on her phone.

She was losing them.

"The best part is," Posey said in her camp counselor voice, "that you have already laid the groundwork for this series with your amazing YouTube channel! I saw your video last night and it was really . . ." She took a beat looking for the word, because she wasn't one to lie. Just one to butter people up, when need be. "It was interesting. I learned a lot about you all. I saw so much potential. Imagine if we posted something on that channel every week!"

"I love this idea!" Yash chimed in.

"Eh," Athena said. "Sounds like a lot of work."

"We'd divvy up duties and it wouldn't be a huge lift," Posey replied. "We had an AV Club with a news show at my old school— with a proper team in place, it's very doable."

"Where's your old school?" Sal sounded bored, scratching at his desk. He seemed like the type of boy who might carve his name into surfaces just to remind himself he existed. Posey had seen his kind before.

"San Francisco," Posey said with pride.

No one responded, except Jeremiah, who said, "I went to SF to see *Hamilton* freshman year and a bike messenger ran over my foot."

Posey closed her eyes a moment, feeling the entire presentation had veered off track. She opened her eyes again and saw several yawns. With a sinking heart, she sped the rest of the presentation up until the last slide that said JUST IMAGINE! and asked Yash to flip the lights back on. He hadn't said a word her whole presentation, engrossed in his project. Posey knew it wasn't the end-all—she played a good long game—but she was discouraged. It had seemed hopeful earlier. She had spent so much time on the presentation. But the team wasn't into it.

"Now can we watch *Tiger King*?" Sal asked Posey, standing up to take the cable from her hand as she disconnected her computer. He said it mockingly, as if she were a teacher, as if she were spoiling his fun.

"I don't know. Aren't you the founder? Aren't *you* the one in charge?" Posey asked, not flinching as their gazes met.

They met and did not part for a good moment or two. Then Posey took her seat, returned her laptop to its case, and focused on her lunch.

Truth be told, Posey felt a bit of a fool. She had worked so hard on the presentation, and the response had been tepid at best. Sal was persistently hostile. Simple misogyny? But no, he clearly had an unwavering deference to Ms. Moses. Though that appeared to be a whole other story. If only she could do a deep dive on *that* situation. Maybe she would. Along with finding out what that whole "investigation" thing was all about.

No one mentioned her presentation for the rest of the lunch period. It was as if it hadn't happened. It was okay. Sometimes things had to soak. But Posey's eyes burned a little when the next *Tiger King* episode started and there was an odd twist of familiar pain in her middle. After a few minutes, while chewing her lunch mechanically, she realized what it was: homesickness. She missed her old life before everything got weird. She missed her old school on the hill, her journalism class, Hannah before Hannah pulled away, the histories she knew that she took for granted. Here, there was no history. There was only right now. It was frustrating. It was terrifying.

When she was packing up, Yash dropped a paper on her desk as he was leaving. He didn't wait to see her response. He kept walking out the door. But it was a lifelike sketch of her, of Posey Spade, in pencil, standing up in front of the class. Posey smiled back at it. Not wanting to injure it with folds, she put it gingerly into her binder and felt a ray of hope beaming inside her even while the rest of the AV Club packed up and ignored her.

She also made a note to herself that Ms. Moses had been in her office the entire time.

And that Sal didn't exit the door with the rest of them but headed back into the hall where his teacher's office was.

FIVE

Wednesday, September 11

For the third AV Club meeting, Posey decided on a different tactic.

At the end of fourth-period English, Posey packed her bag up. The room lit up with the buzz of conversation and students poured out of the sunny classroom to the hallway. Posey made her way to Mr. Hunter's desk. Mr. Hunter was buff and bald and Black; at first glance he resembled someone who might be a football coach. Instead, he was a passionate book lover who teared up when reading poetry to the class. Posey had been in his class only three days and he was already her favorite teacher. To be fair, English teachers usually were.

"Mr. Hunter," Posey asked. "Would you mind if I borrowed your easel and markers?"

Mr. Hunter looked up from his laptop, raising an eyebrow. "What are you up to?"

"Trying to facilitate a brainstorming session for the AV Club. I'll bring it back at the end of lunch period, I promise."

"We have an AV Club?"

"It's relatively new."

"Who's sponsoring?"

"Ms. Moses. I think she teaches multimedia. You know her?"

"I do."

Mr. Hunter didn't offer more, though Posey wished he would. Since yesterday, the sight of Ms. Moses talking with Sal kept replaying in her mind, and she couldn't help but remain curious about this investigation Yash had mentioned on Friday. Posey had even looked her up on social media the day before. Her teacher's account didn't reveal much. All she posted were pictures of pets.

"What's your brainstorming session about?" Mr. Hunter asked.

"I'm hoping to build a news show for the school, with the assistance of the AV Club."

Mr. Hunter smiled. "Interesting. We used to have a school paper . . . that got shut down a few years ago."

"May I ask why?"

"Funding, I'm sure. It's always funding. Surprised they even let us have an AV Club." Mr. Hunter got up and handed her the easel and the markers. "Just make sure you get them back to me right after lunch."

Posey thanked him and hurried out of the classroom with the easel and markers. It was fascinating how teachers transformed once the bell rang. How Mr. Hunter, who was inspiring and full of energy, seemed more subdued and jaded once class was over. *Surprised they even let us have an AV Club.* Who were "they"? The school administration?

The hall outside the classroom was mostly deserted now,

students off to the quad or the cafeteria for lunch. There was a tranquility to the gleaming linoleum floors and the whisper of far-off footsteps, the posters about student elections. At the end of the hall where the stairwells waited, a giant permanent banner gleamed in gold: WILD PINES HIGH CONGRATULATES OUR AWARD-WINNING THEATER DEPARTMENT! There was an entire wall of glass casing filled with pictures of high school plays, ribbons, gold statues, and memorabilia from past productions. There were news clippings of rave reviews and even some glossy magazine photographs of alumni who had moved on to have professional acting careers. Posey wished she had time to stop, but she had to hurry to AV Club to get there in time to have a few minutes before, inevitably, Sal queued the next episode of *Tiger King*.

Down in the basement, Posey turned the corner where their meeting was and heard her name spoken inside. She balked in the doorway and perked up her ears.

"Maybe we weren't excited enough about her time-share presentation," Lexy said dryly.

"It wasn't bad," Yash said. "I think she has some great ideas. Did you know she won, like, a statewide award for journalism at her last high school?"

Yash's defense of her, his interest in her, lit Posey up.

"Yeah, well, her energy is exhausting," Jeremiah said.

"Pfft, you're one to talk," Athena shot back.

"She's just so strange," Lexy said.

"I have a wild idea: maybe you're just judgmental dicks," Athena said. "Maybe that's why she didn't come back."

"Admit it," Lexy said. "She's strange. She has, like, no sense of humor."

Posey was frozen in the doorway, an ill roll in her stomach. This was familiar. She'd been called weird and synonyms of weird by her peers most of her life. She'd been told she was "too much." She was the type of student her teachers had to ask to stop raising her hand, to let others speak. It hurt, it did. But Posey decided to breathe and consider this all a gift: constructive criticism. How often did you get to hear the unedited truth about what others thought about you? Obviously she needed to prove to them that there was more to her, that she could be funny (Posey loved puns!), and that she wasn't always exhausting. She had to work harder at being laid-back.

"Hi, everyone," Posey said with a smile, entering the room. "Sorry I'm late."

Everyone went silent when she walked in and set up the easel. Lexy and Jeremiah exchanged a slightly worried look, as if they feared they'd been overheard. Athena said, "Why, hello, sunshine." Yash waved at Posey and said a bit too loudly, a bit too excitedly, "Hi, Posey!"

"Hey, Posey," Lexy said. "How are you?"

Clearly Lexy was heaping an extra helping of kindness because she felt guilty about what she'd been saying. Either that, or Lexy was a phony—but Posey was an excellent judge of character and she didn't think that was true.

"I'm doing well, thanks for asking," Posey answered. "I was wondering if we could take a few minutes today to follow up and discuss my proposal from yesterday?"

"You are *per-sis-tent*," Jeremiah said as he unwrapped a burger—a sloppy joe, by the looks of it—from its foil.

"I'd love to hear what you feel your talents are so we can strategize about the best use of everyone's time," Posey said, writing their names down the page. When she got to Sal's name at the end, she looked up, realizing his seat was empty. "Where's Sal?"

"Good question," Athena said.

"I wonder if it had anything to do with the mess in Ms. Moses's class today," Lexy said as she scrolled on her phone.

"What mess?" asked Posey.

"It was holy hell in first period today," Jeremiah said as he chewed. "Ms. Moses didn't show up to class and there wasn't a substitute. Principal Vance had to come in while they tried to locate an emergency sub."

"And what would that have to do with Sal?" Posey asked, marker poised in the air.

There was a long silence.

"They're . . . close," Lexy said.

"Some think *too*," Jeremiah said.

Athena took the beanie off her head and ruffled her smashed blond hair around. "What are you, TMZ?"

"I just share what I hear," Jeremiah said, hands up.

This was all so juicy, so intriguing, that Posey fought the urge to run for her binder to take notes. She waited a moment to see if anyone would offer any more information and then focused on the task at hand. The upside of Sal's absence was that she wouldn't have to fight for control of the meeting. That wasn't necessarily a bad thing—she might be able to persuade the group more easily without him resisting her every suggestion.

"So," Posey said, glancing at the clock on the wall, which seemed an enormous eye always cocked in her direction, no matter what room she was in. "Back to the task at hand. What are you all proficient in? What's your background? What AV-related skills do you have to offer?"

The benefit of the earlier eavesdropping was that Lexy now overcompensated by participating in Posey's brainstorming project with uncharacteristic enthusiasm, which seemed to stir excitement in the rest of the group. Lexy volunteered that she loved writing and research and was "decent" when it came to lighting. Jeremiah listed something long enough to qualify as a CV—proficiency in numerous audio-editing programs, a musician, a visual artist, and adept with camerawork. Athena said she was a loser who never belonged in the club in the first place, to the guffaws of the other three, who all claimed in unison she was an award-winning actress. Yash said he could help with computers and data, cameras, editing programs, and graphic design.

Posey took notes frantically on the easel, trying to keep up, her curiosity ratcheting with every entry she made. She wanted to ask follow-up questions, but in a club that had only a lunch period, there was no time for follow-up.

Instead, Posey stood back to survey the easel. It was a marvel, really—the way each person's strengths complemented each other, the sum of which was a talented team that could expertly produce a show. As she stared at her notes, a whole new story seemed to form before her eyes. She could see Lexy writing the news, Jeremiah filming and/or doing sound, Athena reporting it, and Yash editing. The dream of it was a flame that warmed her. A smile spread on her lips, and for the first moment since she'd set foot on this damp campus shadowed with trees and peopled with strangers, she thought she knew her place. And this was it.

It was her gift; Posey knew how to look at an array of parts and put them all together.

"What about you?" Jeremiah asked Posey, balling up his hamburger's foil wrapping and tossing it into a trash can. "Ms. Bossy over here. What are *your* talents?"

"I can do whatever you need me to," Posey said. "I have modest experience and can serve as your backup. But if I were to play a role here—if you all were to try the proposal I laid out for you for a show—I would be honored to serve as director/producer."

"Gonna have to fight Sal for that one, babe," Athena said, with something akin to sympathy.

"Are we actually talking about doing a show?" Lexy asked. She had a way of speaking that was unceasingly loaded with skepticism. And she was on her phone again.

"Can you imagine, though?" Jeremiah asked. "Do a story on Haley *Seabright* and how she never even got suspended for that *fire* she started?"

Some *mmm*s sounded around the room. Posey was piqued, in listening mode, her excitement held back in anticipation, waiting for the enthusiasm to kindle and then turn to a blaze.

"Something on the Noble Youth Club, how about," Yash said as he doodled on a piece of paper.

"Seriously," Lexy said, snapping in agreement. "Buncha racists."

"Whatever. You want to burn it all down, just do an exposé on Mr. Butts and how he's driving a Ferrari on a teacher's salary," Athena said.

Jeremiah put his hands up. "On. *Fire.*"

Posey couldn't contain her smile. It felt glorious. She had no idea what they were talking about—but they were infected with it. She was about to start teasing out these ideas when the doors to the room swung open with a clatter. Everyone jumped in their seats.

Sal stood breathless, backpack slung low on a single shoulder, black shoes black jeans black sweatshirt and a face ghost white. He eyed them with a frightening mix of panic and blankness. Finally, he managed to get the words out.

"Ms. Moses is missing."

SIX

"Ms. Moses is missing," Posey repeated to her dad.

They sat across from each other at Delilah's, the diner on Mile High Drive. The picture window their booth was up against faced the small town's main drag, the row of shops with wooden stoops and hand-painted signs and strung-up lights. Deep-green mountains jutted up beyond the boulevard, and the sky was still stained with sunlight while the moon's smile rose. It was Posey and Peter Spade's most sacred tradition: breakfast for dinner. That and good conversation.

"What do you mean, missing?" her dad asked, whacking a ketchup bottle with the back of his hand. He squirted red on his hash browns.

Posey cut her vegetarian sausage into pieces with a knife and fork. "Apparently she never came home last night. Never showed up to school, either."

"And how'd this come to light?"

"She's the AV Club's sponsor. I heard it there." Posey took a bite, waited until she chewed and swallowed. "I imagine they have to wait twenty-four hours for someone to report it."

"That's a myth," her dad said through a mouthful, poking his fork in the air. "Perpetuated by poor-quality true crime books and movies. You do not need to wait twenty-four hours to report when someone goes missing."

"Really," Posey said, marveling at this fact.

"Anyway, how'd they know she's missing?" he asked. "Teachers are absent all the time. Probably just a rumor."

"I hope so," Posey said. "Though, I don't know, one of the students in the AV Club seems to know her well. Sal's his name."

Her dad raised his eyebrows but didn't talk. Not enough information or too much pancake, maybe.

"Sal said Ms. Moses's husband reported her missing," she went on.

"What, this kid Sal knows her husband?"

She shrugged. "I guess?"

Her dad shook his head, as if he wasn't sure what to make of that. He stared off for a moment, lost in thought. It was one of the most comfortable things about Posey and her father—how they could drift off into their own imaginations in silence and always come back together in the end.

"People go missing all the time," he finally said, meeting her eyes again. "And it's usually nothing to panic about."

"What do you mean, people go missing all the time?"

"Domestic issues," he said, sipping his coffee.

Posey sat up a little straighter, wondering if he was thinking of her mom like she was.

"Financial issues," he went on. "Mental health issues—I once covered a story of an heiress who went missing. Turned out she had something called a dissociative fugue, where you forget who you are. When they found her, she was a hundred miles away, going by a different name."

"How bizarre," Posey said.

"Mmm," he agreed. "Everyone thought she'd been kidnapped by a serial killer. Big story that summer. Someone even wrote the paper, faked a ransom note."

"Why?"

"Who the hell knows. A moment of fame, I guess." Her dad wiped his face with a napkin and stared into the distance again. He had a far-off twinkle in his eye, as if he were watching a movie she couldn't see. To be fair, there was a lot to get distracted by in Delilah's, what with every square inch of the wallpapered walls covered in framed pictures of celebrities who had stopped in at some point over the past forty years. His lips perked up and he raised his coffee cup in the air. The delight on his face made him look so young. "Another splash?"

The waitress with the mole on the tip of her nose and hair piled atop her head came and obliged him with some coffee from her pot. She smiled back at him in a way that seemed like it could be flirtatious. It was like this with Posey's dad—and it was annoying. There was something about him that made women into fools. Even in front of his own daughter.

"Thanks, Sandhya," he said.

"Drinking coffee this late," she said. "You'll never sleep."

"Eh, I never sleep anyway. Hey, this is my daughter, Posey."

"Posey," Sandhya said, smiling. Her lipstick had rubbed off and was mostly now just a ghostly pink line around the edges. "Nice to meet you. Sandhya."

"Nice to meet you too."

When Sandhya left the table, Posey took a moment to drink her water before raising an eyebrow her dad's way and asking, "So what's up with *that*?"

"Oh, you know, I eat dinner here during late nights." He shook his head. "Don't give me that look."

Posey said nothing. She wanted to change the subject too. "Anyway, I've never had a teacher go missing. Sal seemed panicked today. Like he thought something bad had happened."

"Now's a real heck of a time for something to happen in this town," he said. "The sheriff just took his first real vacation in fifteen years. It was such a big deal there was a front-page article about it here."

"Huh."

"Sounds like a good story."

"Yeah," she said. "It could be. But hopefully she just comes back soon."

Posey finished her eggs and fruit cup and looked out onto Mile High Drive. Around the bend, there was a lone office building where the *Sierra Tribune* operated and where her dad would likely spend the next few hours tying up loose ends. The night had settled in and the stars were poking out through the ink-blue sky. It still seemed so strange that they lived here, that this was their home now. She didn't even know what most of those shops were or how exactly to get home from here. It was frightening sometimes to realize how little she knew about everything around her. How small she felt.

"If I wanted to look into it as a story, I wouldn't even know where to start," she said softly.

"You really think it would be safe to look into it?" her dad asked. "You're a bit young to be chasing a missing persons case."

"Daddy, you know I always put safety first. Don't you trust me?"

"I do."

He eyed her extra long, as if sizing her up.

"Well, it's easy." He put his card on the table to pay for their meal. "Just start with the questions. Ask yourself what the questions are that you want to answer. Then poke around and ask them. They'll lead you somewhere. What's her name again?"

"Ms. Moses."

"Ms. Moses," he said, as if the name itself were a puzzle.

SEVEN

Thursday, September 12

Posey had study hall third period each morning. Her teacher, Mr. Suzuki, a hunched man in a sweater vest, read a fat paperback while her classmates scrolled on their phones and whisper-chatted with one another. Usually the chatter of her classmates during academic hours was annoying to Posey, but today, the girls behind her were talking about something deeply interesting. Posey sat with her algebra book open in front of her, but her ears perked.

"Maybe someone killed Ms. Moses."

"You think they *killed* Ms. Moses?"

"What if they *did*?"

"Who is 'they'?"

"The principal and shit."

They giggled. Posey's neck prickled with goose bumps.

"Girl, you've been watching too many telenovelas."

"I'm serious, though. Like remember how Lettie said they were investigating her?"

"They don't kill teachers they're investigating, bitch. How does that even make sense?"

Giggling. Such loud giggling Mr. Suzuki looked up from his book and said, pleadingly, "Really?"

The girls quieted down behind Posey. Posey's piece of paper was still bare, her pencil hovering.

"Sal must be so sad."

"Maybe she skipped town and left him."

"I'd leave town if I were her. I'm surprised he didn't go with her."

Mr. Suzuki stood up, separated the girls, and Posey went back to her homework. But at the top of her algebra homework, she wrote a single word: *Investigation.*

After the bell rang, Posey was hurrying through the busy hall when she bumped shoulders with Yash, who seemed shocked to see her. He wiped the water goatee away from his mouth.

"Hi," Yash said.

"Can we talk?" Posey asked, her fingers circling his upper arm.

"Um, yeah, sure," he said, looking down at her fingers.

A line had formed behind him at the water fountain. "Move it *up*," someone shouted behind him.

Posey put her arm around Yash and led him away, around a corner and through a set of double glass doors into a lush court-yard. They were met with an overwhelming slap of misty air and the scent of trees. There were a few people using the courtyard as a shortcut to get to their next class, but otherwise it was refreshingly hushed.

"We don't have much time," Posey said, exchanging a look with a clock on the wall that she could still see through the glass doors. "But do you have *any* information to share with me about the investigation involving Ms. Moses?"

"Um," Yash said, adjusting his backpack. "I don't know much about it. Just what everyone knows."

"Well, I'm new here, and I don't know anything yet. Can you brief me?"

"Okay," Yash said with a nervous smile.

There was a sweetness of spirit, an innocent glow to Yash that warmed Posey. She smiled back at him encouragingly.

"I heard that there was some kind of issue with Sal that they're investigating."

"They who?"

"Like, the school, the district, an internal investigation. Sal and Ms. Moses got too close or something. I think he was sleeping over at her house." He raised his eyebrows. "Not like that—I don't think it's like that. No one knows exactly why."

"Has anyone asked Sal?" she asked.

"I haven't. I don't know, he can get kind of . . ."

"Prickly?"

Yash leaned in to whisper, as if he were afraid the cedar trees would overhear. "He almost got expelled for punching some guy in the face who asked him about it."

"Interesting," Posey said, noting to herself that Sal was more than prickly: he was punchy. Capable of violence.

"Why do you care?" Yash asked. "I mean—I didn't mean for that to sound mean. But what does it matter to you?"

"Ms. Moses is missing," Posey reminded him. "Doesn't that worry you? I mean, what if we can use our resources to help find her?"

"Oh. So you think you're going to, like, solve the case?" he asked.

A cedar leaf blew on top of Yash's thick hair. He didn't appear to notice it, so Posey reached out and gently plucked it from his head. She studied the cedar leaf in her hand that looked like a tiny green fan—two fans, actually, that merged together. When she pricked her finger on the pointy end of it, it sent a jolt of electricity through her.

"*We're* going to solve it," Posey said.

"We me?"

"We us."

Yash had a look on his face as if he'd caught a whiff of something foul. Posey hoped this was confusion and not disgust.

"But . . . how?" he asked helplessly.

"Yash, we hold incredible power by being members of the AV Club. We can go around asking all the questions we want. The AV Club should do an investigative report, don't you think?"

"Oh," he said, his face relaxing a bit as the meaning sank in. "Yeah, sure. About Ms. Moses being missing?"

Posey nodded. "I'm going to propose this to the group today. That we all start immediately working on a feature. Can I count on you?"

Yash straightened his posture and nodded. "Okay. I don't

know how Sal will feel about it, though. It's kind of his club."

"Well, if he cares about Ms. Moses, I imagine he'd be the first to applaud this idea."

Unless Sal had a reason to *not* want them to chase the story. Which would certainly be interesting. And telling. That in and of itself—Sal's reaction—would reveal whether he was a person of interest.

"True," Yash said. "Yeah, okay."

Posey put a hand on his shoulder. "Yash, I truly appreciate your good nature."

"I . . . I appreciate you too, Posey," he said.

And with that, the bell rang, and the two students scuttled to their classes. But the entire fourth period, as Mr. Hunter led a passionate discussion on *The Great Gatsby*, Posey was jotting furious notes in her AV Club notebook in purple pen. Like her dad advised her, she was starting with questions—the only road to an answer. Why was Ms. Moses being investigated? Who exactly was investigating her? And the day she went missing, what was going on with her and Sal in her office?

EIGHT

Obviously, Posey didn't know Ms. Moses well. But the kindness that Ms. Moses had extended to Posey and the fact she was their club leader made it feel appropriate that Posey and the rest of the club at least put in a little effort to investigate.

Posey strode into the AV Club room that afternoon with a newfound purpose, sliding into the seat beside Yash and giving him a knowing nod as he ate his slice of pizza with a plastic fork and knife. The mood of the room was subdued, everyone gawking at their phones—except Sal, who stared into the screen of a battered laptop while biting his nails.

"Good afternoon," she said as she opened her plastic container of quinoa salad with a *pop*. On second thought, she snapped the lid back on and stood up. The belly butterflies were too active. She couldn't eat yet when there was so much to be discussed. "I have a proposal."

Athena made a noise somewhere between a scream and a groan.

"You got another slideshow for us?" Jeremiah asked without looking up from his phone.

"I hope there are more hedgehogs. Are there hedgehogs?" asked Lexy as she slipped her phone into one of the many pockets on her long denim skirt.

"No written proposal today, this is a verbal pitch to piggyback on yesterday's club discussion here. Yash and I were talking," Posey went on, gesturing toward Yash, who did not respond—he was too busy shoving a pepperoni slice into his mouth with a fork. "We think this group should immediately start working on an investigative report about the disappearance of Ms. Moses."

"Wait—is she really in trouble?" Jeremiah asked.

"Are we jumping to conclusions here? Maybe she just took off for a mental health break and didn't tell anyone," Athena said.

"Anyway, isn't this the police's job?" asked Lexy. "Investigating?"

"They're not investigating," Sal muttered from his seat.

He hadn't even glanced up from the screen he was so rapt with, but everyone stopped what they were doing to listen to him. Sal's presence was like a shadow—he could shrink and slip by unnoticed, or he could balloon into a commanding figure who drew everyone's attention. Posey remembered what Yash said about Sal, that he had nearly been expelled for violence against another student. She had so many questions.

"Do you know why they're not investigating?" Posey asked Sal.

Sal didn't respond to her. It was aggravating, the way he wouldn't even acknowledge the room, wouldn't even give her so much as a look.

"Because the cops are a buncha donut-munchin ham-heads," Athena said in some kind of Brooklyn accent.

"I think that's kind of a stereotype—" Posey started to say, before Jeremiah interrupted with, "She's got *history*."

"Don't act like you're so pure, pissboy," Athena shot back.

The follow-up information Posey wanted, the context she needed to fully understand these statements, was dizzying. Posey shook her head and forged on. "My pitch is this: until Ms. Moses is found, we use our resources to highlight her case. We interview people. We dig into her possible whereabouts."

"Let's be real," Athena said, popping a piece of gum in her mouth. Despite a face with enough makeup to hit the Broadway stage, she was still wearing her pajama pants. "I don't think we need to worry about Ms. Moses. She's a big lady, you know? She can take care of herself. She probably had a *fuck it* revelation and hit the road. Truly, good for her."

"She didn't," Sal said, just above a whisper. Posey wasn't sure anyone heard him but her.

"I don't know," Yash said. "That doesn't sound like Ms. Moses. Does it?"

"I really hope she's okay," Lexy said. "But . . . it sounds like a lot of work. Producing a show, now? And what would we even do with it?"

"Put it on our YouTube channel," Yash piped up, wiping the sauce from his mouth with a napkin. "I don't think it would be that much work."

There he was, her trusty new teammate. Posey flashed him a thankful smile, which he returned, even though his teeth were stained red with sauce.

"It's for a good cause," Posey jumped back in. "Don't we all want to know what happened to Ms. Moses?" A small lightbulb popped in her brain. "You know, my dad works for the paper. He was telling me that the sheriff just took his first vacation in fifteen years. I imagine the department's small, which means they're currently under-resourced. Which means that her case might not be getting the attention it deserves."

"I told you all," Sal said after her, as if to agree. "Cops aren't doing anything."

The room was quiet, a somber hush rolling through it like the moment the wind departs the trees. It was as if the entire club had a collective moment of understanding the gravity of the situation at hand. It wasn't a joke, it was real. Their teacher was missing. The jaws of frightening thoughts clamped over each of their skulls, the horrible possibilities popping into their minds. Ms. Moses had been kidnapped, killed, or wandered into the wilderness. Everyone's eyes shifted from their screens as they exchanged worried glances. Finally, Sal closed his laptop with a loud slap.

Posey had her eyes on him most of all. She had been watching him for a reaction since she walked in, trying to read him. His gaze met hers. It seemed to shine with a steady green-brown anger, an eternal flame. He didn't blink. He just nodded.

"I'm with Posey," he said. "Nobody's doing shit about Mol— Ms. Moses. It's up to us."

Posey smiled at Sal, though he didn't smile back. And she made a mental note of the slip of his tongue. He had started calling Ms. Moses by her first time, Molly, the name Posey had seen on her social media accounts. First-name basis. Intimate talks in her office. What was the story?

"Fine!" Athena said, throwing her arms up in the air. "God-*damn*, you are a relentless little sunflower."

"Is everyone okay with this idea?" Posey asked, looking to Jeremiah and Lexy.

"Yeah, sure," Lexy said begrudgingly. "I'll do it for Ms. Moses. I didn't realize this was such a big deal, and now you have me worried."

"I don't understand what we're doing," Jeremiah said, popping an earbud out. "Did I miss something?"

"We're making a show about Ms. Moses," Lexy said.

"An investigative *report*," Posey corrected her.

"A what in the what now?" Jeremiah asked.

Herding kittens would actually be easier than working with these students. Posey inhaled, exhaled, and stood to cross to the whiteboard. She beckoned to Sal to join her and he did. She handed him a marker, black, to match everything about him. She took the purple one, of course.

ROLES, she wrote at the top of the board.

"Can I ask you something, Posey? Are you a cyborg?" asked

Athena, pulling her beanie down to nearly cover her eyes. "Because I don't know any human who has handwriting that perfect."

"I'm not a cyborg, and thank you. Sal, what do you think about this?" Posey asked, jotting down each person's name and quickly assigning the roles she thought best for them, based on the skill sets they had discussed the day before.

ATHENA: Anchor
LEXY: Writer
JEREMIAH: Graphics / sound
YASH: Editing / postproduction

"What about you and me?" Sal asked her, furrowing his brow.

"Codirectors," she said, meeting his gaze.

It was like a staring contest. His face didn't move and neither did hers. They had reached a stubborn standstill. The moment stretched so long it veered into awkwardness and Athena said, "Are you guys going to kiss?" A champion of staring contests, Posey easily could have won this one. But as a charitable act and in the interest of saving everybody time, she looked away.

"This is how I'm imagining it to play out," Posey said. "You and I grab some interviews, figure out which clips the show will feature and what the narrative is, and perform research. Lexy writes some copy that Athena will either record as a voice-over or video that tells the story between the clips. Yash will edit. Jeremiah will assist with sound and create any graphics we need. I know all this might sound impossible, but I assure you, it's not.

And the more compelling a story we can tell, the more attention we can draw to Ms. Moses's case, and the better chance we have of finding her."

She was edging on breathlessness. Posey stood a little taller and waited as Sal studied what she wrote on the whiteboard and very slightly, almost imperceptibly, chewed his cheek. "Okay."

Amazing that just two syllables, uttered in a deadpan monotone, could give Posey such a lift of spirits. She could feel it—she was winning them over. She was building a real team here and it was all for the greater good.

"What do you all think?" Posey asked the room.

"I'm all for this idea," Yash said.

He already had a pen and paper out and seemed to be taking notes—a boy after her own heart.

"I mean, don't get me wrong, I want to help Ms. Moses," Jeremiah said, cracking his knuckles. "But this is a *lot*, and I actually have a life."

"When and where am I supposed to be recording these voice-overs and videos?" Athena asked.

Lexy's arms were crossed. "Yeah, what exactly am I expected to be writing?"

"Calm yourselves," Sal said, louder than he usually spoke. Everyone immediately listened. "We can iron details out later. Just—are you in or not?"

"I'm in," Yash said.

"Why the hell not," Athena said.

"Tentatively, yes," Jeremiah said.

"Yeah, sure, fine," Lexy said.

Posey was lit with a new inner fire. She looked at the group, at Sal, and at the clock—they didn't have much left of their lunch period. She eyed the boxes of equipment in the corners. No, that was all too complicated. That would eat up all their time and get them nowhere. But then she moved her gaze to their desks, the phones gleaming on every one of them.

"We have to move fast here," Posey said to Sal. "I think it's best we mainly use our phones to record interviews."

"I don't have a phone," he said.

Posey was stunned. "What? Really? Okay, well, we can use mine." She turned to everyone else. "We'll start a group chat for communication on the episode. Does that work?"

They nodded. Posey tiptoed over to her backpack to retrieve her phone. Everyone exchanged numbers—everyone except Sal. Posey's fingers shook a little as she sent the first text to the group:

> testing testing.

"Got it," they all said.

"I'm still not clear on anything, but whatever," Lexy said, plucking a granola bar from a pocket on her skirt.

"It's okay. We can figure it out as we go along. There's a great quote that says, 'Writing is like driving at night in the fog. You can only see as far as your headlights, but you can make the whole trip that way.'"

Lexy raised her eyebrows, appearing to think deeply about the quote. For just a few seconds, the scowl left her face. "Who said that?"

"I actually don't know," Posey admitted. "E. L. Doctorow, I think. I'd have to ask my dad."

"I drove in the fog once," Athena said. "Joyriding in a police cruiser. Ended up smashing the car right into someone's garage."

"Yes, we know," Jeremiah said, sounding bored.

Posey had no idea how anyone could sound bored about *that*—what on earth was Athena talking about? But there was no time for backstory. They had to focus on one thing, and that was diving into Ms. Moses's disappearance.

"Sal," Posey asked. "What do you have going on after school? Would you be available this afternoon to meet about next steps?"

"I have nothing going on," he said.

"Let's meet at the front steps of the school, then," she said.

"Sounds good to me."

Everyone sat in a comfortable silence as the club members ate the rest of their lunches. Posey was starving, devouring her quinoa salad. In the quiet, Posey's thoughts meandered backward, to San Francisco, to what she would be doing now if she were still at Central High. Probably eating lunch alone at a desk in the newspaper room. If it were a year ago, she would be sitting in the bleachers with her best friend, Hannah, but Hannah joined band spring semester and fell in love with her fellow trombone player and everything changed. Posey surveyed the room, the club members who not only tolerated her—they seemed to maybe even like her. They had a group text thread! This was good. This was better than her life in the city.

The bell rang and the AV Club packed it up. Posey was galvanized, unable to think of anything but the next steps. As she stowed her belongings in her backpack, she was already mentally scrawling notes of who they should interview first: the husband, an administrator or teacher from Wild Pines High, or the police?

"See you after school," Sal called back as he ducked out the door.

"Yep, see you then," she said.

The next two periods would be excruciating. Algebra. PE. Who cared about that nonsense when a teacher had disappeared into thin air, there were stories to tell, and mysteries to solve?

NINE

Wild Pines High had one entrance to the school, a set of enormous double doors with a transom window portraying an enormous stained-glass raven—the school mascot, as Posey had learned from football players making the bleating *caw caw* sounds throughout the halls to display their school spirit.

The first thing she had noticed when visiting the school in the summer was how peaceful it seemed, more like a retreat than an educational facility. The creek that ran on the right side of it added a sweet white noise to the creaking sounds of tree branches. Right now, though, there was none of that; there was no tranquility at three p.m. on a Thursday. There was only pandemonium as five hundred students poured out of the doors. Posey stood on the side of the staircase, watching the students flow out onto the emerald sprawl of lawn.

"Hello?" said a voice. "Anyone home?"

She felt a soft tug on her backpack. Sal stood at her side, holding a small, blue-painted ceramic . . . something. It was a bit lopsided and the painting was sloppy.

"What's that?" she asked.

"Oh," Sal said, looking at it like he'd just noticed it was there. "A cup."

"For what?"

"What do you think?" he asked, sounding annoyed. "To drink out of."

Posey could already tell this was going to be an interesting afternoon. This boy seemed volatile. Maybe it was what Yash told her—maybe it was knowing that he'd punched someone hard enough that he faced possible expulsion. She wasn't afraid of him, though. Posey was confident that she knew how to handle difficult people. There was that, and there was also the pepper spray on her keychain in her backpack.

"Okay," she said. "Where do we start?"

"I think we should go talk to Doug. That's Molly's—Ms. Moses's—husband. He's probably home right now."

Posey raised an eyebrow. "Can I ask you something?"

Sal didn't answer, which she took as a yes.

"How do you know so much about her personal life?" Posey asked.

"It's a long story."

"I have a great attention span."

He breathed in deeply without taking his eyes off her. "Look, do you want to go interview Doug or not?"

"I do. Where's their house?"

"Not far. It's on the other side of Mile High Drive."

"That's where I live."

"I can give you the address, we can both drive there?"

"I don't drive."

"Why not?"

Posey shrugged. "I never needed to."

"Okay," he said slowly. "Well, I guess you could ride with me?"

"Sure, thanks."

They were among the last of the human flood to head toward the parking lot, making their way across the lawn where some students were playing Frisbee. This morning when she'd arrived at school, Posey never would have imagined she would be leaving school with Sal Zamora, and that the AV Club would have agreed to dive straight into an investigative report. It was exciting to know that life was so full of surprises. Who knew, maybe by tomorrow, they might crack the case and Ms. Moses would be found? What a relief that would be, to know there was nothing dangerous afoot, to know she was safe. Posey thought about the story her dad had told her about the heiress with dissociative fugue.

"What are you thinking about?" Sal asked her.

It struck Posey as an invasive question and yet flattering that he would care enough to ask. Posey looked at him and smiled. "Dissociative fugue."

"What?" he asked, his checkered Vans squelching the grass.

"Oh, this . . . mental condition that causes people to forget who they are. Some kind of amnesia. My dad was telling me about it."

"That's . . . wild. What does your dad do?"

"He's a journalist. Editor in chief at the *Sierra Tribune*."

"Oh. Right."

"What do your parents do?"

"Nothing."

"*Nothing?*"

"Yeah."

That's all he offered. Her interest was piqued, but Posey didn't press further.

Passing under a tower of pines, the shade dropped the temperature and pricked Posey with a shiver. She followed Sal toward the lot, studying him as she lagged a footstep behind. On the back of his beloved hoodie, the uniform he'd worn each day this week, there was a patch with a skull sewn on. The stitching was neat, tight, careful, and she wondered if Sal had sewn it on himself.

"That lady that your dad wrote about," Sal asked, hands in pockets, eyes glued to his sneakers as they walked along the sidewalk on the parking lot's perimeter. "Did she end up . . . okay?"

Posey fell into step alongside him. "I didn't get the end of the story, but I assume so."

"Because Ms. Moses wouldn't have just *left*," he said. "She wouldn't have done that."

Posey nodded, not sure how to respond. Her breath got shorter, her stomach tightened, and she realized she was thinking of her mother. People left the people they claimed to love all the time. It happened every day. It happened sometimes without reasonable explanation. The realization was like a void opening below her, threatening to swallow her. But like a tightrope walker, she kept herself steady and tried to pay no attention to it. She perked her lips up into a smile.

"We're going to find her," she assured Sal.

He heaved a sigh big enough to move a small mountain and stopped in front of a van, patting it with affection.

"This is Gramps," Sal said.

"Gramps," Posey repeated. "It's . . ."

It was shocking, really. A lot to take in. First, it looked like a relic from the 1970s: light blue, stylish, and long. Then there was the fact it was rusted in some spots and so battered it almost seemed like someone had smashed it with a baseball bat. And were those *bullet holes* in the hood? On top of it all, someone had gone through the effort of painting some kind of beach landscape complete with a sunset and palm trees. The paint was vivid and the mural appeared recent, as if it was meant to cover the damage below.

"It's very unique," she finally said.

He unlocked her door. This wasn't a car with a fob where you beeped it open, it was a key-in-a-keyhole situation. As Sal rounded to the driver's side, Posey checked herself with her hand on the ajar passenger door and realized she was entering a vehicle with a boy who might or might not have violent tendencies and whom she knew almost nothing about. This sounded like it could be the beginning of a news story that she didn't want to star in. She took her phone out, danced a few steps to the front of the van, and snapped a quick picture of the front of it. Her phone was getting one bar, the best her reception could muster in most of Wild Pines, but she sent the photo and texted her dad.

> Hi Dad! I'm going to investigate the
> disappearance of our teacher Ms. Moses
> with my fellow AV Club codirector,
> Salvatore Zamora. We are going to Ms.
> Moses's house, which is somewhere near
> our neighborhood on the north side of Mile
> High Drive. This is Salvatore's vehicle
> and his license plate number. I have my
> phone's tracking on if you need it.

Codirector? Already? he texted back within seconds. Proud of you, Pose. Be safe.

She pocketed her phone in her peacoat and climbed into the passenger seat.

"What was that?" Sal asked her, a baffled look on his face. "Why are you taking pictures of my van?"

"To send to my dad," Posey said, clipping her seat belt. "Just in case."

Sal's hand remained frozen on his keys in the ignition. "In case of what?"

Posey turned to Sal, smoothing her bangs. "Sal, you do read the news, don't you? Bad things happen to young women like me every day."

He gave her a look now as if she were a fool. "What, you scared I'm going to hurt you or something?"

"I'm not scared," she said. "I'm *prepared*."

They locked eyes stubbornly. Sal continued gazing back for a few seconds and then rolled his eyes and started the car, muttering, "Whatever" under his breath.

See? She could win a staring contest whenever she wanted.

The engine rattled and sputtered to life. The inside of Sal's vehicle was as bizarre as the outside, and Posey wasn't sure what this said about his character. The front was separated from the back with a curtain patterned with little bats. A cartoon pinup devil girl dangled from his rearview, a bunch of green bananas sunbathed on his dashboard, and some sort of yellow liquid in a jar sloshed around on the floor between them—Posey didn't want to ask follow-up questions about that one. Next to the jar she really hoped wasn't filled with urine, there was a toothbrush, floss, and toothpaste in a transparent zip-up bag. Perhaps he was one of those rare people so diligent about dental hygiene he flossed and brushed after every meal. Posey realized she had never seen his teeth before. On the rare occasion he smiled, it was tight-lipped.

The two sat in a heavy silence as they inched their way through the parking lot traffic. Eventually, Sal turned on the radio.

"This is Bam Bam Sam kickin' out the jams for the KWPP Wiiiiiild Pines radio," an obnoxious voice boomed from the speakers. "Crankin' the heavy tunes for all you WP goons—"

"Hate that guy," Sal muttered before changing it to a staticky channel with smooth jazz. Though he scowled at it, he left it there. Posey didn't mind it. She preferred music without words, so she could hear her own thoughts loud and clear. Finally, the van made it out of the parking lot and onto the highway road.

How people drove revealed a lot about their character. Sal used his turn signal and obeyed the speed limit, both hands on the wheel. He was a careful, steady driver. She studied his profile as he drove and wondered, with a burning curiosity, what was inside him.

"So," Posey said. "The elephant in the van. What's the real story about you and Ms. Moses? I can't cover this story if I'm walking into it without context."

"She's . . . a mentor to me."

"A mentor," Posey repeated, keeping her eyes on him as he kept his eyes on the winding road. "Could you elaborate?"

"She just, you know, she cares about me. She's helped me get on my feet." He glanced at Posey. "Life hasn't been easy on me."

"I'm sorry to hear that. What does 'helped me get on my feet' mean exactly? Can you be more specific?"

"Look, I know what you're getting at," Sal said, sitting up straighter in his seat. "There's not some *thing* going on between me and Ms. Moses. Don't believe the crap you hear in the halls."

"Then why is there an investigation?"

"Because, I don't know. I don't know why. Someone made some report to admin. They thought they saw something—it wasn't what they thought it was."

Posey's mind flashed back to the familiarity she saw the other day in Ms. Moses's office. She didn't mention it, but the memory was there, percolating.

"Who is 'they'?" she asked.

"I don't know who made the report."

"What did 'they' think 'they' saw?"

"Jesus Christ, Posey," he snapped. "Do you ever stop asking questions?"

"Sometimes," she said evenly. "When people give me satisfying answers."

Sal was silent long enough that they lost the radio signal, and static swallowed the elevator music. He turned it off.

"My parents are fuckups," he said finally. "I always thought I was destined to be a fuckup, too. Last year, things got bad and Mol—Ms. Moses helped me out of the gutter. Literally pulled my ass off the ground with her own two hands. Took me to meetings. Brought me home and made me dinner when I had nothing to eat. Let me crash on her couch when I had nowhere to go. Someone saw me leaving her house one morning and didn't like it and they reported it to admin and then this whole 'investigation' started. Which—they're not investigating shit. Nothing has happened with it since May, when they opened the case. It's just a way to sabotage Ms. Moses."

It was a lot for Posey to take in. She thought about how helpful it would be to have this recorded on her phone the way she did in newspaper interviews, but that would be a tactless ask here and now. Instead, she tried to quickly burn the details into her brain. Hearing Sal's rough backstory stirred her sympathy for him. Now she understood and forgave his prickliness. She didn't say so, but she saw a familiar kind of pain in him.

"And why would they want to sabotage her?" she asked, quieter.

"I don't know. She made a lot of enemies in admin. She's been pushing for an investigation of her own into the theater department's funding."

Posey couldn't stop herself now, this was all too much important information for their report. She took out her phone and was about to ask Sal to repeat what he was saying when Sal pulled up into the driveway of a gray ranch house nestled in the shadows of tall trees. They parked next to several motorcycles in various states of disrepair. The house had Christmas lights strung up despite it being September, and two dark-haired mannequins stood on the lawn, both wearing nothing but oversized T-shirts that said KILLER LIVER in a font and color like dripping blood.

"This is it," he said. "Looks like Doug's not home. I don't know where he'd be. Let's go inside, I'm sure he'll be back soon."

Sal jumped out of the van, slamming the door right as Posey said, "Wait!"

He was jogging toward the house, high-fiving a mannequin. Posey grabbed her backpack and hurried after him. She could hear barking from the backyard.

"If he's not home," she said behind him, following him up the two steps to the porch, "shouldn't we go somewhere else?"

Sal opened the front door and let himself inside, leaving it open for Posey to follow. What on earth was he doing? And wow! People in Wild Pines were trusting. Posey couldn't imagine leaving a door unlocked, but this was some of that small-town living she was still getting used to.

"Sal, we can't just go inside their house," Posey said from the doormat.

"Don't worry about it. I'm allowed. Come check this out," he called back. "And don't let any of the cats out."

From here, Posey could see the living room, its freaky, psychedelic paintings, and a couch covered in a tapestry. Two cats slept on it and another cat slept on a cat tower. There was a wall of records and books and another mannequin, this one also wearing a KILLER LIVER shirt. It wasn't what she would expect a teacher's house to look like. She tiptoed inside after Sal, her heart racing, feeling like an intruder. She'd always wondered what it must feel like to be a detective who got a warrant and was able to enter people's houses, uninvited. Was this the same fear-tinged excitement?

"Sal," she said, closing the door quietly behind her. "This feels wrong."

"You're right. It does feel wrong."

"Besides breaking and entering, what if this guy's dangerous? What if he's responsible—"

"He's not. You don't know him at all. He's like an uncle to me. Come look at this."

Posey followed his voice through the living room and back into a bright yellow dining room. Sal stood pointing at a calendar, where a Persian cat was wearing a knit hat.

"Awww," Posey said.

"No, look at what I'm pointing at." He tapped the page, his

finger on the date Wednesday, September 11, where the word *Anniversary* was scrawled next to a heart. "Yesterday was their anniversary. She wouldn't have left right before their anniversary." His finger moved to Friday, September 13, where the word *Court* were scrawled in the same handwriting. "And she was supposed to take me to court tomorrow."

"To court?" Posey asked.

Sal pulled his hoodie down, revealing his shaggy hair that had been hidden all day. There was something about him that was different since entering this house—as if he had warmed up, his eyes bright. "She's helping me get emancipated."

She had questions but held her tongue. Her heart was still beating wildly from the rush of entering a stranger's house and her knees felt a little weak.

"Sal, I don't think we should be here," she whispered.

He strode over to the refrigerator, opening the door and pointing to a vibrant array of vegetables and fruit. "She just bought all these groceries. Why would she leave if she had just gone shopping?" He gestured to the back door, where dogs barked from the other side. "She has three dogs and three cats, rescues. You think she'd leave them?"

"Sal," she said again, but he'd already closed the door and moved past her into a dark hallway. She heard the *thump* of a cupboard opening.

"All her medication," he yelled. "She has bad insomnia, can't sleep without her pills." She heard the rattle of pills in a plastic container. "She left them here."

"Sal, this is veering into illegal territory," Posey said, raising her voice. She stood at the end of the hallway, refusing to follow him any farther. "I'm not comfortable using any of this information in our coverage, it's highly unethical."

"What about the First Amendment?" he called.

She squinted at the dust in the air. "The First Amendment doesn't protect you if you're breaking and entering."

At that exact moment, the front door opened and a tall, long-haired man stepped into the house. He wore a flannel shirt and ripped jeans. His eyes were wide and shadowed by the bags under them, his face unshaven. He had a mannequin head in one hand and a stack of papers in the other and froze when he saw Posey. The grip of terror that flooded Posey—the feeling that she was in the wrong place at the wrong time—mixed with complete and utter shame. As he stepped closer to her, she exchanged a worried glance with the severed plastic head he held by its long black hair. She knew this was bad. This was very, very bad.

"Who the hell are you and why the *hell* are you in my house?" he asked.

"Um," Posey said, her brain scrambling for an excuse, but coming up with nothing but the truth. She held out a shaking hand. "Hi, my name's Posey Spade and I'm from the Wild Pines High AV Club."

TEN

"Doug, hey," Sal said, popping out of the hallway.

Doug's face visibly relaxed. He set the severed head on a shelf and came over to Sal, doing a fist bump that ended in a back-clapping hug. Posey let out a little breath of relief watching the interaction, putting her extended hand back in her pocket. The faint fine lines on his face put Doug somewhere in the range of forty years old, but there was something about his style and the way he carried himself that made him seem younger. It wasn't any surprise that he and Ms. Moses were married. He also had an air about him that made Posey think it wouldn't be a surprise to see Doug coming out of a cannabis dispensary.

"What's up, brother," Doug said, stepping back. "Hey, Posey." He waved the stack of papers in the air. "So check it out—I was just out getting some flyers made. You think you could take a stack to school tomorrow and pass them around to your buds?"

Posey nodded, still recovering from the adrenaline rush of being discovered in a stranger's house. Didn't this man care that they had entered his house without permission? Apparently not.

Doug handed each of them some flyers and Posey resisted the urge to sniff the fresh ink on the paper. A black-and-white head-shot of Ms. Moses smiled back and Posey got a little pang in her middle at the sight of her.

MISSING!!!
MOLLY MOSES
Age: 38   Height: 5'3"   Eye color: Brown
Hair color: Red   Weight: 125 pounds
Driving a black 2020 Ford Escape
**Tues Sept 7, Molly Moses never returned
home from her night shift @ Pickins
Drugstore. Have you seen her?**

"I'm trying to get these everywhere I can," Doug said.

"Of course," Posey said. "Sal and I will flyer the school tomorrow." She cleared her throat, gently nudging Sal, who was still gazing sadly at the flyer in her hand. "Doug," she said. "Sal and I want to interview you for a report we're doing with the AV Club on Ms. Moses's disappearance. Could we sit down with you for a few minutes?"

"A report?" Doug asked, brow wrinkled.

"We're doing a news story," Sal said. "You know, to get people's attention."

"Man, that's a great idea," Doug said. "Where do you want to interview me?"

Posey surveyed her surroundings—the lamplit living room

that faced the trees, the dining room that faced the sun. The natural lighting in there would make for a much better frame. "Maybe at your table?"

They moved into the dining room, where Doug slumped into a chair. Posey opened her backpack, tucking the flyers away. She retrieved her purple pen and notebook and opened it to a page. Sal looked over her shoulder.

"You want to film or you want to interview?" Posey asked Sal.

"I'll film," Sal said.

"Please don't get me in the shot—just him."

"Got it."

Posey handed him her phone in video mode. She took a seat across from Doug as Sal started recording, walking slowly around the table until he came to a stop. He seemed to be trying to get a much more artistic shot than she would have attempted.

"Are we rolling?" Posey asked.

Sal nodded.

"Doug, you ready?" Posey asked gently.

Slowly, like a man with the weight of the world on his shoulders, Doug took his head from his hands and nodded, bleary-eyed. "Let's do it."

Transcript

POSEY
Thanks for sitting down with us today, Doug.

Can you tell us when you first realized your wife was missing?

DOUG

So Molly works nights at the Pickins Drugstore
off the highway near Blue Mirror Vista, right?
She's got the closing shift, usually home around
ten thirty. When eleven rolled around, I called her
cell—nothing. You know how service is out here,
so I called Pickins to see if I could reach someone
there. It was closed.

POSEY

At what point did you contact the police?

DOUG

I was up all night. I drove to the station as
soon as it opened the next morning.

POSEY

Can you tell me what the police have done?

DOUG

Nothing. They think she left on her own.
They said they'd be investigating and asked me
some questions, but nothing's happened since.

POSEY

What kinds of questions?

DOUG

Well, to me—about our marriage, issues we've
been having.

POSEY

"Issues"?

DOUG

Look, I won't lie, Molly and I hit a rough patch. She's
been working sixty hours a week between both her jobs.

POSEY

So . . . do you think it's possible she left?

DOUG

No. No way.

POSEY

Why not?

DOUG

So many reasons, man. It was the night before our
anniversary. We had reservations at Marceau.

She wouldn't have left her students without saying goodbye. She was going to go to court for this . . .

(Glances across the room)

. . . student of hers. She left her cell at work—where'd she have gone without her phone?
And I've been checking our bank accounts nonstop. She's not spending money anywhere.

POSEY
What about her car?

DOUG
No one's seen her car. It's like she left Pickins Tuesday night and disappeared into thin air.

POSEY
Why do you think the police aren't taking this case more seriously?

At this point, Doug leaned back and crossed his arms, gazing out the back door and shaking his head. Along with the three dogs running to and fro, there was a deck out there and a grill and a clothesline that ran along the railing with T-shirts strung along it. Behind that, it was treetops and skies so bright they seemed to scream blue.

"Can we talk, like, off the record?" Doug asked.

Posey raised an eyebrow and exchanged a look with Sal. He pressed a button on the phone and pocketed it. Her heart skipped a beat at the challenge of handling an off-the-record conversation. If a journalist agreed to go off the record, it meant they ethically couldn't report or even repeat what they heard. It also meant she had established trust with her source.

"Okay," Posey said.

"If anything happened to Molly, I would look at the cops and the school. I bet they're covering their *butts* right now. You get what I'm saying?"

Posey nodded, though it was such a vague statement she didn't quite understand how it fit. She opened her mouth to ask a follow-up question, when Doug's phone started blaring on the tabletop, an abrasive heavy metal song with a singer screaming like they were on fire. It was such a horrid noise and shock to her ears that Posey gasped.

Doug squinted at his phone. "Oh, I've gotta get this."

He stood up, the chair screeching on the floor as he answered the call and ducked into the hallway, shutting a door behind him. Posey and Sal were left alone at the table. He took her phone out of his pocket and slid it back her way again.

"You think that's enough?" she asked.

"For now. We might need to follow up later. For now, I say we head to the police station."

Sal grimaced. "Do we have to?"

"Why are you making that face?"

"The cops aren't exactly members of my fan club."

"And who is, Sal?"

"Harsh," Sal said.

Posey tapped her pen on her paper. She only shook her head. "Listen, act professional. Put your personal feelings aside and approach this neutrally. We'll just ask a few questions and then be on our way."

He didn't protest. As she slipped her backpack over her shoulder, Sal grabbed her phone and held it up in the air. "How about I grab some B-roll real quick?"

B-roll, supplemental footage of a news show. Posey nodded, delighted that Sal was thinking of such things. "Great idea."

As Sal wandered around and took shots of the calendar and a few framed photos of Ms. Moses, Posey stood near the hallway, listening to the tone of the conversation Doug was having behind closed doors. It sounded heated, intense, but she couldn't make out the words.

It was almost four o'clock by the time they left the Moseses' house, and Posey's stomach was grumbling, but she ignored it for the time being.

"Next stop: the police station," Sal said as he started the engine. "You ready, boss?"

"Let's do it," she said.

As they pulled away from the house, she could see Doug's silhouette was in the window, as if he was watching them leave.

ELEVEN

As they drove, Posey watched the wilderness blaze by her window. A doe and her fawns ate grass by the roadside and Posey got a shiver, remembering when her dad almost hit one the other day.

"So you think Doug has nothing to do with Ms. Moses's disappearance," Posey said.

"Think? I know. Come on. You heard the man."

"You know Occam's razor? The simplest explanation is likely the correct one."

"Yeah, well, Occam can kiss my ass."

Posey watched Sal's profile, his glare glued to the road. "You do realize that in most cases when a woman goes missing, it's the husband."

"It's *not* the husband."

"I'm afraid having you reporting this story is a conflict of interest." She took peppermint ChapStick from her skirt's pocket and applied it. "If we were a legitimate journalistic enterprise, this story would be assigned to someone else."

"What are you saying?" he asked, raising his voice. "After

that, you're—what? Suspecting Doug? He's the only person even looking for her right now, how does that make any sense?"

"It would certainly make him look less guilty. If it was him and he were smart, this is exactly how he'd be acting."

"You're joking. *Doug?*"

"Considering that they were having marital trouble, I actually think it's far more likely she might have left to blow off steam—"

"You don't know what you're talking about," Sal said sharply.

Posey sat back, stung by Sal's tone. She wanted to tell him she absolutely knew what she was talking about. Sometimes people had breakdowns. Sometimes they got sick of their lives. Sometimes people ran away and didn't come back.

And get real, sometimes husbands killed their wives.

"I'm going to text the footage to the group," she said quietly.

> Hey all! We got a quick interview with Doug Moses and some extra footage to go along with it. We're heading to the police station now to see if we can get any new information.

Yash texted back right away. Once you're done filming I can edit it together!

Posey smiled. Ahh, Yash. A breath of fresh air.

Lexy texted a thinking-face emoji and asked, What am I doing again?

Posey replied, Lexy, try to work on a narrative. Just a paragraph for the intro and end to sum up the case.

She slipped her phone back into her pocket. Sal pulled into the parking lot of the police station, a brown boxy building that looked like a trailer. There were two cruisers parked outside and only one other car in the lot. This was not a place that saw much action. Posey wouldn't be surprised if a tumbleweed blew by. As she started to open her door, Posey felt a tug on her jacket.

"Hey," Sal said. "Look. I'm sorry. You're right. This is a conflict of interest, isn't it?"

Posey froze, looking back at him, uncertain how to respond.

"So maybe . . . I should stay in the van while you go in there," Sal said. "See, the cops—as soon as they see me with you—it's like, your credibility's going to be in question."

"Geez, Sal. What have you done?" she asked.

"I could write a book, Posey." He sighed. "Cops in this town have nothing to do but bother me."

"Fine, if you don't want to go, I'll do it on my own," she said, hopping out of the van. She slammed the door shut, strode toward the station, and didn't look back.

The truth? She was grateful to take a break from Sal and his incessant negativity. It was like stepping out into the sunshine after shivering in the shady woods.

The police station didn't feel like a police station. Compared to the entire block of austere buildings that comprised the San Francisco Police Department headquarters, the Wild Pines Police Department looked more like a temporary building put in place while a renovation was underway. Inside, it smelled like glue.

There was a banner that said PROTECT AND SERVE in Comic Sans. Comic Sans! Really? Perhaps even more shocking was the woman behind the front desk, who was enormously pregnant and sleeping so deeply in her office chair that she snored.

Well, this was awkward. Posey stepped closer to the front desk and cleared her throat. The woman—white, cropped hair, bespectacled, wearing zebra-printed sweats—opened her eyes and sat up straight, wiping a bit of drool from her hot-pink mouth corner.

"Good morning!" the woman said, then glanced at the clock on the wall. "Good afternoon," she tried again. "How can I help you?"

"I'd like to speak to someone about the disappearance of Molly Moses," Posey said. "I'm from the AV Club at Wild Pines High and we're doing a story about it."

"That's great," the woman said with a big smile. Then, as if she realized the smile was inappropriate considering the circumstances, her face slackened and became more somber. "I mean, it's terrible. It's so terrible to hear about her disappearance. Let me go get the deputy, I know he was out earlier today but I think he's back in his office." She raised her voice to a shrill scream. "*Deputy!*"

It was like a whistle piercing Posey's eardrums. She flinched at the sound.

"Yep," a male voice called from an open door down the hall.

"There's a girl here to see you!" the woman shouted.

"Who is it?" the male voice shouted back.

The woman whispered, "What's your name, honey?"

"Posey Spade," Posey answered.

"Posey Spade!" the woman yelled.

"Who?" he yelled back.

"Her name is *Posey Spade*!"

Posey fought the urge to stick her fingertips in her ears. It was bad enough to have people talking about you like you weren't there—but yelling about you was far worse.

"It's about Molly Moses, deputy!" the woman shrieked. "This girl Posey's from the high school."

A head popped out of a door that couldn't have been ten feet away from the front desk. "Come on in," he said, beckoning her.

Posey thanked the woman and headed into the office. A lanky white man in a tan uniform sat behind a desk and a bulky computer that must have been twice Posey's age. He looked young, twentysomething, but prematurely balding. His desk was neat—a stack of papers and manila folders, a jar of ballpoint pens—but the rest of the office was a complete disaster. Leaning towers of boxes, empty water bottles and to-go food containers on the floor. On the wall, framed certificates were hung crookedly. There was one photograph, and it was of this man with his arm around someone in a giant bear costume.

Wild Pines was truly wild, wasn't it?

"Thanks for taking the time. Again, I'm Posey Spade, co-director of the AV Club at Wild Pines High School. I'm here to ask you a few questions about Molly Moses."

"This for a school report or something?"

94

"Yes," she said, taking out her phone and holding it up in the air. "Do you mind?"

"Oh, on camera?"

"If that's okay?" she asked, with her best, most encouraging smile.

"Sure. Shoot."

As soon as she pressed the record button, she noticed that the deputy seemed to harden his face into something more serious. He stilled himself and looked right at the camera with a grim, tight-lipped frown. It was like watching an actor the second the lights hit them.

Transcript

POSEY

Can I ask what the Wild Pines PD is doing
to investigate the disappearance of Ms. Moses?

DEPUTY

Well, it's only been a couple days now,
remember, but we've been busy looking into
a lot of leads over here at WPPD.

POSEY

Can you be specific? What leads?

DEPUTY

Unfortunately I can't get too into the nitty-gritty,
as this is an open investigation, but we've
interviewed a number of individuals who were
the last to see Molly Moses.

POSEY

What is that number, exactly?

DEPUTY

Uh . . . off the top of my head, I can't tell you.
I'll have to get back to you on that.

POSEY

Is there a plan for a search party
in the works?

DEPUTY

(Pause)
That is a possibility.

POSEY

Is foul play suspected?

DEPUTY

At this point, no. The majority of missing

persons cases end up being domestic disputes.

POSEY

Are you saying you think Ms. Moses left of her own
accord?

DEPUTY

It's possible. If anyone has information
on the whereabouts of Molly Moses, please
contact the Wild Pines Police Department.

POSEY

Are you the lead on this case?

DEPUTY

I certainly am.

POSEY

Is there a reason that you're at your desk today
and not out in the field looking for answers?

DEPUTY

(Laughing)

Well, I hate to break it to you, kid, but even
police officers need breaks. Thank you
for coming in here today, it's been a pleasure.

Posey lingered for an extra moment and then finally pressed the red button on her phone. As soon as she did, the deputy stood and put his Stetson hat on. "Thanks for swinging by, hon. Good luck with your school project."

Hon? If there was one thing Posey hated, it was condescension. The smile on her face was beginning to hurt her cheeks. She nodded at him.

"Thanks for having me, Deputy . . ." Posey mentally slapped herself, realizing she never stopped to ask his name ahead of time. What an amateur move that was for a reporter. She squinted at the shiny, fake-gold badge on his lapel. It couldn't be his name, it couldn't. But it was! ". . . Deputy Butts."

Posey had a formidable poker face, but she almost—almost—burst into laughter as she said his name.

"Walk you out?" he asked cheerfully.

They walked out together, Deputy Butts whistling as they passed the front desk, where the pregnant woman was now on her phone talking about a recipe for egg salad.

"That much mayonnaise? Are you sure? How do you feel about raisins?"

As if the thought of raisins in egg salad wasn't disgusting

enough, Deputy Butts walked behind the desk and kissed the woman's head and said, "Bye bye, shnookums" and she put her hand over the phone and said, "Bye bye, Deputy" before resuming her conversation. The repulsion on Posey's face must have been visible, because he quickly said, "That's my wife, Sherry. Isn't she something?"

Posey nodded and followed Deputy Butts outside, watched him stretch and yawn as he considered the skyline. This didn't seem like a man who was operating with a sense of urgency. He didn't seem like a man in an under-resourced department scrambling to find a lead. In fact, he was moving at the pace of a man who just ate a giant meal and was now ready for a nap.

"You take care now," he said to Posey. "Stay safe."

"I will," she said, chin up, eyeing him for an extra moment before crossing the parking lot. As she did, she could feel his gaze on her back. She climbed into the van, put her seat belt on, and looked out the window. Deputy Butts stood with his hands on his hips and put some Wayfarer sunglasses on. Then he spun on his heel and headed toward his cruiser.

"How was it?" Sal asked, turning down the oldies playing on the radio.

"Weird," she said, sending the clip to the group. "Very."

TWELVE

Her hunger was becoming hard to ignore. Posey proposed that Pickins, the drugstore Ms. Moses worked at, be their last stop of the day. Sal agreed, and they drove the stretch of highway that led to the outskirts of Wild Pines. A shopping center sat in the middle of a meadow: the drugstore, a taco stand, a gas station. As they pulled into the half-full lot, Posey's phone vibrated. She checked her messages. Athena, who so far had been silent in the group text thread, now suddenly came alive and blazing with all caps.

> DEPUTY BUTTHOLE?? THAT SHOULDVE COME WITH A CONTENT WARNING.

Lexy added, ok that clip wtf butts doesn't even seem concerned

Jeremiah chimed in, check me out, club, with an attached audio file.

Sal turned off the engine. Posey put her phone in the air, pressing play, her brow furrowed. An electronic drumbeat hammered in the air with what sounded like a synthesizer and an electric guitar. A high, dramatic voice came in and sang with gusto: *"Wiiiild Piiiines Buuuuzz!"* Then the song ended with an emphatic crash cymbal and the guitar's distortion rang out for a second.

"What *is* that?" Sal asked.

"I think Jeremiah wrote a theme song," Posey said, a smile spreading on her lips. She played it again. She was pleasantly stunned at the gesture, that Jeremiah had thought to do this.

"He's a machine," Sal said. "Seriously talented. He plays every instrument, he sings, he dances. He'll be famous someday, I swear."

That's amazing! Posey texted back with three applauding yellow hands. She slipped her phone back into her peacoat pocket and they headed out of the van.

The sky was starting to darken, the bright last gasp of afternoon sunshine backlighting the trees. Posey and Sal walked up the sidewalk toward the Pickins entrance, passing a row of red shopping carts and a shelf of potted cacti. The automatic doors opened for them with a whisper. There was an explosion of Halloween decorations at the front of the store. A robotic witch cackled at them as they walked past rows and rows of merchandise and gleaming linoleum floors. Posey and Sal exchanged a tired glance, raising their eyebrows, and waited in line to talk to the cashier.

"I'm hungry," Posey said, staring at the Halloween candy.

"Why is everything Halloween already?" Sal plunged his hands into his hoodie's pocket. "It's barely September."

"What's your favorite holiday?" she asked.

"I hate holidays."

"You *hate* holidays."

"Why are you giving me that look?"

"Because no one hates all holidays, that's the silliest thing I've ever heard."

Sal didn't respond, but he bent his neck back to stare at the ceiling as if he was tired of Posey. Honestly, she was getting a little tired of Sal, too. He brooded like it was his brand. He was so frowny and tight-lipped she still hadn't seen his teeth. Hating holidays? Absurd.

"Next," a cashier said.

They made their way to the front counter. Posey fixed a smile on her face.

"Hi, I'm Posey Spade with the *Wild Pines Buzz*," she said, the name just slipping out. "I'm here to ask some questions about Molly Moses. May I speak to you briefly?"

The woman behind the counter was short and ruddy-cheeked, her hair up in a messy ponytail. Posey thought she looked maternal and gnomelike. Her red Pickins vest had the name *El* embroidered on it over the word *Manager*. El looked doubtfully at them. When her voice came out, it was raspy like someone who had smoked all their life. "You're . . . a reporter?"

"Yes," Posey said. "From Wild Pines High School."

"Ms. Moses is our teacher," Sal said.

El shook her head and twisted the crystal necklace she was wearing. "Jesus, isn't it terrible? Isn't it the worst thing?" El pulled a placard that said REGISTER CLOSED and placed it on the counter. "Deb," she called to the other cashier at the end of the row of registers. "I'm going on my ten."

"Don't have too much fun now," Deb called back.

El beckoned Sal and Posey to follow her, leading the way out of the drugstore. Out front, El took a piece of gum out of her vest pocket and chomped it. "So how can I help?"

"Sal," Posey whispered, handing him the phone with her video camera ready.

Sal nodded and stepped back to get a good shot.

"I hope you don't mind us filming a short interview?" Posey asked El. "This is for an investigative report we're doing for school. We're hoping to help find her."

"Fire away," El said. "Anything that I can do for Molly. I'm sick over it, I couldn't sleep last night. Tossing and turning and wondering what in God's name happened to her."

Transcript

POSEY

From what we've heard, it sounds like
Ms. Moses's Tuesday night shift at Pickins
is the last place she was seen. Can you tell
me anything you know about that night?

EL

Well, I can tell you because I was there.

Molly and me worked the closing shift together
Tuesdays. Wasn't a busy night. Never usually
is, I'd been thinking about closing up earlier,
especially since I had to fire that little thief
Abby Frost—Molly was the one who told me
she'd been stealing from the register right
under my dang nose, can you imagine?
I hear Abby's working nights over at Gas Up,
I've got half a mind to go rip her a new one—
Actually, don't air that. You won't air that,
right? That's a whole other can of beans.

Anyway, Moll seemed stressed that night, not
sure why, didn't ask, not my business, I was doing
inventory anyway and not working close to her
all night so what the hell do I know? Here's
the part that's weird: I saw a black truck drive
through the parking lot two separate times
that night. A man was driving it, a guy with
short buzzed hair, and he had this angry look
on his face. Okay and then the next day, when I
heard about Molly going missing, I was doing
some googling, you know, this and that,
and I find this story about Erin Englin—you
know about her?

POSEY

Erin Englin?

EL

Oh, so tragic. The stuff of nightmares. She's this girl who was murdered—strangled—and her body was found on the other side of the highway about a year ago. She wasn't a local, she was a college student in Sacramento, but you know the last person who was seen with Erin? A guy in a black truck with a buzzed haircut.

(Long pause)

POSEY

Are you . . . suggesting that it's possible Ms. Moses was . . .

EL

I'm saying we could have a serial killer on our hands. I pray—pray—it's not true. But I've been sick to my stomach thinking about it.
(She turns to the camera, points directly at it)

You young people better be safe, you hear?

Learn some martial arts. I'm a brown belt.

(El does a high kick)

Because I need to know I can protect myself.

POSEY
Um . . . thank you for the advice. El, one last
thing. She left her cell phone here at work the
night of her disappearance, is that right?

EL
She did. I found it the next morning. Her
husband came to get it and ask questions
when we opened. Later on, cops came
by, watched the footage we have of Molly
leaving the store. They didn't see much.
Molly was parked right there. Then she drove
out and we haven't seen her since.

They wrapped up the interview and El issued another stern
reminder about serial killers, showing them a karate move that
could stun someone's sternum and knock the wind out of them.
Posey felt like she had the wind knocked out of her just listening
to El's rapid-fire monologue. El disappeared back into the glowing drugstore. The sun was beginning to fade, the air was getting
chilly fast. Posey and Sal widened their eyes at each other.

"What the hell was that?" Sal asked.

"I do not know, Sal."

"A serial killer?"

"There was zero concrete evidence to support that."

"Some girl was *murdered*? Do you think that Ms. Moses could actually—"

"I don't, Sal." She stepped a little closer to him, wondering if she should offer him a hug. He looked shaken. Understandably so. It was a wild accusation to throw out there and one that sickened her to entertain. Which was exactly why Posey had to push it from her mind, focus on the facts at hand, and urge Sal to do the same. "Look, we have to try to hold it together. I know that was hard to hear. We're not going to fall down that rabbit hole, okay? I'm sure wherever Ms. Moses is, she's alive, there's no serial killer involved, there's a more logical explanation."

Still, Posey couldn't ignore the goose bumps at the thought of a murderer on the loose. And she could tell Sal was scared.

"The cases sound entirely different. I think it's clear El's not exactly the most reputable source," she said. "You know?"

Though he remained pale with what looked like fear, he nodded.

She glanced up at the glowing Pickins sign and then back at Sal. "Are you going to be okay?"

"Yeah," he said with a sniff. "You're right. The serial killer thing—I mean, it's so unlikely. I can't let my mind go there."

Posey nodded. "How about we call it a night?"

"Okay."

Posey snapped a quick shot of Pickins and the parking spot where Ms. Moses's car was last seen and sent the shots to the group text.

That's a wrap for today, she texted. El said some wild stuff. I wouldn't air the speculation about a serial killer.

SERIAL KILLER?!?!?!?!?! Athena texted back.

Whoa, Lexy said.

Sal and Posey climbed into the van. After they buckled in, Sal looked over at Posey. "I guess I should take you home?"

"If you don't mind," she said. "I live on Blackwood Court, off Ridge Road behind Mile High."

"Sure," he said.

Sal pulled onto the road.

"What the fuck, man?" Sal said, cutting the silence. "I'm sorry, I can't get over this. A *serial killer*?"

"You can't let yourself get swept up by rumors," Posey said, trying to ground the conversation in facts and not emotions. Facts you could control. "El is clearly a woman who watches too many true crime shows."

"The guy in the truck, though?"

"What, because a man drove through the parking lot twice? That's nothing worth reporting. I still think it's most likely she left of her own accord," Posey said as gently as she could.

"'Left of her own accord,'" Sal said mockingly, spitting the words out. "Why do you talk like that? All bizarre and proper? What is *wrong* with you?"

His words were an unexpected blow. Posey had thought that

Sal was . . . well, not a *friend*, exactly, but an ally. The tone he was using reminded Posey of so many bullies she'd encountered throughout junior high and high school who had called her weird, who had also asked her what was wrong with her, who had pushed her around. She'd even overheard the AV Club students talking about her that way! Her heart sank, and she peered out the window at the world darkening quickly to a pitch-black.

"I talk that way because, growing up, I read far more books than I talked to people," she said softly. "I guess that's probably why."

A silence stretched between them. Posey didn't even want to look at Sal. He hurt her feelings. She was done.

Sal sighed. "I'm sorry."

Posey didn't respond. She looked at her phone—no bars of reception.

"Look, I'm sorry, okay?" he tried again. "I actually . . . I like the way you talk."

Posey rolled her eyes.

"You sound super smart," he said. "Or like, I don't know. Old-fashioned. Like you stepped out of a movie from a long time ago."

The compliment helped, a little. Posey still didn't acknowledge his apology. As Sal pulled onto Ridge Road, she glanced down at the mess between them. The jar filled with yellow liquid rolled around and she asked herself, did she really care what a boy who peed in jars said about her? The answer was no. And with that thought, she was fully over the hurt feeling. Posey felt things deeply, but briefly. She tried hard not to hold on to anything resembling a grudge.

"Right here," she told him as they approached Blackwood Court. "The A-frame with the sloped roof."

Sal pulled up to the house, the only one in the cul-de-sac without its lights on. Shrouded in darkness, the front door was barely visible beneath the overhang on the porch.

Bears, Posey's brain whispered. *A whole family of bears is waiting to devour you.*

Brain! Posey thought. *Stop it right now!*

"Well, it's been an interesting day," Posey said in a tired voice.

"I really am sorry," Sal said.

"It's okay. I'm sorry too, about everything. I know it's been a hard time for you." She reached her hand out to shake his, but he just looked at it in confusion, then answered it with a half-hearted fist bump. She glanced at his floor once more and couldn't hold her curiosity. "Sal, why do you have a jar of urine on your floor?"

"Jar of what?" He looked down. "Oh. That's soap."

Posey put a hand to her chest. "Phew," she said.

Sal broke into a laugh—a *laugh*! She didn't realize he was physically capable. "You thought I had a jar of piss just rolling around in my van all day?"

"I really didn't know, Sal."

He did have nice teeth, very nice teeth. Teeth that were mostly straight and white, but not perfect—their slight crookedness only made them more endearingly *him*. Then his face slackened back to its usual deadpan expression. "No. It's soap."

"Well," Posey said, prolonging the goodbye because she was still terrified there were bears on her porch. "I'll be texting everyone to see what we can pull together. Though . . . you don't have a phone."

"Yeah. Guess I'll have to catch up with you tomorrow."

"You live around here?" Posey asked.

"Yep."

"Where?"

"Here."

"This neighborhood? What street?"

He shook his head and turned, opening the curtain behind him to reveal a mattress with a sleeping bag, a box of folded clothes, a box of cereal, and a water bottle. "Here."

Posey felt like someone had punched her. Sal lived *here*, in this van. Which explained the soap, the toothbrush, and toothpaste. Which explained why he had no cell phone. There was something so forlorn about it. This is where this boy slept at night, alone, with no heat and no bathroom and no running water and no one to talk to about his day.

"Sal," she said, with a touch of alarm. "Where are your parents?"

He let the curtain close. "I don't know where they are."

"What?" she said again, reaching out and touching his arm. "How?"

"My parents are junkies, drifters. They're on another plane. Long story. Don't give me that look, like you feel sorry for me—I've been like this for almost a year, okay? I'm doing just fine."

Posey put her hands back in her lap. "So this was why Ms. Moses was helping you get emancipated."

"Yeah."

"Where do you . . . park your van?"

"I used to park at Molly and Doug's but stopped when the investigation started. Now I just do it wherever I can. Not the highway, I'll get bothered by CHP. And a lot of people complain if I park in their neighborhood. Sometimes I park at the shopping complex in Highland, they don't bother me."

"Highland?" Posey said. "Are you kidding? That's like ten miles away."

"Not too bad," he said.

The shock was still ringing through her. "Do you want to park in our driveway tonight?"

"Nah, don't worry about it."

"But we have the extra space. I want you to. I insist, actually, for selfish reasons. Number one, it makes me feel better to know you could hear me scream if I was attacked by bears. And number two, if anything develops tonight with our footage, maybe I could come out and show you."

"It's weird, though," he said doubtfully. "What about your parents?"

"My dad won't care," she said, slipping her backpack over her shoulder. "It's decided—you're staying here."

"You're very convincing," he finally said.

"Yes. It's something I pride myself in." She opened the door and hopped out. "Talk soon, Sal. Are you hungry?"

"I'm all right," he said. "Night, Posey."

"Night."

Posey made her way up the stairs to the house, holding her breath and dashing for the front door. There was so much darkness here. An owl hooted in a tree and crickets sang. She felt as if thousands of beady eyes were watching her. There were bears. And in a flash, she thought of a strangled woman's body rotting in the woods. She thought of Ms. Moses, screaming for her life.

And then she slipped inside her house and locked the door.

THIRTEEN

The group text was exploding.

Posey caught up while eating a piece of seitan jerky at the kitchen table. In just the last hour, Lexy had shared copy for an intro and Athena had recorded the voice-over. They did it all on their phones, the quality surprisingly good. Posey was astounded that the group was working at such a rapid-fire pace—she had expected it to be like pulling teeth to get everyone to work on this project. Ms. Moses clearly meant a lot to them. And like Jeremiah's song, their work was impressive! Lexy's writing was clean, succinct, and Athena's voice sounded like a legitimate newscaster.

Transcript

ATHENA

Wild Pines is a quaint mountain town located
a mile high in the Sierra Nevada mountains.
It's not a place you've probably ever heard of.

It's not a place where a whole lot happens. But
this week, thirty-eight-year-old multimedia teacher
Molly Moses went missing. We'd like to know, in
a town quiet enough you can hear the snow
fall—why isn't anyone talking about it?

Well, we're going to talk about it. We're the *Wild
Pines Buzz*, and today we're presenting you with
our original investigative report asking the
question: "Where is Ms. Moses?" And Ms.
Moses, if you're out there, if you can hear this . . .
please let us know you're safe.

The voice-over continued for another minute, laying out the
facts of Ms. Moses's disappearance, introducing the people who
were interviewed, and then concluded by asking anyone with
information to contact the *Wild Pines Buzz*.

That's fantastic! Posey texted.

Yash texted, Posey how long do you want the interviews
clipped to and which parts should I keep?

Posey fired back her thoughts—keep each interview clip
under ninety seconds maximum so the show could run under five
minutes, feature answers only and not her questions, keep El to
a minimum, skipping all serial killer claims until more research
could be done. They agreed to meet the next day in the usual time
and place, and Posey sighed in relief when her phone went quiet.

She got up, turned on the kitchen lights, and switched the

heat on. Chewing her cheek, she thought of Sal down there in his van. It must get freezing at night. It was heartbreaking and unfair to think he lived that way. Staring at the window that faced the street, it was so dark now she couldn't see anything except her own ghostly reflection. She turned around and got started stir-frying vegetables and microwaving a bag of brown rice.

Posey liked to live every day feeling like she had made the world a better place somehow. Like her existence had made a positive impact, however small. She pushed the vegetables around the pan with a wooden spoon and reminded herself she had done that, she had made the world a little better today. But she didn't feel it. Instead, she was left deflated and exhausted. Sometimes it was like the world was nothing but a tangled ball of problems to be untangled, solved. And it was tiring. She sought perfection, she sought stillness, but those things were not real life.

As she was pouring teriyaki sauce into the pan, the front door opened and Posey jumped like a jackrabbit at the sight of her dad walking through the door.

"You scared me," she said, coming over and hugging him with the spoon still in her hand.

"Smells good in here," he said, taking off his scarf and coat and hanging them up. "You see some bum parked his van in the driveway? If he's still there in the morning, I'm calling in a tow truck."

"It's not some 'bum,' that's offensive. It's someone from the AV Club. I told him he could park it there."

"'Bum' is offensive now?" he asked. "What, it's not PC?"

Posey's dad was highly skeptical of anything he considered censorship, which had resulted in many heated discussions.

"It's just not nice," she said.

Her dad brought a pile of mail to the counter and sorted through it. "Why doesn't he park it at his house?"

"He doesn't *have* a house," Posey said. "He lives in the van."

Unbuttoning the top button of his collar, her dad shifted his attention from the mail to Posey. "What?"

Posey smelled something charred and realized the veggies were still cooking. She ran to the stove and clicked it off. "He *lives* in it, Daddy."

"Alone?"

"Yeah."

"Where are the adults in his life?"

"He's getting emancipated. It's a long story."

Her dad opened his mouth like he wanted to say more.

"Don't worry, Daddy, he seems okay," Posey said.

"Okay," he said, a little reluctantly. "Well, how was your day?"

Her dad set the table and listened as Posey served them food and breathlessly talked about her day. Then the questions started: Did Ms. Moses have any history with the Wild Pines Police Department? Did Doug Moses have a criminal record? What were the last things Ms. Moses did on her phone before she left it at Pickins? Did Posey know what police jurisdiction oversaw the area where Erin Englin's body was found?

"Hold on a minute," she said, finger up in the air, rushing to her notebook and purple pen.

There were so many good questions, Posey had a slight headache. Sometimes, it was like there were no answers in life—just questions that led to other questions.

Speaking of questions . . . Sal.

After dinner, Posey packed up some leftovers in a plastic container. She put on her coat and paced the foyer, letting her bravery build. Pushing the enormous invisible bears out of her brain and finally opening the door to go outside, she hurried down the steps, holding her breath, and knocked on the golden-lit driver window, whispering, "No bears, no bears, no bears . . ."

Sal's head emerged slowly, suspiciously, as he squeezed up to the front seat of the van and opened the door. "Hey," he said.

"Hey. First of all, the team's working on the edit. It's really coming together. I think by meeting time tomorrow we might be able to pull something together."

"Okay," he said slowly, as if he wasn't sure why she was telling him this.

"And here," she said, holding out the food, a fork, a napkin, and a bottle of water. "Just in case you want dinner."

"You didn't need to—"

"I made way too much," she said. "Didn't want to waste it. Did you know Americans waste up to forty percent of their food every year? It's inexcusable. Anyway, it's veggie stir-fry with teriyaki sauce over brown rice."

A beat passed, and then he took it from her.

"Okay," he said without looking up at her.

"Do you need an extra blanket or something? Is there any-thing else—"

"Posey," he said with a little edge to his voice. "I'm fine. Go chill out. I'll see you tomorrow." Then, finally meeting her eyes, he offered a half smile. "Thanks."

She smiled back at him. "Good night."

He slammed his door shut and retreated into his van and Posey raced up the stairs.

Chill out. Posey didn't even know how to chill out. Once she was inside, she glanced at the deck with its fairy lights, the hot tub with a plastic forest-green cover on it. How could she sit out there enjoying a hot tub under the stars when a boy slept in a cold van not thirty feet away? Plus, she had a notebook full of questions. And a missed video call from Lexy. Posey went upstairs to her room and called Lexy back. She sat on her bed and made sure not to have her childhood stuffed animal, a hedgehog named Foo Foo, in the shot.

"Lexy?" she said, surprised that Lexy would call her.

Lexy was backlit, her glasses reflective. She looked like she had a towel on her head and a bathrobe on. "Posey, sorry, is it weird I called? I kinda fell down a rabbit hole and found some info and wanted to share it with you."

"No, go ahead," Posey said, warmed by Lexy's excitement.

"I looked up where Erin Englin's body was found," Lexy said. "It was right off the highway, only like a quarter mile away from Pickins. It happened almost exactly a year ago."

Tapping her pen on the paper, Posey shook her head, her stomach doing a little somersault. "I don't think we should be reporting the serial killer theory. It's irresponsible, there's not enough there."

"Sure, okay. Just telling you." Lexy took the towel off her head and shook her hair. "My other thought was—if you think it's a good idea—maybe following up on the Abby Frost thing."

"Abby Frost," Posey repeated. It sounded familiar but the day had been such a whirlwind, she couldn't place it.

"El said Ms. Moses was why Abby Frost got fired from Pickins. I don't know. Motive?"

"Sure, that's a good idea," Posey said. "Why not? Nice catch, Lexy."

"Thanks."

In the pause, Lexy cleared her throat. "So how are you liking it here in Wild Pines?"

Posey was touched by the question. Not only had Lexy conducted research for their project, but she was taking a personal interest in her. Sulky, bordering-on-rude Lexy! Posey took a deep breath and smiled tiredly. "I think I like it. It's different."

"Yeah, I can imagine. I've spent some time in San Francisco. I loved Haight-Ashbury. All the vintage shops?"

"That area's fun," Posey said.

Posey thought she recognized the book that sat on Lexy's shelf behind her, *Call Us What We Carry* by Amanda Gorman. It was one of Posey's favorite poetry collections. A commonality! Posey suspected she and Lexy had a lot in common. Maybe one day they would be friends, real friends. Maybe they would be like she and

Hannah used to be. In a nostalgic cramp, Posey missed her ex–best friend. Since moving to Wild Pines, they hadn't even texted. But Posey reminded herself that living in the past was pointless. Here and now was what mattered. There were a lot more important things in the world to deal with than feelings.

"Well, thanks for getting all this going," Lexy continued. "I hope Ms. Moses is okay. I'm getting creeped out about all this, what if something bad happened to her?"

Posey nodded. She was worried, too, trying not to let her mind wander too far in certain directions.

"She's the best teacher at our school," Lexy went on. "Like, she actually *cares* about her students, you know? I organized a petition drive last year and Ms. Moses was the only teacher who backed me up."

"What was the petition drive about?"

"There were no vegan options in the cafeteria for lunches. I got a hundred students to sign asking admin to change their menu."

"Did they?"

Lexy smirked, adjusting her glasses. "Now we have the world's crappiest veggie burgers."

"Still, good job!"

"Yeah, I was pleasantly surprised," Lexy said. "Anyway. Just wanted to tell you about some of the stuff I found in case it's helpful for the episode. See you tomorrow?"

"See you then."

Posey hung up. She lay back on her pillow, the day swimming around in her head. By now, Ms. Moses had been missing for almost forty-eight hours. The first forty-eight hours of any missing persons investigation was crucial—it was when evidence was freshest and people's memories were sharpest. The most important next step was to get the first episode out as soon as possible so it could be shared. Maybe more people would come forward, new information would come to light.

Tomorrow. There was no word more beautiful in the English language than *tomorrow*. Tomorrows were when anything was possible.

FOURTEEN

Friday, September 13

"Excuse me, young woman," a voice said. "What do you think you are doing?"

It was minutes before the first bell. Posey stood in the bustling main hallway across from the blinding display of theater arts awards. She was taping her fifth MISSING flyer to the wall when she turned around to behold Principal Vance, her tight curls hairsprayed to a crisp, and her lips sharply penciled magenta. She must have been somewhere around five feet tall, but her navy-blue blazer and pencil skirt, the whistle around her neck on a beaded chain, and her sharp no-nonsense voice that cut through the noise of student chatter made her seem much larger than she was.

"Hello, Principal Vance," Posey said. "My name is Posey Spade. Remember? We met briefly in Ms. Moses's office last Friday."

"Excuse me, Posey Spade," she said. "What do you think you are doing?"

It was one of the most irritating things about adults—always asking what you were doing when they could see perfectly well what you were doing. What she really meant to ask was, *why* are you doing it? But Posey stood up straighter and answered anyway.

"I'm putting up flyers about Ms. Moses," Posey said, pointing to the wall. "Our teacher is missing and we want answers."

Principal Vance began taking them off the wall, one by one, the tape making little *snick* sounds as it ripped. "We do not hang things on this wall. Do you see any other posters, flyers, or literature hanging on this wall? No, you do not. This wall has been freshly painted. I do not want to see any tape marks or, God forbid, thumbtack holes on this wall."

"But the bulletin board is full," Posey said, pointing to the four-by-four-foot corkboard in the corner near the drinking fountain, which had so many flyers on it, it looked like it could explode. "And there's a sign next to the bulletin board that says you can't cover any of the flyers."

Posey noticed a couple of girls in soccer uniforms slowing to point and whisper. People were noticing her interaction with the principal. She tried to ignore the heat rising to her cheeks.

"Can you come with me to my office, please?" Ms. Vance asked, although it was more a demand than a question.

With flyers still in hand, Ms. Vance led the way down the hall, high heels clicking. Posey's heart was racing. She had that gross feeling that she was in trouble, that she'd done something wrong. Heads turned, including Jeremiah, who stood near the bathrooms and mouthed, "What the fuck?" to which Posey could only shrug in response. Ms. Vance got to the ADMIN door at the end of the hall. When she swung the door open, a woman, who had been giggling with another woman behind the front desk, immediately ceased her conversation and both receptionists turned to face Ms. Vance with serious expressions.

"Good morning," one said.

"Good morning," the other said.

"The bulletin board is full," Ms. Vance said sharply. "Does anyone check it on a regular basis?"

The women looked to each other, mouths agape.

"Now." Ms. Vance snapped her fingers. "The time is now."

One of the women got up, stiff with reluctance, and headed out the door to the hall. Ms. Vance led Posey to a glass-walled office that smelled strongly of perfume and shut the door. There was, for some unknown reason, a life-sized cutout of Ms. Vance that stood in a corner next to a file cabinet. There were barbells stacked neatly on a shelf. Her desk had nothing on it but a laptop and a stress ball. No pictures, no personal items, nothing to indicate that Ms. Vance had any sort of a life beyond Wild Pines High. Posey considered herself a master of observation, but she really couldn't gauge Ms. Vance.

"Sit, please," Ms. Vance said, situating herself at her desk and pointing to a wooden chair on the other side. The bell rang distantly and Ms. Vance looked up at the clock on her wall and shook her head. "Still off by seventeen seconds. Unacceptable." She stopped, pulled some rainbow reading glasses from a drawer, and looked over the flyer, moving her lips as she read it. After she was done, she pulled her glasses off. She grabbed her stress ball and squeezed until her fist was white. "Posey, when I consider a decision, I first consider the outcome. And then I consider other outcomes. *Then*, I try to think of the outcomes I have *not* thought of yet. Once I have weighed *those* outcomes, I choose the path that seems least likely to lead to disaster. Do you understand?"

Posey didn't understand.

Ms. Vance sighed. "This," she said, waving the flyer in the air, "*seems* on the surface like a good idea. I get it. I understand the motivation. But it has the potential for disaster. For hysteria. For dis*traction*." Ms. Vance had a very particular way of speaking—a sharp attention paid to every single syllable she uttered. "I want to know where Ms. Moses is as much as anyone else. Believe me. But this? This will only upset people."

"Can you elaborate?" Posey asked, pulling her phone out. "And actually, could I record a short interview and ask you a few questions for a report I'm working on?"

"No. Do not take your phone out or I *will* confiscate it."

Yikes. Posey slipped her phone back in her pocket. "I guess I'm not understanding why I can't put flyers up about Ms. Moses. What if someone at school has information that could help her case?"

"Her disappearance is a personal matter, and we ask that teachers leave their personal matters at home."

"Her husband, Doug, asked me to bring these to school," Posey insisted, pointing to the flyers. "He's desperate for information."

"How do you know her husband?" she asked with an eyebrow raised. Her walkie-talkie gurgled with unintelligible noise and Ms. Vance said something sharply into it and shut it off again. "Listen to me. This is simple. If you start putting up flyers, rumors will

126

fly, students will get distracted, and grades will suffer. We do not need to jump to conclusions and assume the worst. People disappear sometimes. People get angry and storm off their jobs—this is not the first time I've seen it happen. If you are worried about Ms. Moses, talk to law enforcement. Let them do their jobs. And let me do mine."

"What if you at least made an announcement or sent an email—?"

"Thank you, Posey," she said, scrawling a note on an orange Post-it that was as unintelligible as a doctor's prescription. "You should get to class. Your tardy will be excused."

Stunned, Posey stood up with the Post-it trembling on her finger and made her way out of the glass office. The halls were empty now, her footsteps echoing. As she looked up at the banner, the one that read WILD PINES HIGH CONGRATULATES OUR AWARD-WINNING THEATER DEPARTMENT!, Posey turned the conversation with Ms. Vance over in her mind. Didn't Sal say something about Ms. Moses wanting an investigation into the theater department's funding? Was it possible that Ms. Moses made enemies within the school and that Ms. Vance was one of them? Clearly the theater department was Wild Pines High's pride and joy. If you searched their school's name online, nearly all the first page of results were news stories and reviews covering their productions. Posey walked upstairs and joined her biology class, but it was so hard to pretend to care about mitosis today.

She couldn't wait to fast-forward and get to lunch so she could meet with the AV Club again.

FIFTEEN

Posey was shocked to a standstill when she entered the basement for the AV Club meeting at lunch. Not only was she the last one to arrive, but the room was bustling with energy. Sal and Lexy were setting up a green screen that Posey hadn't even realized existed. Jeremiah was busy testing a ring light. Yash was hunched over his laptop at a desk, eyebrows knit in concentration. And Athena stood near the green screen, talking to Jeremiah—though it took a moment for Posey to realize it was Athena in her black blazer, platinum wig, and bright red lipstick.

"Hi, everyone," Posey said, eyes wide.

The room lit up in greeting and Sal beckoned her over. Jeremiah gave her a one-armed hug—how amiable! Posey and Lexy shared a wave. It was as if Lexy's guard was down now, after last night's phone call. Despite the warm welcome, Posey could tell the group was worried. No one was smiling. Ms. Moses's absence filled the air between them like a ghost.

"So we're thinking of filming Athena's voice-over parts today," Sal said.

"It's newsier, right?" Jeremiah said. "Video versus voice-over?"

"Everything shares better online if there's a person, a face, yada yada yada," Athena said. "Plus, come on, I look amazing. I'm a stunner in this outfit."

"And so humble," muttered Sal.

"You know everyone will tune in just to see Athena," Jeremiah said. "For the sheer *drama* of it."

Posey tilted her head. "Sure," she said, though she felt she was missing something.

Athena put her hand on Posey's arm and murmured, "I had a breakdown last year. Very public. Deleted my socials. Whole thing was a BFD. I'll tell you all about it sometime."

"Oh," Posey said, her sympathy piqued. Poor Athena, to have gone through something like that. "I'm so sorry to hear that."

"Yeah, it sucked," Athena said. "I'm okay now, though."

"What can I do?" Posey asked the group.

"I think we've got this," Jeremiah said, with something like surprise in his voice. He turned to Athena. "We ready, Drama?"

"Shut the fuck up and yes, I'm ready," Athena said sweetly.

"Silencio," Jeremiah sang to the room. "We're about to shoot."

Posey's heart raced as she stood, crossing her arms, and watched. It was unusual, this feeling of standing back and having nothing to do. It made her a little bit itchy. She wanted to ask more questions about their plan and give input but there was no time for discussion, because filming was happening.

"Hello, Wild Pines, I'm your host, Athena Dixon, and this is *Wild Pines Buzz*," Athena said with a tight smile and a voice that could pass for a professional news anchor's. "And you'd better stick around because our beloved multimedia teacher Ms. Moses is missing and we have the exclusive investigative report. And Ms. Moses, if you're out there, if you can hear this . . . please let us know you're safe."

Mesmerized by her performance, Posey stood silently and watched as Athena recorded the intro and rerecorded the voice-over portions that she'd sent the day before. At the end, she recited a new plug that Posey hadn't heard before, one that emphasized how important Ms. Moses was to all her students and urged everyone to take action by coming forward with any new information, and subscribe, comment, and share the post. Athena said all this with complete confidence and poise. There wasn't a single mistake or a single "um"—it was so polished that Posey was convinced Athena was an incredible actress by this performance alone.

"That was fantastic," Posey said, applauding.

"Yeah, good job, Drama," Jeremiah said.

"Thanks, Posey. And Jeremiah, I'm going to kick you in the nuts."

"Hostile," Jeremiah said with the point of a finger.

Sal went to look over Jeremiah's shoulder at the footage when Yash, who had thus far been working in such solitary silence Posey forgot he was there, spoke up.

"Um, Posey?" Yash said. "I think we have a problem."

While other people in the world might hear the word *problem* and sigh, whenever Posey heard the word *problem*, she gleefully interpreted it as an opportunity. Posey took a seat next to Yash to peek at his laptop. He appeared to be editing a video. She recognized the footage from her interview with Doug.

"What's the problem?" she asked.

Yash expanded the screen so she could get a closer look. He pointed at Doug's chest. He was wearing a flannel shirt, two buttons unbuttoned, and the top of the word KILLER was visible. You could see only half the letters, but anyone who looked hard enough would notice it there and know what it spelled.

Posey sucked in a deep breath. It seemed to be one of the many KILLER LIVER shirts that had been on every mannequin and hung in his front yard. But how could she have not noticed? How could she have sat there asking him questions and not read the word peeking out of the top of his shirt?

"Oh dear," Posey said. "That's not a good look."

"I tried to crop it," Yash said with an apologetic smile. "This is the best I could do."

Posey bit her lip and considered her options. They could ditch Doug's interview footage, but then they wouldn't have much meat for the show. They could refilm, but they had so little time and she wanted to get this out today while it was still fresh—when you're dealing with a missing person, time is too precious to waste. What would her dad say? That was usually Posey's default when she didn't know what to do. His advice would be practical, straightforward, and objective. He would tell her to air the footage. Her job was to report the story as straight as she possibly could. Doug was wearing that shirt the day of the interview. That was the truth.

"It's unfortunate," Posey said to Yash. "But we have to air it as is. We could blur it, maybe, but researching how to do it, and with what tools, would slow us down. It's not noticeable unless you blow it up into full screen."

"Why is he . . . wearing a shirt that says that?" Yash asked, baffled.

"A very important question, Yash, thank you for asking it. Sal," she called, beckoning him over.

Sal broke from his conversation with Jeremiah and ambled over, hands in his hoodie pockets. Not that it was important in any way, but Posey couldn't help but notice that Sal was clean-shaven and that, as he leaned over her shoulder to see Yash's laptop, his dark brown hair looked soft as if he'd just washed it. If he lived in his van, where did he shower? Where did he use the bathroom? But Posey forced her focus back to what mattered right now.

"This shirt," Posey said, pointing to the screen. "I didn't ask yesterday, but what's the deal with these shirts?"

"Shit," Sal said. "That's his band, Killer Liver. Damn. How did we not notice?"

"I swear it wasn't visible when I first saw him," Posey said. "Maybe it came unbuttoned?"

"He wears those shirts everywhere." Sal stood up and closed his eyes a moment as if he was collecting himself. "I should have seen it. Can you crop it?"

"This is cropped already," Yash said.

"I don't think I need to explain why this is problematic," Posey said. "But we have to air this footage, Sal."

"What's up, club?" Jeremiah said, coming up behind them.

"This," Posey said, pointing to the screen.

Jeremiah squinted. Then he put a finger to his chin. "Does that say what I *think* it says?"

"It's his band," Sal said flatly. "Killer Liver."

"That is a *very* unfortunate choice of attire. Also . . ." Jeremiah dropped his voice to a whisper. "That band sucks. Have you heard them?"

"Yes," Sal said at the same time that Yash and Posey said, "No."

Jeremiah did a performative shiver. "Anyway, Yash baby, I just AirDropped you the green screen footage."

"Thanks," Yash said.

"What are you putting on the green screen?" Posey asked.

"I drew a logo," Yash said. He clicked to another tab, revealing a striking, full-color picture of a bee and the words *Wild Pines Buzz* in a Courier font. It was a strange logo—artistic, as if it deserved to be hung on a wall and contemplated deeply rather than used as a logo for a low-budget high school news show. It took a long, wondrous pause before Posey decided she absolutely loved it.

"Yash, it's *beautiful*," Posey said.

"Yeah?" he asked, smiling at her praise. "Check this out."

He opened another tab and played an animated version of the logo, where the bees flew away and Jeremiah's song played—guitar and singing "Wild Pines Buzz!" with rock-star gusto.

"Siiiick," Jeremiah said.

Posey glanced at the clock. "We have less than a half hour. When do you think we can turn this around?"

"I have multimedia after this," Yash said. "Ms. Moses's class? There's, like, a substitute and everyone's just been working on independent projects. I might be able to finish it and upload by then. I have everything edited, I just need to drop in the green screen footage."

Posey was tempted to ask to see his edit, but there was a bead of sweat on Yash's forehead and he kept glancing at the clock. Sometimes being a strong leader meant trusting other people with their jobs and not micromanaging every detail.

"Thank you so much for all you're doing," she said to Yash, then glanced around the room. "Thank you everyone, seriously. Maybe someone with information will see this and be able to help us figure out where Ms. Moses is."

"It's important," Athena said as she took her blazer off and slipped back into a fake-fur coat. "Ms. Moses is one of the only decent teachers at this garbage school."

"She really is," Lexy said as she ate a banana. "So Posey, after this, what's next? Are we going to start on another episode, or . . . ?"

Posey nodded. "I don't think we stop until we find her."

"We should interview Doug again," Sal said, biting his nails. "I don't want people thinking he's a killer because of some stupid shirt."

"We can drop a comment in if someone says anything and explain that's it's a band shirt," Posey said.

"But still, a second interview anyway. He's her husband, he's probably got more info than anyone else," Sal said.

"What about the phone?" Lexy asked, sitting on the edge of a desk. "What if we could report what her last texts were?"

"Yeah, doesn't hubs have her phone?" Athena asked from a desk across the room.

"Good point," Posey said, remembering her dad had suggested the same thing. "We could do that. And Abby Frost—the woman who Ms. Moses got fired."

"Can we just take a moment to acknowledge how *messed up* it is that a teacher has to work a second job to begin with?" Jeremiah said, cracking open a soda.

"She was saving for something," Sal said. "That's what she told me."

Posey turned to Sal. "Saving for what?"

He shrugged. "Didn't say."

Adjusting her glasses, Lexy cleared her throat and said, "What if she was saving, like . . . to take off?"

"Wouldn't that be the fuckin' twist?" Athena said, eating a slice of pizza on a napkin that seemed to have appeared from nowhere. "All this and she just hightailed out of here?"

"That seems to be what Ms. Vance thinks," Posey said. "I spoke with her today—there was no sense of urgency from her whatsoever."

"You talked to *Vance*?" Sal asked.

"Oh yeah, what *was* that?" Jeremiah asked.

Everyone was rapt, the room quiet. She could hear a fluorescent bulb flicker.

"Don't leave us hanging, sunshine," Athena said. "Do tell."

Posey summarized her frustrating meeting with the principal that morning. No one seemed surprised, but they all fell into collective thought about it.

"You need to interview Butts," Athena said.

Jeremiah laughed one loud *ha*. "Sorry, that name will *never* stop being funny."

"I did," Posey said. "Deputy Butts was as unhelpful as Vance."

"Not Deputy Butts," Athena said. "*Mr*. Butts. Theater teacher. Head of the department."

Posey didn't say anything as the information sank in. It seemed like everyone watched her, waiting for a reaction.

"Mr. Butts," she said slowly. "Theater teacher. The one Ms. Moses was looking to investigate?"

Four nods. Yash had long ago put his headphones on to edit and wasn't listening. Posey admired his hyper-focus.

"They're brothers," Athena said.

"The Butts brothers," Jeremiah said, hooting with a laugh. "Sorry. How can I *not*?"

"Why didn't you tell me this?" Posey asked Sal.

He shrugged. "I thought you knew?"

Posey pulled her notebook and purple pen out and jotted notes. "Okay, yes, obviously we have to interview him. Sal, we should interview him first thing after school."

"I doubt he'll do it," Sal said. "We can try, though."

"Can I come?" Lexy asked. "I have nothing to do this afternoon. I could turn copy around way faster if I'm there."

A volunteer; Posey's heart swelled. "Of course!"

Athena put her hands up. "I will absolutely fucking not be joining you."

"Me either. Work," Jeremiah said.

"We'll stay in touch via text. Hopefully in a few hours the episode will be posted and then—who knows?" Posey asked. "If a lot of people watch it, maybe a bunch of new leads will come in over the weekend."

The room sank into silence. Sal stared down at the linoleum and looked like he was going to cry. Posey breathed deeply. Of course, she wasn't a psychic, nor did she even believe in psychic abilities. But Posey had a feeling everyone's thoughts were something like hers right now: calculating how long Ms. Moses had been gone. Trying not to think of the nightmarish possibilities that come when a woman goes missing. Realizing the emergency of the moment. Beaming something like a prayer into the universe that the show would lead them to the truth.

SIXTEEN

Posey suffered through algebra, only half paying attention as she jotted down questions for Mr. Butts in her AV Club notebook. Covertly, she also searched him online with her phone on her lap. It seemed the Butts family—she would not laugh when she wrote that down or said it aloud, she would *not*—had been in Wild Pines for several generations. Deputy Butts and Mr. Butts's father was Mayor Butts, whose father was State Senator Butts. (It wasn't funny. It *really* wasn't.) The family obviously held a lot of power in this area. Posey imagined they could disappear someone if they wanted. The question was, *would* they?

If she went on gut instincts, Posey still predicted that the most likely scenario was that Ms. Moses had left Wild Pines voluntarily. She hoped that was the case. But journalism wasn't about gut instincts. In fact, her dad once told Posey about a study that showed that people who relied on gut instincts were more likely to believe in fake news. Reporting was about facts and only facts. Posey needed to forge on assuming anything was possible, even something as far-fetched as the Butts family being responsible.

Or—*gulp*, she hated to admit it—a serial killer.

Uneasily, she made a note in her book to conduct more of her own research on the Erin Englin case this weekend.

Her phone vibrated in her lap and she gasped when she saw Yash post "It's almost uploaded!"

"See something interesting there, Posey Spade?" asked her teacher Mr. Sandino, a white man who barked rather than spoke and looked like he could play the part of a Mafia henchman in a movie.

"Oh," Posey said, heat rising to her cheeks. There was a no-phones policy in every class and he'd caught her in the act. The whole room rubbernecked to see her there in the back row. "Yes. I apologize."

"Gimme," Mr. Sandino said, hand out.

"I'll put it away—"

"What part of 'gimme' don't you understand?"

There were some giggles and whispers as Posey rose and reluctantly handed over her phone, dying inside from three things at once: embarrassment, guilt because she broke the rules, and a desperation to not miss what was happening in the group thread. Their episode was almost up. They actually pulled it off, they did it! Yet she was expected to sit here and pretend that the quadratic equation mattered at a time like this. Posey was almost sick to her stomach the rest of class until she recovered her phone.

After fifth period, Posey stepped into the girls' room and locked herself into a stall. She pulled her phone out of her backpack and checked the group thread.

Yash texted, It's up! and shared the YouTube link.

Athena replied with a row of clapping hands and then added, I KNOW THIS IS BANANASVILLE BUT I'M THINKING OF REVIVING MY INSTA AGAIN JUST TO GET THE WORD OUT BOUT THE EPISODE

halleloo!!!! Jeremiah texted along with a fire emoji. nature is healing! and then a rainbow.

Lexy texted, whoa

Once again, Posey felt like she was missing the context in their cryptic chat, but she had to remind herself there was time to fill it in. Right now she had only six minutes to watch this four-minute-and-fifty-six-second episode. Posey's heart hammered as she pressed play, putting her phone close to her face to tune out the echoey noises of the bathroom—laughter, murmuring, flushing, the hiss of sink faucets. She listened and watched her screen with such deep focus that the entire world disappeared around her.

In her seventeen years on this blue-green earth, Posey had accomplished a lot she was proud of. She wrote countless articles for her school's newspaper and once, when both the editor in chief and deputy editor were out sick, she assembled the entire edition herself. In junior high, she had written a poem that was selected to be read aloud at that year's graduation ceremony. Summer after freshman year, she and Hannah volunteered at a cat shelter. And last year, she was on the ballot for Most Likely to Succeed, and though she didn't win, it was an honor to have been nominated. But this here—this five-minute investigative report constructed by an entire team that *she led*—she had never felt so proud of anything in all her life.

It wasn't perfect. There were some choppy edits. The sound during the interviews had a lot of background noise. You could see the ring light in Athena's pupils and one of the text overlays that showed their missing teacher's picture said "Ms. Mose." And Posey was undecided on whether the logo and song intro were corny. But you know what? It was their first episode. It wasn't high art, it was a high school news report. Posey's dad had once told her that a story didn't need to be beautiful, it just needed to do its job like "a good shoe." This first episode of *Wild Pines Buzz* was certainly a good shoe.

Surprisingly, there were a hundred views on it already and two comments. One was from someone named Ainsley and it said, What?! This is the first I've heard of this! And another from cheese-fart2029 said the husband's shirt omg is this fr. Posey shook her head at that one—she really hoped the comments wouldn't focus on Doug's shirt. But still, comments! When she worked on the school newspaper, it enjoyed a small print run and was shared schoolwide as a PDF. There were no comments, no instant reactions, no data to see how many people you reached.

Posey was yanked from her thoughts when the bell rang. Quickly, she peed and then went out to wash her hands. She was going to be late. Being late was the stuff Posey's nightmares were made of. She headed for the door but there was a girl standing in front of it. A white girl with a puffy jacket, one of the ones who had called her a "biohazard" the first day of school, staring at her with icy-blue eyes that contrasted strikingly with her light skin.

"It's Biohazard Girl," she said. "What the hell you doing in that stall all that time? You constipated?"

A very invasive line of questioning. This girl was setting off Posey's inner alarm system. She'd always been a target for bullies, and bullies were one breed where her greatest strength—her intelligence—usually proved useless.

"I was watching an episode of a news show that I'm part of," Posey said. "It's about Ms. Moses."

"Yeah, I heard she's missing," the girl said, as if the subject of their missing teacher was boring. Her ponytail was so tight it seemed to stretch her face back a little. "I don't know. You're the one walking around all bloody and shit. Maybe you killed her."

"That was ketchup," Posey said, offended.

The girl laughed. "I'm joking! Geez, you can't take a joke?"

Great. Not even a week in and Posey already had a nemesis and a derogatory nickname. Posey hurried through the halls, through the courtyard, and out to the cacophonous hellscape known as the gym.

SEVENTEEN

When the last bell rang, Posey's heart sang along with it. She raced to meet Lexy and Sal. Outside the front doors, among the rushing crowd of students, she spotted Lexy, who waved wildly at her from the veranda. Posey was beginning to see there were layers to Lexy; underneath her skeptical exterior, there was a childlike earnestness.

"Hey," Posey said breathlessly. Down on the lawn, a group of students in cheerleading uniforms cawed like ravens.

"Did you see? Oh my God, did you see?" Lexy asked, holding her phone up.

"See what?" Posey asked.

She hadn't looked at her phone since the bathroom. She had been too busy playing a pathetic game of volleyball in the gym.

"We're going viral. It's, like, *exploding* in real time." Lexy showed her the screen of her phone. Her hand was shaking.

The video had two thousand views and sixty-three comments.

"What?" Posey asked in complete disbelief. This had to be a mistake. How could anything get two thousand views in an hour?

"Watch this. I'll refresh." Lexy reloaded the screen and now the video had over two thousand and three hundred views. Within seconds, hundreds of people had watched the video. Unbelievable. Posey couldn't even wrap her brain around it.

"Holy . . ." Posey said, trailing off.

". . . shit?" Lexy finished for her. "The comments already have tons of leads. Everyone thinks it's Doug. One guy said he drove by and saw Doug cleaning out his car with bleach yesterday morning. I—I don't even know how to handle this; what do we do with all this information flooding in?"

"Where's Sal?" Posey asked, looking around. "Does he even know the episode's up?"

"Probably not. You know Sal, he lives full-time in his head."

Posey scanned the thinning crowd for a boy with poor posture and a black hoodie, but he wasn't there. Glancing through the front door, the giant clock said class had been out for almost ten minutes.

Lexy was scrolling her phone. "Okay, so Athena shared it on her Instagram page. That's why it blew up so fast."

"She must have a big following."

Posey squinted at the parking lot to look for Gramps. Maybe Sal had already left without them. But there it was, at the same corner of the parking lot it was at yesterday.

"Yyyeah, Athena has over a hundred thousand followers," Lexy said.

Posey startled at the number. "Really?"

"Mmm-hmm," Lexy said, lowering her voice even though

144

there wasn't anyone there. Students had poured out of the building and scattered like spilled marbles in every direction—the grass, the parking lot, the thicket surrounding the school. "Do you know what happened?"

"I don't," Posey said. "But it's okay—"

"Athena's an absurdly gifted actress. She's also ridiculous when it comes to makeup and cosplay and all that. She went viral freshman year for doing these spoken-word lip syncs from movies where she was in full costume. Seriously, now that her account's back up you should watch them all. She's brilliant."

"I'm not surprised to hear that, she seems immensely talented," Posey said.

"Athena had a breakdown last year. It was *wild* because she was all over social media and everyone watched it happen in real time. We all didn't know what to think because it started off fun and just like, okay, this is Athena being Athena. Wacky rants and bizarre monologues while dressed up in character. But then it got bad fast. She stopped coming to school. She shaved her head on livestream, posted videos of herself claiming she was untouchable because she was some kind of reincarnated angel and *then*—" Lexy paused to clutch Posey's arm. Posey was rapt, waiting for her to finish.

Lexy dropped her voice to a whisper. "—she posted nudes of herself on Snapchat and ended up getting suspended from school and had charges pressed against her."

Posey avoided gossip at all costs. It usually had an air of meanness to it, and it was often peppered with misinformation.

But to think that Athena went through all that—it was stunning, and she couldn't help but ask a follow-up question.

"*Charges?*" Posey repeated. "For what?"

"Possession of child pornography."

Posey's brain hurt; there were actual pains in her forehead from all this. "For . . . pictures of herself?"

"For pictures of *herself*," Lexy said, letting go of Posey's arm. Lexy stood up a little straighter and her voice resumed its normal volume. "So after that, she got help, she's much better, but she deactivated her account, I assumed permanently. And she quit theater."

"Why quit theater?"

"Embarrassment? I don't know."

Suddenly so much made sense as Posey breathed in the fresh woodsy air and processed the information. First, there was Athena's hair that she always kept covered. In glimpses Posey had caught of Athena's hair, it looked to be about four or five inches long. Human hair grew about six inches per year on average, dating her breakdown to approximately nine or ten months ago. Second, there was the reluctance to be part of the group interviewing Mr. Butts today. Athena didn't want to go anywhere near the theater department.

"So that's why Jeremiah called her 'Drama,'" Posey said.

"Yep."

"Is there something between those two, by the way?" Posey asked.

Lexy shook her head. "I doubt it. Jeremiah used to date her

brother back in the day. She's like a sister to him. Hey, here comes Sal. Um, hello, why are you so late?"

Sal's resting expression always seemed to have a hint of rage, but right now, he was emanating it. His teeth were gritted.

"Let's *go*," was all he said, and headed down the stairs without stopping.

Lexy and Posey exchanged a glance and then followed him down the many steps and to the sidewalk that skirted the parking lot.

"Excuse me, aren't we interviewing Mr. Butts?" Posey called after him.

"I'm going to the faculty lot," he said with the tone of voice a petulant child might use when speaking to their mother.

"You're acting hella weird, what is wrong with you?" Lexy said.

Posey so appreciated this quality in Lexy, that she was willing to say whatever needed to be said out loud. She didn't hesitate or overthink it like Posey did. She just blurted it out. But Sal didn't respond. He was walking so fast he was huffing and puffing, and Lexy and Posey broke into a jog to catch up. Finally, they took a right into the thick shade of cedars, which led to another staircase going down that had a weathered sign that read FACULTY PARKING ONLY. Sal stood, pulling his backpack straps and scanning the lot.

"He's gone," Sal said.

"What? How do you know?" Posey asked.

"You see a red Ferrari?" he asked.

"What about the theater lot?" Lexy asked.

"I had ceramics last period and I could see the lot from the window," Sal said, tucking his hair behind his ears. "Whole lot was closed off, they're repaving or something."

"What's Plan B?" Lexy asked Posey. "Try to track him down? He lives in my neighborhood, like six houses down from me."

"We could do that," Posey said. "We could also find Abby Frost. Either of you know anything about Abby?"

Lexy and Sal shook their heads in unison.

"Okay," Posey said. "Sure, let's try to see if we can catch Mr. Butts at home."

The three of them turned around and headed back to the student parking lot, which had emptied considerably in the past few minutes. Only a dozen or so cars remained. In a pickup truck bed, a couple was engaged in such intense kissing it looked like they were eating each other's faces. How on earth anyone could enjoy such a lewd public display of affection was as much a mystery to Posey as where Ms. Moses had gone.

"Get a room," Lexy said loudly as they passed the couple. "You're gross."

The couple didn't stop their make-out session, but Posey smiled at Lexy, who had voiced the thoughts Posey was too polite to say aloud.

"You don't have to be an asshole, they're just having fun," Sal said as he pulled his keys out and opened Gramps's passenger door.

"I'm not," Posey said, snapping her attention back to the van.

A sudden heat flushed her cheeks. She cleared her throat, and Sal shook his head at her as if she were silly, something like a smirk almost dancing on his lips. Then he heaved himself up and inside Gramps. "Hold up, I need to make a third seat."

"*This* is what we're riding in?" Lexy asked, eyeing the side of the van. "Um . . . I have a Tesla."

"You want to drive?" Posey asked.

"Yeah," Lexy said.

"Oh," Sal said, pulling back out. "Gramps not good enough for you?"

"Save your gas money," Lexy said with what sounded like an edge of sarcasm. It was hard to tell with Lexy—she spoke with a bite in her tone regardless of how sincere she might be.

Sal closed the door and slung his backpack on his shoulder again. "Fine, let's go ride in your *Tesla*."

Despite the many bumper stickers (*MEAT IS MURDER, ABORTION IS HEALTHCARE, SCIENCE IS REAL*, rainbows and protest fists), Lexy's car was so new it smelled like she'd just driven it from the dealership. They climbed inside and the dashboard lit up like a spaceship. Posey settled into the passenger seat and Sal sat in the back.

"Oh my God, we're almost at ten thousand views," Lexy said, showing Posey her phone. "I mean, I know I shouldn't focus on this, but it's bonkers."

It was the YouTube page for their first episode. And indeed, it showed that they would soon be breaking *five digits* in views in a matter of hours. That had to mean something. It had to mean, with an audience that large, someone out there must have answers. What if Ms. Moses herself somehow saw the video, wherever she was?

"Sal, did you see this?" Posey asked. "We didn't tell you! The episode went live. I think it's—it's going viral or something?"

Lexy turned to Sal. "Athena reactivated her Insta account and shared from there."

"Yeah, I know," Sal said, staring out the window. "That's why I was late. Ms. Vance just found out about the episode and she was grilling me about it."

Posey's mouth dropped open and she twisted around in her seat to address Sal. "She was?"

He nodded once and gazed out the window as if he was watching a movie in his head. He was aggravating. What was with him? What went on inside him that made him so . . . unreadable?

"I said it was the AV Club, that's all I said," he told them. "I said I hadn't even seen it yet and I didn't have a phone."

"I'm sure Vance is shitting her pants," Lexy said, clipping her seat belt. "As she should. Hello! A teacher is missing."

"What else did she say?" Posey asked.

Sal shrugged. "That was it."

"She should be thanking us," Lexy said as she pulled out of the parking lot and back onto the highway.

"She should," agreed Posey.

Lexy turned on her stereo and a woman thrashed on an acoustic guitar and sang mournfully about no one understanding her. Lexy drove a little too fast, was a fan of the California stop, and tailgated. She used her horn twice to hurry cars that waited at a turn too long. Not that Posey was critical of Lexy's driving, it was just something she noticed. She felt a lot safer in the passenger's seat of Sal's van.

Rather than continue up the highway toward Mile High Drive or past it to Posey's neighborhood, Lexy made a sharp turn up Silver Springs Circle. Posey had never been this way before. The road was windy at first, sharp corkscrew turns with barely enough room for two cars to pass one another. Each house they passed seemed larger, more elegant than the last, until the road opened up a bit and they drove past a golf course and country club that had an incredible view of the valley. It was gorgeous here, so lush and green—Posey could hardly imagine what it would be like when the snow started later that fall.

After the golf course, Lexy slowed down at the end of the road. There was a kiosk there that said SILVER SPRINGS CIRCLE RESIDENTS ONLY. Lexy rolled her window down and waved at the attendant at the kiosk, a white man in a security uniform and a hat like an old-timey policeman, who waved them into the gated neighborhood.

EIGHTEEN

All the houses in Silver Springs Circle were alike: storybook-style architecture, towers and turrets, stone paths and streams running through the properties. Mr. Butts's house was no different, except it had a large stone placard on the front that said THE BUTTSES' ABODE and boasted a life-sized stone statue of a frowning man with what looked like a baseball-sized planet earth in his hands.

"That is really creepy," Sal said, stopping to contemplate the statue.

"I think that's, like, his great-grandpa or something," Lexy said.

"He's ugly," Sal said. "He looks like his face is melting."

In the driveway, Posey noted a vehicle under a car cover, a glimpse of red paint peeking out near the back tire. It was roughly the size and shape of a Ferrari. "He's home," she said.

"Can I have your phone, Pose?" Sal asked. "I want to get some footage of this place."

Posey nodded, unexpectedly touched by the fact Sal had so casually called her "Pose"—a nickname her dad and Hannah both used with her. Sal had no idea, maybe he had just called her that on accident. But it gave her an affectionate flutter to think she was on a nickname basis with him already. She handed him her phone and smiled. He met her eyes and though his lips didn't smile back, his eyes did.

"Thanks," he said, and stepped back to film the exterior of the house. Lexy and Posey waited a moment for him to finish and then the three of them walked up the path to the front door, which had a gold BUTTS placard on it. To each their own. If Posey'd had such an unfortunate surname, she wouldn't be proudly screaming it from her front door. Sal was filming behind them as she rang the doorbell, and an extended chiming version of Beethoven's Fifth Symphony sounded. After what seemed like an eternity, the door opened, and a white man stood in front of them in a button-up shirt, slacks, and slippers. He was balding on top with a limp gray-brown ponytail and a clipped beard.

"Alexa Kennedy," he said, surprised. "What are you doing here?"

Posey glanced at Sal, who was still filming, but doing it in a way that looked like he could just be looking at his phone.

"Hi, Mr. Butts," Lexy said. "I'm sorry to come here like this."

"It's quite the surprise," Mr. Butts said.

Behind him in the living room, Posey couldn't see much—a fire in the fireplace, a bookshelf with leather-bound books, an easy chair.

"We're with the AV Club," Posey said. "My name is Posey Spade. We wanted to ask you a few questions about the disappearance of Ms. Moses."

"I know nothing about it. I'm not the man to ask." He put his hands on his hips. "Are you filming me without my consent?"

Posey turned to Sal and waved her hand as if to say, stop it. After a moment, Sal pocketed the phone again.

"So you're the ones—you're the students behind that You-Tube video?" Mr. Butts's gray eyes danced. "The AV Club. Ms. Moses's pet project. You all did that?"

"We did," Posey said. "You saw the episode?"

"It's making the rounds," he said. "You know . . ." Mr. Butts shook his head and sputtered out something like a sorrowful little laugh, something like a sigh. "I—I realize you're scrambling to make sense of her being gone. I get that." He made his hands into a little tent and met their eyes, one at a time—Lexy, then Posey, then Sal. "But not everything's a . . . you know, a Netflix show, a—a story worthy of a true crime podcast. In all probability, let's face it, Ms. Moses likely just up and ran away."

"We don't think that's what happened," Posey said.

"Off the record?" Mr. Butts said, dropping his voice. "You know she had . . . mental health issues." He fixed his gaze on Sal. "*You* of all people should know."

"Mental health issues," Lexy repeated slowly. "Meaning . . ."

"You draw the conclusions," Mr. Butts said, putting his hands up.

"What the fuck are you—" Sal started to say, but Posey reached back and squeezed his arm as hard as she could to stop him. Thankfully, it worked.

"I'm sorry, Mr. Butts, what exactly are you implying?" Posey asked as amiably as she could to make up for Sal, who stood behind her like a grenade missing its pin.

"Look, I can't talk about open investigations," Mr. Butts said. "But if you take a look at what Molly Moses was facing, I would get out of town and stay out of town, too. Some could say I might not even have a lot to live for anymore. That's all I'm saying. You want to know more? Ask that guy." He pointed to Sal. And in one second, Mr. Butts's entire visage changed. His face darkened, his eyebrows furrowed, his smile disappeared. "I don't appreciate students coming to my property uninvited. It doesn't look good. Do it again, Alexa Kennedy, and I'm going to have a chat with your dad and with Silver Springs security."

"Sorry," Lexy whispered, visibly shrunken by the threat.

The door closed, the lock clicked. The three of them stood in silence, absorbing the shock of it. Then they turned and headed back down the path that led to Silver Springs Circle.

"What was he saying about her mental health?" Posey asked. "Is there anything we should know, Sal?"

"She had depression," he said, an edge to his voice. "Who doesn't?"

I don't, Posey thought. But that would be a tactless response, so she bit her tongue.

Maybe Sal was a depressed person. Maybe his condition was part of what bonded him to his teacher. But that was speculation, not fact; Posey needed to stick to the truth. The exchange with Mr. Butts swam in her mind. The brief discussion was unhelpful, bordering on hostile. Then again, Posey could understand him not appreciating three students showing up to his doorstep on a Friday afternoon. If Ms. Moses had depression, if she was facing a humiliating investigation and the town thought she had an inappropriate relationship with a student, her marriage didn't seem great, she was working two jobs . . . she left her phone at work and didn't return for it. It all just seemed to heap up in Posey's mind and point to a possibility she foolishly hadn't considered: suicide.

Posey didn't say anything about what she was thinking. Sal and Lexy didn't speak either, which made Posey wonder if they were all thinking the same unsayable things. How depressing would that be, to find out Ms. Moses had ended her own life?

"He's such a dick," Sal finally said.

"He really is," Lexy agreed. "Also did you smell his breath? Halitosis city." A wild rabbit scampered over the road in front of them and Lexy's voice rose two octaves. "Awww!"

"Your name's Alexa?" Posey asked.

"Yeah." Lexy sighed. "Like, every device in our house is powered by Alexa. So when I was a kid, they decided to call me Lexy instead. Less confusing."

"So basically your family chose a robot over you?" Sal asked. "That's harsh."

"Welcome to the Kennedy family," Lexy said.

Speaking of which, Lexy explained she had a strict dinner protocol with her parents, where they ate dinner together virtually every night at six. Her dad was at the tech campus where he worked in Cupertino and her mom was in Hong Kong on business until November. They ate together via Zoom and she couldn't miss it, so Lexy apologized and said she couldn't do any more interviewing tonight.

"That's all right," Sal said. "I'm pretty zonked."

"I'll call you later tonight, Posey," Lexy said. "We'll catch up about next steps?"

"Works for me," Posey said.

Lexy drove them back to the school parking lot, where Gramps sat alone in the sea of asphalt. It was getting to be twilight already, the sun a blaze of orange through the tall trees. Posey shivered in the night air as she jumped out of the Tesla and waved goodbye. Lexy peeled a little rubber as she pulled back onto the highway. As soon as Posey climbed into Sal's van, he cranked the heat and blew out an exasperated sigh.

"What's that mean?" Posey asked.

He gave her a look, raised his eyebrows. Right now, in the low light, his eyes seemed greener than before. "*Man*, she gets on my nerves."

"Lexy?" Posey asked, surprised. "Really?"

"You saw how she was about Gramps, right? 'I have a *Tesla*.' Kiss my ass."

Sal pulled onto the highway and switched his headlights on. Though he was being over-the-top, Sal's ranting was out of character for him. She allowed him to continue, interested in knowing whatever was inside him whether she necessarily agreed with him or not.

"Now you *know* I'm on some list. I'm on the record, coming to a teacher's house—you know how bad that looks for me, under the circumstances? I do not need to be in any worse with admin right now than I already am. Bet you anything I get pulled over this week by Deputy Butts just to mess with me for coming to his brother's house."

"Are you serious?" Posey asked.

"Hell yeah, I'm serious. Half the time I find a place to park for the night I wake up to him whacking my window at the ass-crack of dawn and telling me to 'Move along, now.' And it got so much worse after the investigation started. You think that timing's a coincidence?"

"You can stay in my driveway again," Posey said.

He didn't answer. "Hate that whole fucking neighborhood, those families up there, all that money, those smug smiles, I just—I hate them all."

"*Hate*'s a strong word," Posey said.

The word itself left a bad taste in her mouth. It wasn't something Posey liked to feel and it wasn't something she was comfortable seeing in other people. Looking at Sal right now, it occurred to her how close the words *hurt* and *hate* were.

Suddenly, Sal wrenched the steering wheel to the right, shocking Posey so much she let out a tiny gasp. He pulled over onto the shoulder of the road. The van came to a screeching halt and then, like an animal in pain, Sal let out a giant roar and gripped the steering wheel and shook it. He thrashed in his seat and made a whimpering noise while Posey was frozen as a corpse in her seat, jaw unhinged, watching him, not computing what was going on. Then she heard his sniveling. She wasn't sure what to do.

"Sal," she said, reaching out and putting a hand on his shoulder. He stopped thrashing, his hands on his face.

"Sal, it's okay," she said, then immediately rethought her statement as she pulled her hand away. "Actually, it's not okay. Nothing's okay."

"Where the fuck is she?" he asked, pulling his hands away from his face and revealing blotchy, pink-stained cheeks and bloodshot, teary eyes. "Why would she do this? *Nothing makes sense.*"

His pain, so raw, so on display—it made Posey squirm as she met his stare. Her helplessness hurt. She wanted to make this better for him, but she couldn't. And even though she knew that it was okay to cry, Posey herself would never. She held her tears and let them out behind closed doors and then washed her face so no one would know. Emotions were wild and frightening things.

"You're right," Posey said. "Right now, it doesn't make sense. We're going to make sense of it, though, Sal. We're going to figure this out."

"She wouldn't do this to me," he said, wiping his eyes on his sweatshirt. "She wouldn't *disappear* like this." He slouched, defeated, and faced the wheel again with both hands on it. "I kept hoping she'd be back today."

"I'm sorry," Posey said.

She felt very stupid uttering a feeble two-syllable word like *sorry* as if it would make a difference. Of course it didn't. It was like tossing a stone into the sea.

"We were supposed to go to court," he said.

"Right," Posey said, remembering the calendar.

"If they wanted, cops could pull me into a group home or a foster home like *that*. The only reason they haven't is because they know I'm working on getting emancipated," Sal snapped. "Finally, finally, I was going to legally be on my own. Molly was going to take me there. She helped me file the paperwork, she was the one walking me through the whole process. . . ."

"Listen, I know she was your support person. But no matter what happens with Ms. Moses, you can still get emancipated," Posey said. "Right?"

Sal had a glassy ten-yard stare. The torment had left him and now he was blank. Posey almost put her hand on him to try to gently stir him from his trance but wasn't sure if he wanted to be touched right now.

"What if she did just leave me?" he said to the air, as if he were trying it out. "What if she left us?"

"That would be awful," Posey said.

"Everyone leaves me," he said.

He didn't say it despondently. He said it assertively, like a fact. The boy looked broken. Posey tried to control the feeling inside her, but it was like a vise was on her chest, cranking tighter and tighter. Then he turned to her, their eyes locking.

"My parents left me," he said.

Posey knew this already—after all, he lived in a van and was looking to get emancipated—but hearing him say it made her hurt for him.

"How old were you?" she asked.

"Oh, it was a process. They left me over and over again. Couple of junkie drifters who just bum around the country. Sometimes they blow through town and then blow right out again."

"My mother left me when I was a toddler," she said. "She had postpartum issues and went on vacation and never came back."

"Wow, Posey," he said, sitting up straighter. "I had no idea."

"So Sal, I understand," she said. "I know it's the worst thing in the world when people leave. But we don't even know that Ms. Moses left yet, okay? Don't give up hope."

It might have been the longest staring contest yet. They were still looking at one another, though something resembling curiosity had softened Sal's gaze. There was something warm and sweet running between them. She wouldn't call it romantic—it was trust, pure and simple.

Not that it mattered, but he lost the staring contest.

"Okay, so then what's next, boss?" he asked as he started up the van. His voice perked up. When they pulled back onto the road, it was as if the whole thing had never happened. "Abby Frost? I was thinking about how El said she worked nights now at the Gas Up. Let's see if we can find her there."

"Smart," she said, pointing at him.

And off they went.

NINETEEN

Posey didn't know what the "Gas Up" was. Naturally, she assumed it was a gas station. She wasn't wrong—it was a gas station, there were pumps and cars—but at first glance it sure didn't *look* like a gas station. On the road signage, there was a metallic clown head with glowing eyes and a glowing red nose next to the cursive lettering that said GAS UP! That same giant clown head was also on the front of the convenience store. It looked . . . vintage. That was a nicer way of saying it. Like an amusement park for clown lovers built half a century ago. As they pulled up to park in the small side lot, Posey gulped.

It was fine. It was only a gas station. Posey was not afraid of clowns. She let out a breath when they were right outside the convenience store and Sal gave her a look, his hand on the glass door that had a big, blown-up picture of the same clown on it. He hesitated before pushing the door open.

"What?" he asked. "You okay?"

"Yep, doing great!" That seemed a bit much, considering the

circumstances, so Posey walked it back by saying, "Doing okay, actually. Just okay."

He continued giving her that look she knew so well, that "you're a weirdo" look.

"You want to give me your phone and we'll do the usual?" he asked, holding his palm out.

Posey nodded and handed it over.

"You sure you're okay?"

"Yep! Ready, let's go."

As Sal pushed the door open, a clown-honk doorbell announced their entrance. To Posey's horror, the first thing to greet them was entire shelves of clown merchandise. Coffee mugs shaped like clown heads, fishbowls full of clown noses, clown T-shirts, clown keychains, clown shot glasses, clown earrings, clown baseball caps, clown coasters and beer koozies. It was dizzying. Was it hot in here? That must be why she was breaking a sweat.

"Are you sure you're okay?" Sal asked Posey.

She realized she was standing frozen in the middle of the store and gaping at the horrible clowns.

"I'm not really a huge fan," she whispered.

"Of clowns."

Sal snickered at that. On the one hand, it was nice to see his teeth again, it had been a while. On the other, he was laughing at her expense. If she were a meaner person, she would kick him right now. Not hard. Just soft enough to surprise him. But Posey instead glared at him and hissed "Never mind" and led the charge to the counter, now fueled with a renewed fire of annoyance.

The employee who stood behind it appeared to be only a few years older than Posey, though the woman was quite the picture: white, with brown hair so wild and frizzy you'd think she stuck her finger in an electrical socket; heavy, raccoon-like eyeliner around wide, buggy eyes, and beneath one eye, the tattoo of a crooked little star; a red vest with GAS UP embroidered in cursive. Posey never wanted to judge, and maybe it was the circus music soundtrack . . . but at first glance, this woman looked unhinged.

It only occurred to Posey then that they were interviewing a woman who could possibly be responsible for the disappearance of their teacher. Who could, very well, be dangerous. Posey met the blinking red eye of the security camera and felt a flicker of comfort at the sight of it.

"Hello," Posey said to the woman with a smile. She folded her hands on the glass counter displaying lottery tickets. "Are you Abby Frost?"

"Me?" Abby asked. "Um, yeah. Why?"

"I'm Posey and this is Sal and we're with the *Wild Pines Buzz.*"

Abby, chewing a large wad of blue gum, had the placid look of a cow chewing cud. "Huh?"

"We're doing an investigative report on the disappearance of Molly Moses," Posey said. "Could we ask you a few questions?"

At the sound of "Molly Moses," Abby's expression darkened. She stood up straighter and huffed out a sigh. "What's this for?"

"It's for a news show we have," Posey explained. "We're

students at Wild Pines and we're interviewing people in her life, trying to figure out where she went."

"How long's she been gone?" Abby asked. "Bet she just jetted, you know, 'cause of what was going down." She leaned in and dropped her voice. "I heard she was doinking one of her students."

Posey looked at Sal, whose expression hadn't changed. But Posey could see he was clenching his jaw so tightly his muscle bulged beneath his cheek.

"That's fascinating. I hadn't heard that," Posey said, giving Sal a little nudge to stay calm. "Could we ask you a few questions?"

Abby thought about it for a second and then shrugged and stood up. "Yeah, sure. Does my hair look okay?"

Posey thought it looked like Abby had perhaps just escaped a tornado, but she nodded and said, "Yep."

Though his jaw was still clenched, Sal started filming.

Transcript

POSEY
Abby, can you describe how you know Molly Moses?

ABBY
Um, yeah. She and I worked together over at Pickins,
you know that place? Yeah. (looks at camera)
And all you all out there? Take note that Pickins is a

discriminating place. A place where certain
religions are not respected. And I'm going to be
talking to my lawyer about it. You hear? Yeah, I got
a lawyer now. A good one. You know that guy on
the billboard up the highway, the Santa guy?

POSEY
Abby, how did you know Molly Moses?

ABBY
I'm getting there, okay? (looks at the camera
again) Because speaking of discriminators,
Molly was number one, you know? At Pickins,
she harassed me and spread lies about me
shoplifting, which, no, wasn't what happened—
she got me fired. And now I'm here at the
Gas Up, sleeping on Mama's couch again,
and it's all Molly's fault this happened. And
so I hope she ran herself out of town. And if,
Tad forbid, something did happen to her?
Well, I believe that's her destiny.

POSEY
Can we back up and can I ask about this claim that she
was the reason you were fired? Can you explain what
happened exactly?

ABBY

Look, some items fell into my purse. Wasn't
my doing. Gravity put them there.

POSEY

Items?

ABBY

Actually I'd better not talk about this any more
without my lawyer present.

POSEY

Anything else we should know about Ms. Moses?

ABBY

Just that she's a liar and a bigot and she's
probably run herself out of Wild Pines because
she doinks her students. (points to camera)
If you're watching this, Molly, you'd better
stay out of Wild Pines for good.

TWENTY

Posey and Sal sat in silence as Gramps sped along the highway toward town again.

"Well, we're not airing that," Sal finally said.

"No. No we're not." Outside the window, it was so dark now that all Posey could see was her own reflection. She shifted her gaze to the glowing light of the radio tuner on the dash. "She really broke the fourth wall there, didn't she?"

"Yeah. She was out there."

Posey chewed her cheek as she mentally reviewed the interview. First of all, *doinking* was a word for sexual intercourse? Really? Second, she saw how Sal had tensed up when Abby said it. And even though she was inclined to believe Sal that there was nothing like that going on between him and his teacher, she couldn't help but entertain the possibility. Third, Abby's animosity toward Ms. Moses was palpable. Finally, there was the Tad stuff—what on earth was that about? While none of the details of her interview could be believed (some things "fell" into her purse, really?), the one takeaway for Posey now was this: there were quite a few people who were delighted to have Ms. Moses gone from Wild Pines, and Abby was one of them.

"My head is spinning," Posey said. "I need to eat. You want to go get breakfast for dinner?"

"That's okay," he said. "I have Cup O' Noodles and stuff."

"Cup O' Noodles?" she said in horror. "That's not a healthy dinner."

"Yeah, well, when you're living on a hundred bucks a week, it's what you get."

Posey wondered where his money came from. Was someone sending it to him? Was it financial aid from the government? But she didn't think it was her place to ask.

"Oh." Out the dash, she could see the string of lights peeking through the dark forest. It was Mile High Drive with its lantern-shaped streetlamps and fairy lights strung up between trees. "Listen, I'll pay for breakfast for dinner. We need to discuss everything. And I haven't had reception for a while now, we need to check on the episode."

After a beat, he said, "Okay." And then, "Thanks, Pose."

There it was again—"Pose." She couldn't help but smile.

In Delilah's, the lights were blindingly bright and the Supremes were cranking on the jukebox. Posey and Sal sat side by side at a booth and Posey pulled out her phone. Now that her reception had returned, she got a notification that she had missed forty-three messages on the group text.

"Jesus," Sal said when he saw it.

Posey scrolled through it, hoping there was some lead about

Ms. Moses. Maybe she'd come home! But unfortunately, that wasn't the case. "It's all about the episode taking off." She squinted. "Yash's compiling all the comments in a spreadsheet so we can look for tips." She put her hand to her heart and took in a deep, satisfied breath. "I do love a spreadsheet."

"Of course you do," Sal said.

Posey opened YouTube and refreshed the episode page, waiting for the tiny numbers to update. When they did, she balked.

They were at *twenty thousand* views.

"Sal, look," she whispered, pushing her phone to him for a closer view.

He spent a moment squinting at the screen as if he were reading a foreign language before finally saying, "Wow."

"Have you even seen the episode yet?"

He shook his head. "I'll watch it later. Honestly, I don't even care about the episode. I just want her to come back."

She nodded, pushing the phone away. It was silly, wasn't it? To care about the numbers on the screen when the whole goal of the project was to find Ms. Moses. She wondered what Ms. Moses would think about all this if she were here. Maybe she'd be proud of them for producing something like this. Maybe she'd be angry that they were nosing around her life and broadcasting it on You-Tube. Posey didn't know her well enough to make an educated guess—all she knew was Ms. Moses was kind, she was welcoming, and her story deserved attention.

"I want that too, Sal," she told him, straightening her fork, knife, and spoon on its napkin.

The waitress arrived. It was Sandhya again, the one Posey met the other night. Posey found it odd that her dad had made friends with a waitress. But after taking their orders on a pad and slipping it back into her apron pocket, the first thing Sandhya asked was where Peter was.

"Probably working," Posey said. "He works late most nights."

"Ah," she said with a hint of disappointment. "Tell him I said hi."

Posey gave a tight-lipped smile as she watched Sandhya walk away, noticing the mermaid tattoo on the back of her calf below her poodle skirt. Posey didn't understand what compelled human beings to disfigure themselves for something like a permanent cartoon mermaid.

"That lady has the hots for your dad," Sal whispered in a sing-song voice.

Turning her head, Posey glared at Sal. "Stop it."

He grinned, exposing his teeth to her for the third time—not that she was counting. "She has the hots for your dad and it bugs the shit out of you."

"Sal Zamora, you do not know the first thing about what's inside me," she said, sitting up straighter.

"I think I have some ideas," he said.

Suddenly, Posey became aware of how close the two of them were sitting. Of the fact that they were squeezed together on one side of the booth, their legs touching, his hand only inches from hers on the table. She got up and moved to the other side, across from him.

"Can we stay focused, please?" she said, pulling her notebook out of her backpack along with her purple pen. "Next steps. I need to send those interviews—"

"Club!" someone belted out, interrupting Posey.

Looking up, Posey spotted Jeremiah waving at her from the cash register. He had a plastic bag of food dangling in his hand and was striding toward them. He looked even taller than usual from this angle.

"What's up, club?" he said, sliding into the seat next to Posey and nodding to them. "Any word on Ms. Moses?"

"Nothing so far. We've been out chasing interviews," Posey said. "The video has a ton of views, hopefully there are clues in the comments. I haven't had a chance to read them."

"I just put, like, a hundred flyers up around Mom and Pop's store." Jeremiah reached into the plastic bag to pull out a French fry and pop it into his mouth. "Who'd you interview?"

"Abby Frost," Sal said. "At the Gas Up."

"Ah, Clown Hell," Jeremiah said. "Funsies. She have any good info?"

"No," Posey said. "She was . . ."

"She's a Tad freak," Sal said.

"Ohhhhh." Jeremiah's eyes widened. "Okay."

"What's a 'Tad freak'?" Posey asked.

"They're this group—" Sal started.

"They're a cult," Jeremiah corrected him, fishing out another French fry. "Y'all want a fry? Where's your food?"

"It's on its way, we're good," Sal said.

"A cult?" Posey asked, straightening up, intrigued.

"Yeah, they live up Blue Mirror Vista. There's a compound." Jeremiah checked the time on his phone and stood up. "Shit, I have to go back to the shop. What's the plan this weekend?"

Posey was bursting with questions—a cult! Come on, that was juicy. But she swallowed them for the time being. "I guess Sal and I will keep interviewing?"

"I have work tomorrow," Sal said. "You'll have to go without me."

Sal had a job? There was so much she still didn't know about her club colleagues.

"The problem is, I don't have a mode of transportation," Posey said.

"She doesn't drive," Sal explained to Jeremiah.

"You don't have your *license*?" Jeremiah said in horror.

She shook her head.

"You might want to get on that. Our bus system's a *joke*. Anyway, I'm off tomorrow. I have practice at four but if you want a partner in crime, I'll meet up with you."

Posey was touched by the offer. "I'd love that," she said to Jeremiah. "I have some ideas. I'll text you?"

"Yep." Jeremiah stood up and stretched. "Catch you later, kids."

He went out the door, singing along with the jukebox song so loudly heads turned. Posey admired his confidence—she couldn't even manage a solo in choir class at her old school.

Their breakfasts for dinner arrived. Sal and Posey must have both been starving, because they ate for a few minutes in silence. Finally, Posey wiped her mouth and asked Sal about his job.

"I work over at a mechanic's shop at the end of Mile High Drive," Sal said. "Molly and Doug got me the job. I work weekends."

"Fixing cars?" Posey asked.

"Yeah. Learning to."

"That sounds fun."

"It's okay."

"Can you tell me about the cult thing?" Posey asked. "Number one, there's a cult here? And number two, how do you know Abby's part of it?"

"Yeah, you don't see the Tad freaks much in town unless they're at the grocery store picking up supplies or something. They live full-time up on their compound doing . . . whatever they do. But you can always spot them because of that star tattoo under their eye. Or former members. There are a few of them around here."

"So Abby must be a former member?" Posey asked, sipping her cocoa. "She mentioned sleeping on her mom's couch."

"Yeah, guess so."

After finishing up, Posey paid the bill and they climbed back into the van that was starting to feel comfy and familiar to her. She shivered at the bite of the cold night air and hoped that wherever Ms. Moses was, she was warm.

"I can't wait to read the comments Yash compiled," she said as Sal pulled Gramps onto the road. "I'll go through them all tonight and highlight anything worth following up on, maybe start a new sheet with interview prospects and who our interviewee priorities are this weekend. Do you have an email address?"

"Yeah. But I mean . . . I don't always have an internet connection. So it might be a bit before I see something sometimes."

"Sal, maybe we should consider investing in a burner phone for you, at least, while this investigation is happening. What if I find out where Ms. Moses is and I can't reach you?"

"Your energy is exhausting sometimes."

"I'm going to choose to hear that as a compliment. If you'd like to stay in our driveway again—which you're more than welcome to—you can hook up to our internet. The network is 'House of Spades' and the password is 'integrity.' You are staying in our driveway again, right?"

He was silent. Everything was so dark as he pulled onto her street that she couldn't see anything but the misty road ahead of them in the headlights.

"Sal?" she asked as he pulled to a stop. At first, she wasn't sure why he was stopping. Then she realized they were in front of her house. It took time, getting used to a new house. When she looked up the stairs at the cabin nestled in the pine trees, she had to remind herself it was home.

He didn't answer her. He didn't turn off the engine, either.

"Are you not staying here?" she asked, trying to read the silence. She couldn't see anything except for the shape of his sweatshirt hood.

"You're really sweet," he said. "Everything you're trying to do for me, it's—it's nice. Buying me dinner and letting me sleep in your driveway and offering to get me a phone, but . . ."

"But what?" she asked, her heart dropping.

"I can't, like, keep accepting things from you. You know? I have to figure out how to do this on my own. In a way it's like the whole reason I got in trouble—and who knows? Maybe the whole reason Molly's missing now—maybe it's because I was relying on her too much." His voice caught in his throat. "I got her in trouble, you know? Whatever happened to her, I feel like it was me depending on her that made it happen."

"Sal," Posey said firmly, unclipping her seat belt so she could reach across and rest a hand on his shoulder. "None of this is your fault."

"Don't tell me that. Come on, I'm not stupid," he said. "I'm the reason she was being investigated. If she skipped town, it was to run away from me."

The hurt changed his voice. It made it small and tight. Both of his hands were still on the wheel, as if he didn't notice her hand there on his shoulder, or maybe he didn't want her touching him. She wasn't sure what was too little or too much sometimes. She pulled her hand back into her lap.

"And what if she didn't skip town and what if she didn't run away?" she asked softly. "What if something happened to her and we can help find her?"

"What if it's too late?"

"What if she's out there and she needs help and no one but us is even looking for her?"

A long pause settled in the car, over the low grumbling of the engine. Posey thought she had won the "what if" game but she still hadn't won this argument entirely, not until he parked his van in her driveway again. She didn't understand why it mattered to her so much that he stayed here, why she didn't want to let him go.

"Sal, it's selfish, everything I'm doing for you. Me feeding you, me wanting you to stay in the driveway. It's not pity. It's me needing you as a partner. I can't do this alone. I can't do this if I can't reach you. You're my Watson."

"What does that even mean?"

"Sherlock Holmes? Don't tell me you don't know who that is."

"Oh."

"You're my Watson," she repeated.

"Look, I have plenty of other places to go. I mean, if worse comes to worst, there's always Doug—"

"Are you serious? Number one, the school investigation. Number two, that is a complete conflict of interest when it comes to our story. You can't do that, Sal."

He blew out a long sigh, one that signaled victory to Posey and lit her up like a bulb. He turned the car into her driveway and parked it. Sometimes dealing with Sal felt a bit like luring a stray cat. There was a skittishness to him that made Posey feel as if he might run from her at any second.

"Do you . . . Do you want to come upstairs?" she asked.

"No thanks."

"Not even to use the bathroom?"

"Nah, I'm good."

"Where do you . . . go to the bathroom?"

"Good night, Posey."

"Or shower? Where do you shower?"

"You ever notice that the word *nosy* rhymes with the word *Posey*?"

It was not the first time this observation had been shared with her. Posey stopped her line of questioning and instead asked for his email, programming it into her phone. She reminded him of her internet network and password, then took a deep breath and jumped outside.

"Good night, Sal," she said.

"No need to say good night," he muttered. "I'm sure I'll be hearing from you in the next ten minutes."

Rude. She had planned on waiting at least a half hour before emailing him. Her feelings for him were on such a spectrum—she wanted to hug him and she wanted to wring his neck. Posey had never known anyone who made her feel both things at the same time. She didn't utter another word to him, just jutted her chin up, slammed her car door shut with extra *oomph*, and sprinted up her stairs.

TWENTY-ONE

After a quick shower, Posey sat on her bed in her robe and caught up on the group text thread. The video's viral growth seemed over, the video plateaued at twenty thousand views. Posey took a few minutes to call Yash. To her sheer delight, he had already highlighted the most promising YouTube comments in a color-coded system and pasted them to a new page in the spreadsheet.

"Yash, you are an absolute rock star," she told him.

"I am?"

"This spreadsheet is super helpful."

"It is?"

"I'm sending the group some files of today's interviews. We won't be using Abby's, there's nothing there. But there's a little bit of footage with Mr. Butts. I don't know, we should see if Lexy has ideas for how to string a narrative together."

"I'm worried sick about Ms. Moses," he said. "Reading through the comments—there's some, like, unsettling stuff in there. Like R-rated stuff."

"I know. Comment sections are a sinister place sometimes."

"When are you thinking we drop the next episode?"

"This weekend, I hope, if we can."

"Okay. I babysit both afternoons but I can just put on a movie for the kids or something so I can edit."

"Rock star," she repeated.

"Wow, Posey. Thank you. You are . . . a rock star as well." He cleared his throat. "Did you—did you read all the comments yet?"

"I'm scanning the ones you highlighted right now."

"I highlighted people who said something that could be helpful or who might have more info, you know, people who seemed to be local and we could follow up with? Most of them are just saying they think she left town on her own, like she ran away. Those are highlighted in green. Some are saying they think Doug had something to do with it—those are highlighted in yellow. One person said they thought they saw her at the Gas Up that night and that's the only one in red."

"The Gas Up?" Posey repeated.

"Then there are the ones I highlighted in gray," he went on. "All talking about a serial killer—do you really think that's what happened? Because that is, like, terrifying."

"No, don't let yourself get sucked into a conspiracy theory."

Posey was still stuck on the Gas Up comment. She found it in the spreadsheet and read it back to herself, mouthing the words silently.

topdawg408: pretty sure i saw her pull into the gas up that night around 10 something when i was there with my girls (my toy poodles, i breed if anyone is looking for poodles!! link in bio)

👍 👎 **Reply**

"I'm going to digest this spreadsheet for a bit," Posey said. "You going to be okay?"

"Yeah. I was looking up statistics to comfort myself. Did you know that the vast majority of missing persons cases get solved within a short period of time? One article I clicked on said about ninety-nine percent of cases."

"That's encouraging," she said. "Thank you for sharing that with me. Talk soon, Yash."

"Oh. Okay. See you."

Posey hung up. There was so much humming in her mind that she got up and paced her room, padding the carpet in her bare feet. She wished she could make a murder board like they did in crime shows—photographs and news articles and pins with colored threads connecting all the pieces.

Wait, though. What if instead of a murder board, Posey made a *Jamboard*?

The revelation stopped her in her tracks and prickled her fingertips. Why hadn't she thought of this earlier? Posey's enthusiasm for Jamboards was up there with slide presentations and spreadsheets. She sat on her bed again and opened her laptop and, in a flurry of typing and copying and pasting and moving a rain-bow of virtual Post-it notes around on different pages, she created a master document for the AV Club. It had pages for each person they had spoken with so far. In pink notes, she added standout or suspicious quotes, e.g. for Abby, she added the line, "If you're watching this, Molly, you'd better stay out of Wild Pines for good." In green notes, she described the relationship Ms. Moses had to each person, e.g. for Mr. Butts she said, "Wild Pines fac-ulty, theater department, possibly hostile." In yellow, she detailed follow-up questions, e.g. for Doug, "Ask to see MM's last texts."

On another page, Posey put a picture of Ms. Moses taken from the Wild Pines High website. She sectioned off three different cor-ners of the page. Each section was titled:

LEFT OF HER OWN ACCORD

MURDER   SUICIDE

She pinned Post-its detailing "evidence for" in purple and "evidence against" in orange. She exhausted all possibilities and sat back, nearly breathless from how fast she had been working since she started the Jamboard an hour ago. It was interesting to note that, on this most recent page she'd been working on, the sec-tion with the most purple was "left of her own accord" and the one with the most orange was "murder." The third section, "suicide," had the fewest Post-it notes, period.

That said something, didn't it? So far, Ms. Moses leaving of her own accord appeared the most probable conclusion, and murder was the most far-fetched conclusion. But that was already what Posey had thought. Maybe this was confirmation bias. Posey googled *confirmation bias.*

> confirmation bias: the tendency to interpret new evidence
> as confirmation of one's existing beliefs or theories

Hmm. Her dad often spoke of how important it was for journalists to avoid confirmation bias. If Posey already had a hunch that Ms. Moses wasn't murdered—was that the reason why the evidence affirmed this? She tried so hard to ignore her hunches when reporting a story, but it seemed impossible. To be impartial was like trying to be perfect. You can try and try and try and you'll never quite get there. Posey knew this well.

She was suddenly so exhausted.

Posey lay back on her bed and closed her eyes for a moment. She could feel a headache coming on, which happened sometimes when she stared at a screen too long. She must have drifted off, because when she opened her eyes again her alarm clock revealed that nearly an hour had been stolen by a nap. Ugh, naps! Such a literal waste of time. She groaned and sat up. Her computer was dinging with a weird noise, which is what woke her up. They were instant messages coming in through email.

deadinside1234: posey?

deadinside1234: helloooooooo

deadinside1234: *screams into void*

Posey narrowed her eyes at the screen and typed back:

msposeyspade: Who is this?

deadinside1234: it's sal

She smiled.

msposeyspade: Oh! Hi.

deadinside1234: what's goin on?

msposeyspade: I was just making a Jamboard for us.

deadinside1234: wow fun

Sarcasm? Posey couldn't tell. It seemed the line between sarcasm and sincerity was razor-thin with this boy. She decided to assume sincerity until proven otherwise and forged ahead.

msposeyspade: How's van life?

deadinside1234: cozy

msposeyspade: Did you watch the episode yet??

deadinside1234: yeah

deadinside1234: the comments 🍌

msposeyspade: Yash made a spreadsheet to organize the comments!

deadinside1234: yall so organized

deadinside1234: lemme see the jamboard

Posey sent Sal the link and waited for his response. After about five minutes her computer dinged again.

deadinside1234: thanks for making that, good stuff

That's it? All that A+ work and *that* was his response? Sal was definitely the classmate who did absolutely nothing when assigned a group project. It was fine. Sometimes she preferred working with people like that because it meant she could easily assume the role of leader.

msposeyspade: No problem!

"Hey," her dad said from the doorway, startling Posey.

He looked tired, his hair windswept. It was almost nine, which meant he had been working for nearly twelve hours. Posey stood up and gave him a giant hug, squeezing tight. She loved the way he smelled—like soap and cinnamon.

"Hi, Daddy," she said.

They pulled apart and he tousled her hair. "Whatcha up to?"

"I was just chatting with Sal."

"Ah." Her dad rubbed his chin. "Wait—the guy in the van?"

Posey nodded.

"The van parked in our driveway right now?"

Posey nodded again.

"Is he . . . chatting with you *from* the van?"

Posey nodded a third time.

After a pause, he said, "Your generation is very strange."

"Funny, I think the same about yours."

Her dad smiled and leaned against the doorframe. "So. How was your day?"

"We put the episode up!" she said, grabbing her phone. "You want to see?"

"You mind if I go eat something first? I'm starving."

"I'll make you pancakes," she said, grabbing her computer to follow him back downstairs.

When Posey showed her dad the episode, he watched it with deep consideration, chewing his pancakes. At a couple of points, he said "Hmmm" as if he wasn't sure about it. Jeremiah's wailing vocals in the song at the end of the episode made him chuckle.

"It's good," he said simply, shutting her laptop. "That's a good pilot."

Posey sat across from her dad, braiding her hair. She blinked back at him. In the silence, the wind sang a haunting song and rattled the kitchen window.

"And?" she said.

"It was good, Posey. Some of the transitions could use a little . . . something. You know? A bit jarring."

"Yes." She finished her braid, snapping the band into place, the end of her hair like a little paintbrush. Getting up, she grabbed a pen and small yellow pad of paper from a console table. Every room in their house had pens and paper scattered about—both Posey and her dad were prone to fall down rabbit holes of thought that suddenly needed to be captured and written down. She took her seat again and uncapped the pen. "What else?"

"There was very little about who Molly Moses was as a human being. You want this story to have legs, you need us to understand who she was and what she meant to people. I realize you don't have a lot of time there—but sprinkle in some talking heads, you know, students, family, people saying how much they mean to them."

Posey was writing so fast her hand cramped up.

"Some major details were missing. Like when was the missing persons report filed? Did her husband file it? Things like that."

Her cheeks flushed. She felt a little foolish for not asking these questions. She wrote down *missing persons report!*

"Other than that, Pose, I'm impressed." Her dad stood and turned to the kitchen to wash his dish. "Twenty thousand views for something you all slapped together in what—a day? That's nothing to sneeze at."

"Thanks, Daddy," she said.

Her dad was always encouraging, but not exactly generous with praise. Once, when Posey had written a poem in junior high school she was particularly proud of, she gave it to him to read. He put on his reading glasses and sat with it. Ten minutes later, he handed it back to her marked up with a red pen to point out her typos and grammatical errors.

"I like it," is all he'd said.

She had been disappointed at this response, but then she

corrected her errors and submitted it to a school contest and guess what? She won. Her dad wasn't interested in being her cheerleader. He wanted to be her coach.

Posey tore the page of notes from the pad and gave her dad a hug and thanked him. She'd do better. She'd dive deeper. Tomorrow.

Bright, shining tomorrow.

TWENTY-TWO

Saturday, September 14

6:05 AM

Concern for our teachers and students

Dear Wild Pines High community,

This week, we were shocked to learn our multimedia teacher, Ms. Moses, was reported missing. We are deeply troubled by this news. The safety and health of our staff and students' physical and mental health remain our top priority.

While we currently do not have many details about the case, we will be working closely with law enforcement in their investigation. We urge any community members with information about the case to contact the Wild Pines Police Department directly.

When a person goes missing, especially a teacher, it is natural for the community to speculate and for rumors to fly. Let us all remain levelheaded and wait for details before jumping to conclusions. We will continue supporting our students and faculty during the investigation and updating our community with any new details.

Sincerely,

Valerie Vance
Principal
Wild Pines High

Interesting. Very interesting. Posey chewed her oatmeal as she sat alone at the table, staring at the email on her phone. She forwarded a screenshot of it to the group text and was surprised when Athena responded right away.

👀 I know a CYA move when I see one

CYA? Posey texted back.

cover yo ass, Athena texted. episode made the rounds and now she had to respond. what's the plan today?

Jeremiah and I are going out for interviews, we'll touch base after that. Sal's working. How about you?

> stupid group therapy all morning. free later tho. can't believe she's been gone four days now, officially worried over here

Same, Posey said.

It was like a cloud cast over Posey. Four days. Four days was bad in any scenario. If someone were lost in the wilderness, the human body was unlikely to survive dehydration that long. If Ms. Moses was the victim of a kidnapping, she could be in grave danger. If it was—*shudder*—a homicide, the first seventy-two hours were crucial in an investigation to protect the integrity of evidence. But Posey couldn't let the grip of doubt squeeze the hope she held on to dearly. For all she knew, there were new discoveries. Maybe Ms. Moses had used one of her credit cards since she'd last interviewed Doug. Maybe the FBI had been contacted. Maybe Doug had even heard from her since her disappearance—which was why Posey needed to get dressed and ready to chase a second interview with him for updates.

"Hey, Posey," Jeremiah said when she climbed into his car. It was a white sedan that smelled of the artificial cedar tree hanging from the dash. The back seat was packed with crates of records. Jeremiah seemed more subdued than usual, tired maybe. He wore a jean jacket, one dangly earring, and he might have put some pink in his afro—or maybe it had been there and she was just noticing it now. Jeremiah was a good-looking guy. He had wide eyes and freckled light brown skin and when he smiled, it was like lights turning on in a room. But what really made him something special was his confidence. Posey was someone who had to work hard to keep up her confidence, but Jeremiah's seemed to just come naturally. He pulled onto the road, one hand on the steering wheel. Punk music quietly played on the speakers. "Cute house. Cute dress. You're just a little button, aren't you?"

"Um, thanks," Posey said as she fastened her seat belt.

"I need to stop by the shop real quick before we get started, and I also need to get caffeinated because I am not a morning person and I'm *not* feeling it yet."

"The shop?" she asked as he pulled on the road.

"My family owns the record slash bookstore on Mile High. You know, The Vinyl Word?"

Posey loved puns and she loved bookstores, so she was immediately smitten. "That's wonderful! No, I haven't been there yet. Your family owns it?"

"Yep, almost fifteen years. It's cool. We have shows and stuff. My band plays there sometimes."

"I didn't know you were in a band."

"Guitar and vocals. We're called Pissy Goblins."

"Pissy Goblins," Posey repeated doubtfully. "Sounds . . . interesting."

"This is us, actually," he said, turning up the stereo.

During the remainder of the five-minute drive to The Vinyl Word, Jeremiah sang along with every lyric with an alarming amount of passion for someone who claimed to need caffeine. One hand was on the wheel, yes, but the other held an invisible microphone that he sang and/or screamed into. The song was about wanting to set the world on fire, which seemed a bit of an extreme sentiment. Posey sat stiff in her seat, uncertain how she felt about this impromptu performance, especially when the car drifted into another lane. Soon they were on Mile High Drive, passing the many shops, fairy lights glowing in the early morning fog. The diner and the Wild Pines Market had cars parked in front of them already, but almost everything else was still closed at nine thirty a.m. The song ended along with the accompanying performance, Jeremiah parked, and then they hopped out.

"What'd you think?" he asked.

"That was . . . very energetic," she told him.

He raised one eyebrow at her as he slammed his door shut. "Soooo . . . you didn't like it."

"No, I—"

"'Energetic'? I know a euphemism when I hear one." Jeremiah opened the back door and grabbed a crate. "Grab one of these and follow me?"

Posey did as she was told. The crate was shockingly heavy. He led the way up the walkway to the storefront, which had a window with a disco ball and a display of paperbacks and LPs. Inside, the store was absolutely packed with records on the left side and books on the right. It had a yin and yang feel to it—the left side's walls were covered in posters among the record shelves, while the right side was painted white and airy and hung with art.

"What kind of music are you into, Posey?" Jeremiah asked as he unloaded the crates near the long wooden counter where the register was.

"I don't really listen to music," she said.

Jeremiah stopped next to the counter, leaning an elbow on it to study her. It was as if Posey had told him she was half alien. "Excuse me?"

"I just . . . I don't know, I don't think to put music on very often."

"How can you—" He closed his eyes and shook his head. "Give me strength," he whispered. Then he opened his eyes again. "Different strokes. It's fine."

"I love books, though," she said, gesturing to the right side of the room. In fact, if they weren't on a mission right now, she would ask if she could look through the shelves.

"Nerd," he sang affectionately. "Okay, let's get going."

Luckily, there was a café open on Mile High Drive that they hit up after leaving the record shop. It was adorable, hardly big enough for them both to stand in—a cat café attached to a "feline sanctuary" that wasn't open yet. Posey put a mental bookmark in to revisit here when the sanctuary hours were open. Perhaps she could convince her dad to adopt a cat now that they were settled.

Back in the car, Jeremiah turned the sound of his own voice in the stereo down and sipped his "cappy," which was apparently what he called a cappuccino. He explained that The Vinyl Word was the combined life dreams of his parents. His mother was a writer who longed for her own bookstore. His dad, a musician, had always wanted to own a record store. Finally, they decided to own one store together, sliced perfectly in half.

"What do you think of Wild Pines?" he asked. "I mean, quite the contrast from San Fran."

"It is a contrast. I like it, I think. Do you?"

"I mean, sure. Lived here all my life. It's gorge. It's funky. I do plan on getting out as soon as I freaking can, though. I'd like to go somewhere a lot bigger."

"Understandable."

"I'm sure you notice there's a bit of a, shall we say, melanin deficiency in this town. So there's that."

Posey nodded. "Yes, it's definitely not as diverse as the Bay Area."

"I mean, people are generally super accepting. But living in a small place, one of the only families with a white mom and Black dad—I just feel it sometimes."

"I hear that," Posey said.

Their conversation halted as soon as the Moseses' house came into view and they saw the two police cars out front and—count them—three police officers. Yellow crime scene tape circled around an old pickup truck, flapping in the wind.

"Oh sheeeeeeit," Jeremiah said, slowing down the car. "They've got the whole WPPD up in here."

"Park across the street," she said excitedly. "We should get footage of this, whatever it is."

He pulled his car to a stop in front of another house. As they surveyed the scene across the street through the car window, Jeremiah whispered, "I feel sick. What is going *on*?"

Posey, too, was a little nauseous at the sight. It certainly looked like something from a true crime show. They were gathering evidence—for what crime, exactly? She had to wonder what development had occurred since yesterday. A tow truck arrived at Doug's house just then, backing up into the driveway behind the pickup truck. Jeremiah pulled out his phone and covertly shot footage through the window as they waited in the car and watched. Deputy Butts was there, directing the tow truck, waving his arms like someone on an airport tarmac.

Doug was there, too, in an outfit identical to the one the other day—same flannel, same jeans. He paced the lawn as he spoke to another police officer and gesticulated toward the tow truck action.

"He looks up*set*," Jeremiah said.

"He certainly does."

"Why would he be upset? Do you think . . ."

"I don't know." She googled "Molly Moses" on her phone in the news section but nothing came up. "I don't see any big developments. You'd think if a body was found, it would have been reported."

Jeremiah's jaw dropped and his voice rose in both pitch and volume. "If a *body* was found?"

Posey gazed at Jeremiah. He looked like someone had slugged him in the stomach. She recognized that feeling written on his face. She was stunned too. It was like this all was suddenly becoming real at the sight of the police and crime scene tape. Ms. Moses hadn't simply run off; this was far bigger, far more sinister than that.

"She *can't* be . . ." Jeremiah didn't even finish his sentence. He sat back and put both hands on the wheel and looked ahead at the road through his windshield instead of at the tow truck, which was getting hitched to the pickup. "Like, who would do that? Honestly. Ms. Moses was the nicest person. She was real, you know? She *cared* about us. She was helping me with my college applications, she was going to write me a letter of rec, she can't—this can't be happening."

Posey had noticed the subtle flip from present to past tense. She was watching hope drain from this boy's face in real time. It was something, it really was. Jeremiah seemed impenetrably assured until now. But this was messing with him. It occurred to Posey that the deeper they got into this investigation, the more this was bound to happen. Their entire team, save Posey herself, was one walking, talking conflict of interest. It was up to her to hold them all together.

"Take a breath, Jeremiah," she said. "We don't know the story yet. That's why we're here. We're going to get the story."

He inhaled and exhaled. "Yes. All right. Centering myself."

The tow truck started driving away and Posey flapped her hands, saying, "Film this! Can you get this? Get this!" as Jeremiah whined, "Omigod, I'm trying, I'm trying" and after dropping the phone on the floor and shrieking, he managed to film a clip right as it was driving away.

Posey realized she missed Sal. They had chemistry. Not *that* kind; just, you know, platonic chemistry. With Jeremiah, it was the usual awkwardness she felt with so many people. With Sal, it had become easy.

"Okay, let's remain calm," she said to Jeremiah, putting a hand in the air. "We got this footage. Let's go see if we can talk to Butts and get some details before they take off."

"Wait—I don't want to talk to police. We're talking to *police*?"

"Jeremiah," she said as steadily as she could. "We're journalists. This is what we do."

"Ma'am, that man has busted me for public urination. I do not think he's about to take my ass seriously."

"Public urination?" she asked.

"We live in the woods! It was during Wildfest this summer!"

Posey stopped herself. There were some stories she could leave untouched, some context that could remain unknown to her. This was one of those times. But—really? Was she about to have to go do this alone yet again? Was everyone in the AV Club a juvenile delinquent?

"On top of that, come on, you read the news," Jeremiah said. "I'm not about to become a hashtag this morning."

Posey suddenly became aware of her insensitivity—asking a person of color to jump into the fray of a police scene. "You're a hundred percent right. I'm sorry for not thinking of that. I'll be right back, okay?"

Posey stepped outside the car and took a minute to get her phone filming. She got some B-roll, as Sal always thought to do— which helped those awkward transitions and allowed for some variety in the footage they featured, like her dad had suggested. Then she jogged across the street, her breath visible as smoke in the air as it puffed from her mouth. Right now, one of the police cruisers was pulling away. Deputy Butts was getting into the second cruiser. Doug stood on his doorstep with a frown on his face, gaping at the yawn of space where his pickup truck had been and where now nothing but yellow police tape was left.

"Deputy Butts!" Posey shouted as she approached the cruiser. "May I have a word with you?"

Deputy Butts, who was halfway in his car by now, was clearly shocked at the sight of Posey there in her peacoat with her phone already filming him.

"Again, I'm Posey Spade, *Wild Pines Buzz*. I have a few questions—"

"Please," he said, holding a hand up. "I'm a bit busy."

"What was going on?" she asked, her hand shaking. "Why was Doug Moses's truck towed?"

He reached toward his door handle. "This is an open investigation. We're not currently sharing details at this time."

"Has—has Ms. Moses been found?" she asked. "Is there evidence of foul play? I would suspect so, considering the crime scene tape—"

"Go play reporter somewhere else, hon," he said. "This isn't a fun little school newspaper gig; this is a serious investigation."

The word *hon* was so enraging to her, he might as well have thrown a lit match on a pile of kindling. She jutted her chin up. "Any comment, then, on the fact your brother had friction with Ms. Moses? Do you think that his—shall we say—*adversarial* relationship with her might mean you leading this investigation is a conflict of interest?"

Saying it, she knew she was a bit of a hypocrite. "Conflict of interest" might as well have been the AV Club's name at this point. But this man was a police officer. He was leading an investigation that meant life or death for a missing woman. It seemed like a question that deserved asking.

Deputy Butts stared at her, his hand still on the door handle. His lips hardened into a line. She didn't know him but she could tell, by the way his eyes changed, that her question had dug into him. Well, good. She expected him to flare up, raise his voice, maybe get out of the car and lecture her. But instead his face changed again and he just snickered at her and slammed his door shut. As he started the car and pulled away, he put his siren on for a split second for no apparent reason at all.

Posey's hand was still shaking as she turned her phone off. There was nothing there. Nothing that could be used. But the interaction had crawled beneath her skin and she had a feeling it had crawled beneath the deputy's skin as well.

On the porch, Doug stood and yelled, "Hey. Can I help you?"

Posey saw Jeremiah across the street, who was watching through his window with a deer-in-headlights look. He pointed toward Doug and then made an exaggerated shrug, then did some kind of circle gesture with his hand. She had no idea what this meant. She ignored him and walked across the lawn to where Doug stood, next to a mannequin.

"Oh," he said with an edge of disappointment. "It's you."

Had he been expecting someone else? Posey held her hand out. "Posey Spade again with the *Wild Pines Buzz*."

Doug eyed her hand but didn't shake it. "Where's Sal?"

"Working," she said, sliding her hand back into her coat's pockets.

"Ah."

From this close, Posey could see the two-day beard that had grown in patches on his face, the greasy hair, and she could smell his sour breath. He looked like a man who was quickly unraveling.

"Your video, dude," he said. "Really wish I hadn't let you interview me."

"Why?" she asked.

"Because," he said, "now all these—these people I don't even know are messaging me saying they think I killed my wife. You know how fucked-up that is? On top of—of—not knowing what happened to Molly, I'm being accused of—of—"

His voice broke. He sputtered a sob, snot coming out of his nose, which he wiped with his hand. It was disgusting but she supposed acceptable considering the circumstances.

"And now they took my fucking truck," he went on, as if it were somehow her fault. "I can't even look for her! No one's looking for her and now I can't even go around looking for her because they took my fucking truck!"

Posey was torn. She wanted to film this interaction badly. But that would be tactless, right? The man was sobbing in front of her. The man lost his wife and couldn't find her. Swallowing, Posey offered a soft, feeble apology before she asked as gently as she could, "Why did they take your truck?"

"Because I cleaned the interior. The seats. I deep-cleaned it the day before yesterday because I was scared what they'd find in there would be . . . I don't know, *suspicious* to them. And then I guess cleaning it was suspicious, so now they're coming and taking my truck and claiming this is a crime scene."

What? Posey was dizzy trying to figure out what he was saying. He wiped his eyes on the cuff of his flannel and pointed at the empty spot where his truck was.

"Why did you clean your truck?" she asked. "What were you scared they could find?"

"There were bloodstains in there." He pointed accusingly at Posey. "Old ones. Bloodstains from when I cut my hand open this summer. I cut it bad, drove myself to get stitches, covered the mess in the truck with a blanket. But after she disappeared, I was just worried—I didn't want to look guilty. You know how that would look. Search a guy's truck and see all that blood in the passenger seat when your wife's missing . . . it, like, doesn't look good."

"No," she agreed. "It doesn't look good."

She glanced back at Jeremiah, who was in the car on his phone.

"I've gotten like no sleep," Doug said. "I've been driving around looking for her, doing what the police should have been doing this whole time."

"And there's no new action in her bank accounts or anything?" Posey asked.

"Nothing."

"Doug," she said. "Me and Sal and everyone in the AV Club want to help figure out where she is. What were the last texts on Ms. Moses's phone? Maybe there's a clue there?"

Doug sighed. "Okay, so that's another thing. I fucked up. I shouldn't have done it but I freaked out the day she went missing. I erased her texts. Butts took the phone as evidence today."

Slowly, Posey asked, "Why did you erase her texts?"

"I—we were fighting, we were saying stuff I wouldn't want people to read. I just—I didn't want that to be a thing people saw. So I erased them."

Posey wasn't sure how to respond. She really, really wished she was filming this and wondered if her sympathy for Doug at this heightened emotional time was getting in the way of her objectivity. And she didn't know what to make of him. He was visibly troubled and haggard. Honestly, he looked five years older than when she had seen him two days before. And he was making some *very* poor decisions—cleaning his truck and erasing the text history with his missing wife? Giant red flags. He was either a fool or a killer trying to get away with murder; possibly he was both.

"Doug, can I film this?" she asked, taking out her phone. "Please? To help the case? I wanted to ask you about when you filed a report—"

"Nuh-uh," he said, hand up. "I'm not filming anything. Listen, I love Sal. He's like a nephew or something. He's welcome in my house anytime. You? I don't know you. I don't trust you. I don't like how you, you know, made me look on that show of yours. I don't want to be any part of whatever it is you're doing. I've got enough problems, thanks."

His pocket blared suddenly with atrocious screaming and guitars, and Posey realized it was his phone.

"I have to take this," he said.

And in a split second, he had gone inside the house and closed the door. She heard the dead bolt's *snick*. He locked it. He locked his door. Well, that said something. Posey stared at the front door, at the mannequin next to it who wore a KILLER LIVER shirt but no pants. There was a knot in Posey's stomach so giant she was heavy with it. She had a bad feeling, one she hadn't had while investigating the story until now. The crime scene tape, the suspicion of Doug that was building based on the facts, everything just seemed to point to foul play now. And to Doug.

Back in the car, Posey scooted into the passenger's seat, slammed her door, and immediately regurgitated the entire conversation to Jeremiah. She told him the bizarre story about cleaning out Doug's truck, the fact he erased Ms. Moses's texts, his hostility toward being on camera and being on the show, and the way he locked his door at the end.

"Guilty," Jeremiah said. "He's acting so *guilty*. What if he did something to Ms. Moses?" His voice rose in pitch. "What if he *killed* his *wife*—"

"Okay, okay," Posey said, putting a hand on Jeremiah. "It's— we don't know that—"

"Look at him!" Jeremiah said, pointing toward the Moseses' house across the street, where they could see Doug looking at them through the living room window. "That is a *guilty* man!"

As if he could hear them, Doug closed the curtains.

"Jeremiah, let's maintain professionalism," Posey said.

"I'm just stating my opinion. Come on, between friends. *Guilty.*"

On the one hand, Posey was irritated by Jeremiah's rash judgment. On the other, she was surprised and flattered that he called her a friend.

"You really think he killed her?" she asked.

"I sure *hope* not, but I do think there's more to the story with him. Listen," he said to her, showing her his phone. "Text thread's blowing up because a search party for Ms. Moses was just announced. There was a press release from WPPD and Vance just sent an email out to the entire school."

"Seriously?" she asked. "What time?"

"Starts in less than an hour," Jeremiah said. "Everyone's meeting in the empty lot next to Pickins."

"Let's go."

"I don't feel good," he said, not starting the car.

"About . . . ?"

He collected himself, putting his fingers together like a little tent. "This sounds terrible because it *is* terrible but I don't want to find her body."

"Nobody wants that, Jeremiah."

"I mean, I can't even look at a dead mouse. And I just . . ." He started the car and sighed. "I can't believe this. Ms. Moses deserves better than to be one of those murdered ladies on true crime shows who everyone says lit up the room. You know?"

She nodded.

"Last year in her multimedia class, I made this short film," he said, a smile spreading, a wistful twinkle in his eye. "This cute li'l thing about my parents' shop that they could put online, about how I practically grew up there, how my parents started it, our legacy, our family story, our enterprise, you know? My sister, she's three years older than me—she works there now full-time. It's always just been, like, *assumed* that after I graduate I would too. Ms. Moses, she saw this corny thing I made about a literal mom-and-pop shop, and she, like, sensed that there was more to it all. She said to me, she said, 'You know, Jeremiah, there's a big world out there with your name on it. Don't ever forget you're the director of your own movie.' And I don't know why, that just—that meant a lot to me. It was like, she saw this thing in me—this *potential* that I had never really thought about. She gave me permission to think about another life. She started showing me colleges and art schools and was like, you should go for it."

"She sounds like a fantastic teacher," Posey said.

"Yeah." He wiped beneath one eye. Posey couldn't tell if it was his eyeliner being smudged or if it was a tear. "Anyway. So yeah. *I* certainly don't want to find her. I don't want anyone finding her."

"You want to sit this one out?" she asked. "It's totally okay if you do, for any reason at all."

"No, no—like, I know she'd do this for me. I want to go. I want to be part of it."

"Let's go then and hope for the best," she said.

On the way to the search party, Jeremiah put Killer Liver on the stereo. Horrific! Guitars so distorted and drums so fast it was hard to even find a melody. It was torture to her ears. Posey wasn't sure how much of it she could take. She squinted at the song titles. "Bludgeon Dungeon"; "Bloodbrain"; "Disemboweler"; "Murder Is Fun." She sat back in her seat and shook her head. A man who was now a person of interest in his wife's disappearance wears a shirt that says "killer" on it in an interview; cleans out his car because there was blood in it; wipes his wife's text history; and literally has a song called "Murder Is Fun." It was all too much. It was a very bad look for Doug. In fact, Doug Moses was one very bad look. And they had to report it all in the next episode—along with whatever awaited them at the search party.

TWENTY-THREE

She didn't say so, but Posey was scared, too.

She had never been part of a search party before. As they drove through the forest and along the stretch of highway that opened onto a spread of meadows and fields, her stomach got tighter and tighter, as if a screw inside her was getting turned with every passing second. In the distance, she recognized Pickins, its red sign up in the air, and let out a little gasp at the crowds and the full lot next to it. There was even a news van with a crane in the air—real press, real reporting. Posey felt like a mouse entering a gladiator battle. A joke, a girl with her phone and her notebook and purple pen, calling herself a journalist. But then she heard Deputy Butts's voice in her head saying, *Go play reporter somewhere else, hon. This isn't a fun little school newspaper gig; this is a serious investigation.* An inner flame was lit. Posey corrected her posture and took her phone and began filming out the passenger window as Jeremiah looked for parking outside the vacant lot of the pumpkin patch, which had a sign in front of it that said FULL.

"Damn, community showed *up*," Jeremiah said.

"They sure did," Posey said. "There must be a hundred people here."

"At least."

Jeremiah found a parking spot about fifty feet away from the entrance to the lot, tires crunching on the gravel as it pulled to a stop. The two of them jumped out of the car and eagerly started walking a path behind other people headed toward the action. Posey didn't recognize anyone within eyeshot, but she did hear some human voices singing a distant raven *caw*, so she assumed there must be at least a few of her classmates here. She kept her phone steady and got a quick panorama shot to show the size of the crowd they were heading toward.

It was unreal. Posey didn't know how to process what she was seeing. Yesterday no one was talking about Ms. Moses being missing. The deputy was dragging his feet, the school administration was oddly silent. And now the police were towing trucks and collecting evidence as if a crime had happened and Wild Pines High was sending emails to rally support for the cause. Today half the town showed up to form a search party and there were actual news stations covering it. What had happened? What invisible force had snapped its fingers to change it all?

As they entered, Posey noticed there was a particular feel to the gathering—something carnival-like, but also funereal. It was crowded and yet relatively quiet. There were a few people wearing bright orange shirts that said VOLUNTEER on them. Posey spotted Ms. Vance in a pencil skirt and pumps, speaking to a reporter with a microphone near a table full of water bottles.

"*Now* she's talking to reporters," Posey said, nudging Jeremiah. "Yesterday she was bothering Sal about our video and telling me not to put up flyers about Ms. Moses. And today she's talking to reporters?"

"That woman has a visceral hatred for teenagers," Jeremiah said. "I'm not even kidding. Oh! Athena's right over there. *Athena! Athena Murielle Dixon!*"

He yelled so loud Posey flinched and at least a dozen people turned around. Athena, who was talking to someone Posey didn't know, turned at the sound of her name and appeared incredibly annoyed. She was wearing a beanie and a long trench coat, hands deep in her pockets. She stalked over to where Posey and Jeremiah stood near a stack of hay bales.

"Jesus *Christ*, you are obnoxious," she hissed at Jeremiah as she hugged him with one arm. "What is wrong with you? You think I want the entire world to know my middle name is Murielle?" She pulled away from him and faced Posey with a little bow. "Hi, sunshine." She sighed a big, theatrical sigh. "Well. Search party. This fuckin' sucks."

"I'm so sick right now," Jeremiah said. "I might spew, not kidding."

"Let me guess: no breakfast. Coffee on an empty stomach," Athena said to him. When he didn't respond, she shook her head. "You never learn, boo."

"Why are you even here? I thought you had your little group therapy thing."

"Eh, mental wellness can wait."

Looking around, Posey felt overwhelmed, uncertain where to begin, who was in charge. This was a big scene she hadn't exactly expected. She spotted two police officers she recognized from Doug's house but didn't see Deputy Butts. Nor did she see Doug. Posey felt a light *tap-tap* on her shoulder. She turned around and Lexy was there, waving at her. She wore overalls and had her hair in lopsided pigtails.

"Hey," she said. "I've been here for, like, twenty minutes looking for you all. Does no one check their texts?"

"Sorry. It's been hectic," Posey said.

"We saw some *shit* this morning," Jeremiah said.

"Do tell," said Athena.

Jeremiah briefly and theatrically described everything that happened at Doug's house. He described it so well it was like he was actually there and not sitting in the car the whole time—but Posey didn't say that. Lexy and Athena gasped and the group started debating in low voices whether Doug could have done something.

"I definitely think we need to explore Doug as a person of interest in the next episode," Lexy said.

"Sal is not going to be a fan of that idea," Jeremiah said.

"Tough shit," Athena said. "Sal's in way too deep with both the Moseses. Moseses? Is that how you say it? Moses-ees? Anyway, point is, he can't be deciding on what direction we take."

"He's literally the codirector," Jeremiah reminded her.

"Posey's the director today. Sal's not here. Where is Sal?" Athena asked suddenly. "And where's Yash?"

"Right here," Yash said.

Everyone, Posey included, turned in surprise to see Yash standing there, pulling his backpack straps. He had a baseball cap on and had clearly just applied sunscreen, as he had streaks of it on his cheeks.

"Creeper," Athena teased him.

"How long have you been standing there?" Lexy asked.

"A while?" he said. "My mom dropped me off."

"I thought you were babysitting," Posey said, still shocked that he had appeared like a rabbit from a hat.

"I am, at one. Anyone need sunscreen? I also brought protein bars."

Everyone took a protein bar and devoured them in solemn silence. It tasted like berry-flavored cardboard. But Posey appreciated that Yash packed his bag so thoughtfully.

The gang was all here, except Sal. She thought of him working and oblivious that all this was happening. It didn't feel quite right to be here without him—then again, like Athena said, maybe Sal was in too deep with this and it was better he wasn't here.

Posey led the way to an orange-shirted woman with a clipboard who stood near the entrance. She looked frazzled, a bit sweaty, curly hair blowing around her face.

"Hi, is this where we sign up for the search party?" Posey asked.

"It is," the woman said with sadness. "Are you students of Ms. Moses?"

The group nodded.

"Thing is, I'm sorry, you have to be eighteen to join." She turned away and sneezed. "Excuse me. Allergies. Legally, we can't have minors in the search party."

"Oh," Posey said, her heart sinking. She turned to the group. "Is anyone here eighteen?"

No one answered, except Jeremiah, who raised his hand after a long pause.

"Okay, you," the woman said, beckoning Jeremiah over and giving him a pencil and the clipboard. "Go ahead and sign up."

"I'm doing this *alone*?" he nearly shouted.

"You'll be assigned a team," the woman assured him.

Jeremiah signed his name on the form with the flourish of a star signing an autograph. "I'm doing this for Ms. Moses," he said, probably more to himself than to anyone else.

"You've got this, Jeremiah," Lexy said.

"Go over there," the woman told Jeremiah. "That group standing near the haystack? No, not that haystack. Not that one either. The other one, back there, near the scarecrow. Yeah. That's your group."

Jeremiah straightened his posture, flipped up his jacket's collar, and tightened his scarf. "Well . . . goodbye then, children."

"Text us!" Athena shouted after him.

"Get footage!" Lexy yelled.

They stood watching him go for a minute. She thought she could feel a collective relief in the air—her remaining team members had secretly hoped they didn't have to look for a body. Understandable. Posey took this opportunity to talk to the woman

213

with her hair blowing everywhere, who spoke into a walkie-talkie that she put back into a sparkly fanny pack.

"Who organized this search party?" Posey asked.

"The sheriff's office," the woman answered. "But it's been a group effort. I know Ms. Vance at Wild Pines High was also instrumental in getting all these folks together."

Posey's eyes panned across the many groups forming and convening in huddles. She felt envious of them and resented the fact she was excluded from being a part of something so momentous due to her age. It wasn't fair. Eighteen couldn't come fast enough. There were so many things she couldn't wait to do: vote, serve on a jury, serve in public office. Now she could add "joining a search party" to the list.

A shrill noise cut through the air and everyone's attention snapped toward the sound as it continued—*beep, beep, beeeeep.* It was coming from about thirty feet away, where Deputy Butts was standing atop some haystacks next to a slumped scarecrow. He had a megaphone in hand and his Stetson hat on.

"Attention!" he yelled.

People made their way closer to him to listen. Posey and the rest of the AV Club remained near the back, exchanging glances with phones ready in hand, uncertain what to do since they weren't technically allowed to join the search.

"Thanks everyone for coming out here today and gathering to help us find Molly Moses," Deputy Butts said into the megaphone. "We've formed six groups to search the area surrounding the shopping center, which is the last place Molly Moses was seen. Some of this search will go down the highway, where we'll be checking the areas adjacent. A few quick pointers before we get started. Each team is assigned one part of the grid. The team leader's got the map for you all to follow. Remember to go slowly. Give everything a good look. Okay? If you see anything suspicious, you're going to use some of that neon tape your team leader's got—can you all hold them up?"

Six hands jutted up from the crowd, all holding rolls of hot-pink tape.

"That's it. You don't touch anything, you don't move anything, you just mark it for law enforcement to come take a closer look. And you take a picture of it, too, and you'll send that to us. Watch your step and don't forget about obstructions like cliffs, trees, rocks, ditches. And some of these areas, you know, you might see some wildlife, so be prepared for that. Make sure you're all wearing appropriate clothes right now, pants and sneakers. This place is filled with snakes and ticks and bobcats, so, you know, take caution."

As Deputy Butts continued laying out the rules that didn't apply to her because they wouldn't let her join the search party, not that she was bitter or anything, Posey could see Jeremiah with his group—he was easy to spot being so much taller than all of them. Jeremiah's mouth was agape and his hands were on his cheeks and he was mouthing, "Snakes?!" Posey moved her gaze to study the crowd around him, searching for familiar faces. So many people were here. Even people who didn't seem to be big fans of Ms. Moses, like Mr. Butts, and that strange woman Abby from the Gas Up. She saw Doug now in one of the groups, wearing one of the volunteer shirts and looking ready to cry.

"Let's all have a moment of silence," Deputy Butts said into the megaphone. "For Molly Moses—a teacher, a beloved wife, a pillar of the community."

The weight of the moment clenched Posey's heart and she beamed good thoughts into the universe about this kind woman who touched an entire community. *You're okay, Ms. Moses. I know you're out there and you're okay and we're going to help find you.*

"Go forth with focus and fortitude," Deputy Butts declared.

The swarms of people dispersed. In the hubbub, she recognized right away the sweatered arms waving at her from the other side of the crowd. She gasped. Of course he was here.

"Daddy!" Posey turned to the AV Club. "Excuse me. I have to go talk to him. You all—walk around, grab footage, whatever you think would be helpful. We'll meet back here in ten?"

After agreement, they dispersed in different directions. Posey went running straight through the now-emptying lot to her father and threw her arms around him. She didn't know why, but something about the sight of him here in this sad and strange scene was exactly the comfort her soul needed.

"Daddy," she said, pulling away. "You're covering the story?"

"Me and everyone in the tri-county area." He reached over and picked something out of her bangs. "Piece of hay," he said, showing it to her before chucking it on the ground. "What do you think of this circus?"

Posey looked over her shoulder, making sure no one nearby

could hear them. But there was no one nearby—the search parties were now heading in different directions, beginning in the field behind the lot. The only people left now were reporters and a few volunteers and police. Oh, and Ms. Vance, touching up her lipstick near the news van and using her phone as a mirror.

"It's so weird," she said to him. "This all happened so fast. Yesterday no one we talked to took this seriously, and now . . ." She gestured toward the search parties that were heading toward the surrounding field. "I'm worried that there's more to this than they're letting on."

"Like what?" he asked.

"Well, Ms. Moses's husband's car was towed by the sheriff's office this morning. I saw it happen."

"Interesting. Doesn't mean anything necessarily, though, without more details."

"I talked to him right after—the husband. Doug. He admitted there was blood in the truck but claimed it was his."

Her dad cocked his head. "Now *that's* interesting."

"I just don't understand what happened that changed everything so fast," Posey said. "I mean, I'm glad that people are finally caring she's missing, and that they're looking for her. But it doesn't make sense to me."

"My guess is that your little video going viral yesterday lit a fire under the city's ass to actually do something about the case. Public pressure's a beautiful thing—when used for the right cause."

Her dad took gum out of his pocket, the same cinnamon kind

he'd been chewing on the job since he quit smoking sixteen years ago. He offered Posey a piece and she shook her head.

"When I got in this morning, the video was all the office was talking about," he said. "We were trying to figure out our angle. We're a weekly, so we can't hit this like a breaking news piece. The search party seemed the best framing for us. You know, how the community comes together at a time like this." He put a hand on her shoulder. "We're citing your show in the piece."

Posey felt her face flush. This was, perhaps, the highest honor she'd ever been awarded in her short stint on this planet. A citation. A source. Her own father, editor in chief of a real actual newspaper, was crediting *her* news team in their reporting.

"What are you citing?" she asked.

"A few quotes from your interviews." He patted her back. "You've done good, kid. Keep up the good work."

"Trying to. They wouldn't let most of us join the search party because we're minors," she said. She spotted Athena looking bored on her phone as she sat on a haystack, with Lexy staring at her as if deep in thought, and then Yash wandering around with his phone taking shots of the search parties that were getting farther and farther away. She blew out a sigh and shook her head. "I don't know how to feel. On the one hand, I hope they don't find anything today. On the other—"

"Sorry, Pose," her dad said, holding up his phone as it glowed and vibrated in his hand. "This is one of my reporters. Have to run. Talk later. Breakfast for dinner?"

"Sure," Posey said.

But she said it to the air because her dad was already racing away from her, saying, "Where the hell have you been all morning?" into his phone in a voice she was sure glad wasn't for her.

Posey could feel a bad mood trying to push its way in and it took all her mental strength to push it back. First, there was the ever-present fear about whatever happened to her missing teacher. Then there was the disappointment of showing up to a search party and being told she was too young to join. There was her dad, who never learned the art of a proper goodbye. There was Deputy Butts, who was strutting around with his megaphone and sunglasses on, and who stopped a moment just to give her a stare and tap his sunglasses and then point at her, whatever that was supposed to mean. Lastly, there was the matter of her empty stomach. Not one to get hangry, Posey instead got sangry. When she hadn't eaten enough, sadness crept in, so she joined Lexy and Athena and Yash at the haystacks and asked if they had any interest in wrapping up for now and breaking for lunch.

"Yes," Lexy and Athena said in unison, then looked to each other in surprise.

"Lunch?" Yash said with a crestfallen expression. "I packed more protein bars for everyone. And jerky. Seitan jerky?"

"No offense, buddy, but those bars tasted like ass and forgive me if 'Satan jerky' isn't exactly whetting the ol' appetite," Athena said. "Which is my way of saying, yes, let's go get lunch."

"I can't. I need to get back to my house by one," Yash said.

"I'll drop you off," said Lexy, holding her key fob up in the air. "Meet you two at Delilah's?"

Athena's car was a modest, champagne-colored sedan. From the outside, it looked like one of so many forgettable cars you might pass on the road. On the inside, it was the most filthy, disgusting vehicle Posey had ever seen. Athena threw three empty soda cans, a to-go box, and a black banana peel on the ground to make room on the passenger's seat. Then she brushed away what looked like a thousand cracker crumbs. Posey hesitated before climbing in.

"I'm sorry, sunshine, yes, this is your chariot for the evening. The afternoon. Is it noon? Anyway, get in."

Posey swallowed and climbed in, focusing on the dashboard and not looking down at the floor where she could feel garbage squelching and crunching under her Mary Janes. And the *smell*. The stench was horrid.

"Maybe I should wait here for Jeremiah," Posey said, trying not to breathe through her nose.

"I already texted him, he knows we're leaving."

Athena started the car. Something that sounded like a self-help spiritual audiobook came on the speakers. It was a German man saying, ". . . must transcend the ego and earthly identity . . ." Athena flipped it off and said, "I've been listening to that same book for a week and I'm sad to report I still have an ego and a head full of problems."

The car pulled onto the road so quickly Posey felt herself yanked back in her seat.

"Anyway," Athena went on, "Jeremiah might be there all day for all we know. Better for us to move ahead without him. That was a bizarro scene back there, right? It's like the whole town woke the fuck up."

Posey didn't want to take credit for the wave of action they were seeing, but she did feel a little flicker inside remembering what her dad said when she saw him—that their show lit a fire under the city's you-know-what.

"I hope they don't find anything, though. I can't let my mind go there, you know? I just keep telling myself Ms. Moses is off in some tropical location drinking mai tais and living her best life."

"I hope you're right."

"Look, there's something I want to talk to you about," Athena said, pulling a lollipop from the visor above her. She discarded the wrapper by flicking it toward her feet and started sucking the candy as she kept talking. "Salvatore. Love the guy. But . . . I have questions."

"Like what?" Posey asked.

"Okay. All right. This is between us, right?" Athena asked. "This stays in this car."

"Sure," Posey said, honored that Athena trusted her with confidential information.

"First off, teatime: he shouldn't even be working on these episodes with us. Yeah, yeah, I know, he's the director of the club, he's got the title, he's the founding member. Don't care. It's weird that he's working on this when he could be a suspect."

"Suspect?" Posey said it so loudly it neared a shriek.

"I said what I said. Salvatore's got a very, shall we say, *questionable* relationship with Ms. Moses. I happen to know a couple of things." Athena pulled the lollipop out of her mouth. "I'm sorry, this is disgusting. I think it's grape. I need to . . ." She grabbed a tissue from a box that sat between them in the console, wrapped a tissue around the lollipop, and threw it behind her. Posey was agape but Athena didn't seem to notice. "Anyway. The investigation. Let's start there."

Posey waited for Athena to go on. This conversation felt more like a monologue than a dialogue, which was fine with Posey. Posey was an excellent listener. But something in her was tightly coiled at the mention of Sal, at the hint that there was information coming that might change her view of him.

Athena continued. "The school's investigation is kind of bullshit—I mean, on the one hand, right, okay, I get it, but I do think it's been blown out of proportion. Could be retaliation because of funding issues or whatever. That's a hundred percent my opinion, by the way. Just me and my bitter-ass feelings about the theater department. So take it with an assload of salt."

An assload of salt? That sounded painful. But Posey continued listening.

"All they have in that investigation is 'inappropriate relations' between Moses and Sal because, what? Yoni Gomez saw him coming out of her house one morning? You and everyone else at WPH, Yoni. That could have a hundred legit explanations. Dude's practically homeless. His parents are deadbeats. He couch surfs."

Get to the point, Posey thought, trying to send telepathic messages as Athena zipped down the road at ten miles an hour over the speed limit.

"But what *I* know that the people doing the investigations don't know is this: there *was* something going on between Ms. Moses and Sal. Or is, or whatever."

Posey almost rolled her eyes. It was tiresome, these rumors about Sal and Ms. Moses. He had explained everything. The woman was his lifeline, a guardian figure, she was helping him get emancipated. Didn't people understand?

"And how do you know that?" Posey asked, crossing her arms in front of her chest.

"Because," Athena said, pulling into the diner's parking lot so fast she burned rubber. She parked on the line between two spaces and pulled the keys out, the car coming to a standstill that suddenly felt so loud and suffocating. "I saw them making out with my own two eyes."

TWENTY-FOUR

The shock of it. The idea that something like that, something immoral and illegal like that, was going on—it was too much for Posey to bear.

"They didn't," Posey said simply, reaching for the door.

"Oh, but they *did*," Athena said.

Posey put her hand back in her lap. As Athena's words sank in, really sank in, Posey felt her heart sinking too. What Athena said was gross, was wrong, and it changed everything. Posey didn't want everything to change. But while Posey the Person didn't want to hear about this, wanted to deny it, Posey the Journalist needed to turn the feelings off like a faucet and step it up. This was huge. She took a deep breath. A deep, rancid breath that smelled like sweet rot. She would have liked to hear this somewhere fresh air was available, but this was the kind of conversation that needed to be contained.

"Tell me the story," Posey said.

"Okay," Athena said, turning to her. "It was prom night.

Community center. And man, it was wild. The theme was bubbles and there were bubble machines everywhere and Jeff drove his Jacuzzi truck and I went with this girl Maddy, she was a senior, lots of drama, an ambulance was called, that's another story. Anyway. You ever tried Molly?"

"Moses?" Posey asked, lost.

"Never mind, my innocent child. Where was I? Right. Prom. So after my date left in an ambulance—"

"What ambulance?"

"Doesn't matter. Let me skip to the good part. So my dad comes and picks me up. I get in the car. We drive home. The old man chews me out when he sees my red eyes. Blah blah blah, irresponsible, can't trust you, you're grounded, blah blah blah."

"What about Sal and—"

"I'm getting there. Patience. So while my dad's blah-blah-blahing, I'm tuning him out and staring out the window of the car as we go down Mile High Drive, not thinking about anything. Probably dreaming about sandwiches or something. Man, I love a good sandwich. And then I focus my eyeballs for a sec at the stoplight and realize I'm staring at a parked car outside the liquor store and that I know the car—black SUV with tons of KILLER LIVER bumper stickers—and I expect to see Ms. Moses and her hubby, Doug. But instead, as the car pulls to a full stop at the light, I realize that it's actually Ms. Moses and *Sal*. Hanging outside a liquor store on prom night. Then, right as the light turns green, my dad guns it and that's when I could see them and it totally looked like they were making out. I gasped so loud my dad thought I was having an asthma attack. I didn't tell him what I saw. I knew he'd just say I was high out of my mind."

"You were intoxicated?" Posey clarified.

"Posey, it was *prom night*," Athena said.

Posey swallowed. "Describe the . . . making out."

"Describe the—what do you want? I was twenty feet away on a dark night and I was in a moving car. It looked like they were glued together at the head or whatever, you do know what making out is?"

Posey considered the story and how this shifted Ms. Moses's disappearance. She chewed her cheek and tried to ignore the odd way her throat burned at the thought of this.

"So Sal working on this with us? Not the best idea, methinks," Athena said. She flipped her visor and popped another lollipop into her mouth, balling up the wrapper and throwing it behind her this time. "I don't think they're a *thing* thing, but I do know boundaries seem to have been an issue. For all we know, she left to escape the rumors about it. Fucking grape again, disgusting." Now she threw the lollipop behind her.

"What are you implying?"

"Nothing. I'm just *saying*."

"What are you expecting us to do with this information?"

"I don't know. Report it?"

"But report what exactly, Athena?" Posey noted the frustration that was sneaking into her tone and she told herself to cool it down. "That you thought you saw them making out one night three months ago? How does this fit?"

"I don't know what to do with it, you're the expert producer reporter investigative journalism person. Use me as an anonymous source if you have to."

"Anonymous sources should only be used as an absolute last resort to protect a source and when the information is truly credible. This can't be used, Athena."

"Well, then just keep it in mind as background info, I don't know."

Posey shook her head as the details swam around in her mind. Could she really take the word of someone who was intoxicated and in a moving vehicle on a dark night? Eyewitnesses were often wrong anyway.

"Did you tell anyone what you saw?" Posey asked. "Admin at school, a teacher . . . someone?"

"You are the first person I've shared this with," Athena said.

"But why wouldn't you tell someone? And why would you stay in AV Club after what you saw?"

"Because . . . I don't know. Maybe part of me doesn't believe myself. I thought I saw it but I don't want to believe I saw it." Athena's eyes widened. She had eyes such a pale shade of blue they were like ice. "Ms. Moses is the reason I still go to WPH. Early last year, after I went off the deep end, she appealed my expulsion. She went to bat for me. She convinced me to come back and keep going. And when everyone at school treated me like the freak I am when I came back from ye ol' mental hospital, she gave me a space to hang out at lunchtime with the AV Club and I learned a few badass video skills." Athena sighed. "I fuckin' love Ms. Moses, man. It's that simple."

Posey chewed her cheek. The details were like a tsunami threatening to overwhelm her. How on earth was she supposed to make sense of this, to shape it into a story? It was too much. What she wanted most of all was to talk to Sal about this, but Athena made her pinkie swear she wouldn't say a word to anyone and Posey took pinkie swears very seriously.

"I am hungrier than a hippo," Athena said in a more upbeat tone. "Hey, there's Lexy. Ready for lunch?"

"Yes," Posey said, although she couldn't feel her appetite anymore. She opened her car door and stepped out into the cold, sunshiny day.

TWENTY-FIVE

Delilah's was the busiest Posey had ever seen. They had to wait for a table, lurking in an area near the hat racks and pinball game that pulsed with red light.

"Buncha bnb-holes," Athena whispered to Posey, gesturing to the six men in polo shirts wearing sunglasses inside the restaurant who waited ahead of them.

"What?" Posey asked.

"You know, city people get their little Airbnbs online and come out here for the weekend." Athena shook her head. "Just wait till snowy season."

"What are you whispering about?" Lexy asked loudly.

"Nothing," Athena said, waving.

"Did you know Yash has seven little brothers and sisters?" Lexy said.

"Jesus," Athena said with a grimace.

"Wow," Posey said.

"His house was like a day care," Lexy said.

Posey thought about Yash—his ability to tune them out when

they all worked in the room together, the snacks he packed for everyone. It all made sense now. Yash had big brother energy.

Right after getting seated, Lexy took out a composition book and a pen and put it on the table. As if she were a mirror image, Posey was on the other side of the table doing the same thing—only her notebook and pen were purple instead of black. Athena looked between the two of them in wonder.

"You came *ready*," she said. "What's next?"

"We've got to figure out the narrative for episode two," Lexy said. "Obviously we're going to talk about the car getting towed and the search party."

"I texted Jeremiah for an update, by the way," Athena said. "He just texted back, *This is the worst party I've ever been to.*"

"Have they found anything?" Lexy asked.

"No, thank Goddess," Athena said, slipping her phone back into her sweatshirt pocket. "Hey, pssst, Lexy—can you pass the sugar packets?"

"You don't have anything to put sugar into," Lexy said slowly, pushing the plastic container Athena's way.

"I sure do. It's called my mouth," Athena said, wiggling her eyebrows. She plucked a sugar packet out, ripped the top off, and downed the whole thing.

"You are chaos," Lexy said with a half smile. Then she cleared her throat and turned her attention back to the page. Her expression darkened and she looked up. "Do you—do you think any of this matters?"

"What do you mean?" Posey asked.

"What we're trying to do for Ms. Moses?" Lexy said. "Making these episodes?"

"Well, we have to do *something*," Athena said. "I mean, of course I keep telling myself Ms. Moses is off enjoying an impromptu Hawaiian vacation or whatever so I don't lose my mind down a rabbit hole of worry but—but if one of us was missing, don't you think she'd shout it from the rooftops and look for us herself?"

"She would," Lexy said.

Posey nodded in agreement.

"So, there. It's our duty," Athena said. "Plus, how proud is she going to be when she comes back and sees the club finally got off our asses and did something?"

"True," Lexy said. She took a deep breath and let it out. "So, okay. I was thinking the three of us could go through the highlighted comments together, the ones Yash put in that spreadsheet?"

"Yes, great idea," Posey said, taking her phone out.

"Oooh yeah, those *comments*." Athena ripped open a tiny plastic container of half-and-half and sipped it with the poise of a queen at teatime. "Did you see the psychic lady? We should totally follow up on that one."

"Psychic lady?" Lexy asked at the same time as Posey said, "Missed that one."

The server, a very stressed and sweaty man with large biceps and an underbite, took their order and left. While they waited for their food, the girls read some of the comments out loud.

231

ms_sheila_dunlap: ms. Moses was my teacher in hs and recently I saw her at Pickins and I was so surprised to see her working there. I asked if she was still at WPHS and she said she was, just working nights for a little extra cash, and I asked what she was saving for and she said "a new and better life." she seemed tired and we laughed but it was a weird thing to say and only a couple of weeks later here she is missing. what do you think that means?

 **Reply**

▼ **3 Replies**

> **reply from monsieur_farthouse:** derpidy derp obv she just left yawn why is this even a news story
>
>  **Reply**

> **reply from rockclimber1258:** But according to this video, she's not spending her $$$ so . . . . where is she then?
>
>  **Reply**

> **reply from selflove_selfcare:** SHE'S NOT SPENDING MONEY ACCORDING TO WHO? HER HUSBAND!!!! OH YEAH LETS BELIEVE WHAT HE SAYS!!! HER HUSBAND KILLED HER YOU FUCKIN IDIOTS!!!!!
>
>  **Reply**

"That selflove_selfcare person is, like, *hostile*," Lexy said.

"Oh yeah, that yelly bitch is all over every thread," Athena said. "But did you see *this* one?"

Athena showed them her phone. It wasn't one of the comments that Yash highlighted. It said:

> **tiffany_the_psychic_witch420:** I have psychic abilities;
> last night, molly moses reached out to me in a dream;
> she said, "you will find my body" and was holding a
> baby deer and then she did a cartwheel; please DM
> me for more; i am available for seances, blessings, hex
> removal, tarot, palm readings, etc.
>
> 👍 👎 **Reply**

"So did she do the cartwheel with the baby deer in her arms, or . . . ?" Lexy asked with a deadpan expression that made Posey think she was trying hard not to laugh.

"I actually think we should follow up on this," Athena said. "Seriously. You know sometimes the FBI works with psychics, right?"

Posey couldn't tell if Athena was being serious. She really hoped not.

At that moment, their food arrived: a vegan BLT for Lexy, a grilled cheese with tomato soup for Posey, and for Athena, a club sandwich so tall she had a hard time fitting it into her mouth. But what she said earlier during her long-winded story about The Make-Out Session That May or May Not Have Happened was true; she did seem to have a passion for sandwiches. Posey had never seen someone moan and devour food like that in her entire life. As Posey ate her grilled cheese in silent witness, she almost felt as if she was watching something sensual, something she shouldn't be watching. Lexy watched as well with something resembling skepticism, squinting through her glasses at Athena's performance.

"My God, woman," she said. "You and that sandwich need to get a room."

"I want to marry this sandwich," Athena said, her mouth full of food.

"You are so disgusting," Lexy said with a smile.

Posey didn't want to jump to conclusions, but Lexy seemed to have a special smile just for Athena. Once upon a time, Hannah had a smile like that for Posey. A smile that held a private little world of promise. Posey and Hannah would be in the middle of some tedious lesson in physics and Hannah's smile, beamed at her from across the room, would make Posey tingle all over. But after Hannah got together with Miles, the smile disappeared along with everything else. Posey got a shiver in the middle of the restaurant and swore she could almost taste Hannah's strawberry lip gloss for a moment. Her spoon clattered to the floor.

"Sorry," she said, picking it back up. "Um, anyway, obviously we won't be following up on the psychic."

"Why not?" Athena asked indignantly.

Posey didn't dignify the question with a response, instead turning to Lexy and asking, "What do you think about maybe having some kind of featured comments section where we show some of these comments onscreen? Obviously we don't have the time to follow up on all of them. But maybe the ones that seem credible could be shown at the end of the episode?"

"I like that," Lexy said, wiping her mouth with her napkin. "It's, like, a little audience participation."

"Right? We're making this a collective investigation."

"Why aren't we going to talk to the psychic again?" Athena asked.

"And there are a bunch of people just saying they're thinking of her, they're praying for her. . . . I don't know, could be nice to show a couple of those?" Lexy continued.

"Sure, showing the community support," Posey said.

"Hello? Psychic?" Athena asked.

"Oh my God, we are not going to talk to the psychic. *Focus,*" Lexy said.

Posey stole a glance down and noticed that, underneath the table, Athena's leg was rubbing against Lexy's. She inhaled sharply. Okay, so there was a flirtation going on between them. Hopefully it wasn't going to get in the way of the investigation. Posey took a sip of water and decided to pretend she hadn't seen it.

"All right," she said. "So we have Doug, we have the search party, we have some comments. That's it?"

"For now, yeah. I mean, if we want to get an episode up today, maybe we should run with what we have before it goes stale," Lexy said.

"Okay. Can you write up some notes and send them to Yash? I think he has all the footage already. They're in the group thread."

"I can do it now," Lexy said, taking out her phone.

"Have we considered Wild Pines Sasquatch could be responsible?" Athena asked in a low, conspiratorial voice. "Right around the time Erin Englin went missing, there was a Sasquatch sighting. A lot of people online thought there might be a connection."

Posey shook her head. It was becoming apparent to her that Athena was an excellent anchor, but not exactly a trustworthy source for reality-based journalism. Psychics and Sasquatches! Which was almost a relief. Because that meant that maybe, just maybe, she was wrong about what she thought she saw between Sal and Ms. Moses.

TWENTY-SIX

After lunch, the girls banged out a quick script on notebook paper and decided it was time to part ways. Lexy had a virtual piano lesson and Athena was going home with the script to film her anchor portion of the episode. Posey could have assisted, but declined for two reasons: one, she needed a break from Athena's energy. Two, she would do anything to avoid ever getting into Athena's car again. It was the stuff of nightmares. Instead, Posey accepted a ride from Lexy and headed home to check if there were any updates about the search party. The only thing Jeremiah had texted the group so far was a picture of a dirty thong and a crushed beer can he had found in his search. Posey thought that was highly unprofessional and chose not to react to it.

"You okay?" Lexy asked as she pulled up to Posey's house to drop her off.

Posey was staring at the empty driveway, asking herself why she had an equally empty feeling inside.

"Yeah," Posey said, a bit hoarsely from all the talking she'd been doing these past couple of days. "Just tired, you know?"

Lexy watched her as if she knew there was more going on and didn't know how to say so. Likewise, Posey wanted to ask Lexy what was going on with Athena and didn't know how to ask. It seemed easy for Posey to communicate about work, about facts and data. But to talk about feelings was like fumbling through a foreign language.

"I know," Lexy said. "I could barely sleep last night. My anxiety's through the roof."

"You have anxiety?" Posey asked, surprised.

"Like, horrible."

Posey marveled at Lexy's placid expression. Just more evidence that you truly never know what's going on inside another person.

"I'm sorry," Posey said. *Sorry* felt silly as it left her mouth.

"Hey, at least my anxiety has something useful to spin its wheels about now, right? Instead of me torturing myself over what I said in class a thousand times." Lexy played with one of her many bracelets on her arm. "Anyway. I'll reach out after my lesson's done, okay?"

Posey wished she had some experience with anxiety and could offer some wisdom, but she didn't. She made a mental note to read more about it later on WebMD so maybe next time she could offer a more intelligent and helpful response.

"Thanks for everything, Lexy," Posey said. "You know—I really like working with you."

"I like working with you too," Lexy said. "We're the dream team."

Posey smiled. *The dream team.* She liked that.

"Hope you have a good lesson," Posey said as she hopped out of the car.

"Chopin," Lexy said, rolling her eyes. "Pray for me."

Athena sent her portion of the episode to the team in record time. In the footage, Athena transformed back into her anchor-woman alter ego—that blazer, platinum wig, and red lipstick. There was no green screen this time, so Athena filmed instead on her back deck, where the wind picked up in her headset mic and made certain parts hard to hear. It would have to do. Yash got the footage, texted On it! within seconds, and the episode was posted to the *Wild Pines Buzz* account by four p.m. that afternoon.

By then, Jeremiah had updated the group that the search party ended at sundown and as far as he knew, no trace of Ms. Moses had been found.

Posey stayed glued to the YouTube page, refreshing the episode to see the numbers tick up. It was picking up views, thanks to Athena promoting it on her Instagram account.

Posey could almost feel the dopamine surging through her system. She'd done research, she knew that the brain produced dopamine, that rewarding, feel-good chemical, when people got attention on the internet. But of course, this wasn't some narcissistic internet performance, this was an investigation into her missing teacher. The numbers mattered because the *story* they were telling mattered. Because the more views their show got, the better chance someone with information about their teacher would see it. Posey ate a bowl of cereal for dinner (her dad unsurprisingly texted to say he was working late again) and scoured the new comments for anything promising.

As Posey noticed earlier, today the winds had shifted and this shift was reflected in the comments of episode two. Yes, the psychic spammed the account and selflove_selfcare went on all-caps tirades about how Ms. Moses was murdered by her husband again. But there was a certain feel to the comments today, as if the citizens of Wild Pines had collectively recognized the gravity of Ms. Moses's disappearance and earnestly wanted to help. Pickins customers ruminated over their interactions with her in the store. Wild Pines students posted a range of remarks—most were supportive and concerned, but a few were ugly and said she was having an affair with a student, which was why she left. Posey scrolled past those.

But the most interesting comment was left by mel_mcbeal, a childhood friend of Ms. Moses who now lived in San Diego. Mel dropped a paragraph saying she hadn't heard from Ms. Moses in months, but Ms. Moses called her in the past few weeks and was distraught.

"Distraught." What did that mean? Posey DMed the woman and asked if she could interview her, leaving her phone number and her title, *Posey Spade,* Wild Pines Buzz *Director.* Yes, Posey secretly gave herself a promotion. Let's be honest, she was the de facto director now, considering her problematic codirector. Posey turned her ringer up, in case the woman called back, but the only sound coming in was chatter in the group thread. Ugh, Athena was talking about Sasquatch again.

With a quick search of the internet, Posey learned that there had been quite a bit of press today. Local news as far away as South Lake Tahoe had posted about the search.

Professional reporters were now chasing the story and their write-ups and video clips were worlds more polished than the AV Club's. But what set the *Wild Pines Buzz* apart from the rest of the media was what was happening in the comments. Most of the news shows didn't even *have* comments sections. This was the *Buzz*'s uniqueness—the participation factor. The entire community was alive in the comments section, coming together to argue, to conspire, to express their support, to offer clues. That was something special.

Posey's train of thought was derailed when a loud knock sounded on her front door. By now, it was dark as ink outside the windows. Her first thought was that it was her dad, forgetting his keys. But her dad rarely forgot anything. Plus, he would have texted, and she would be shocked to see him home before eight. Her next thought—*gulp*—was that it was a murderer. But that was ridiculous. Posey got up in her slippered feet and peeped through the peephole.

It was Sal.

TWENTY-SEVEN

Posey took a step back. Sal, of all people, right now? She really didn't want to talk to him right now after what Athena had told her.

He knocked again.

Posey's blood pressure rose as she wrung her hands. Okay. There was a problem right now, a real problem. See, Athena told Posey about The Make-Out Session That May or May Not Have Happened, and Posey's view of Sal had shifted. As dubious as Athena might be as an eyewitness, Posey wasn't sure she could trust Sal. She wasn't sure what his relationship was to Ms. Moses. But where it got complicated for Posey was this: Posey promised Athena she wouldn't tell anyone, so she couldn't talk to Sal about it. And here's where it became an utter, stinking mess: Posey not only loathed lying, she was terrible at it. How was she supposed to continue working with him knowing what she knew, unable to hide her true feelings, and honor her promise to Athena at the same time?

He knocked louder now.

Posey took a deep breath and opened the door and did what she always did: hoped for the best.

Sal's hair was wet and he was clean-shaven, as if he just showered. He was in his usual black sweatshirt and black pants. Though he didn't smile, his green-brown eyes twinkled a little when she opened the door. She saw the way he first glanced at her hedgehog slippers and her flowered dress before his gaze landed on her face. He had a brown bag in his hand.

"Hi, Sal," she said evenly.

"Hey. The new guy never showed up, I had to work late. You get my messages?"

Posey shook her head. She hadn't opened her email, she had been too absorbed in other windows on her computer.

"There was a search party?" he asked, a slight shake in his voice.

"Yes. They didn't find anything."

"Why didn't anyone ask me to come?"

"How was I supposed to do that, Sal? You don't have a phone."

She sounded colder than she meant to. Trying to act normal with this boy after hearing Athena's story was already a challenge.

"You know where I work," he said. "You could have called the shop."

"Actually, no, I don't know where you work. You never told me the name."

"It's Friendly Auto," he said in a most unfriendly tone.

"Well, now I know."

"What's up with you today? You have this *look* on your face."

"This is just how my face looks."

"It didn't look like that yesterday."

"Today's a different day," Posey said.

She was still holding on to the doorknob and was becoming aware of the awkwardness creeping between them like an odious fog. For the first time, she lost the staring contest, looking past him at the sliver of a moon in the starry sky.

He shook his head. "Um, okay. I brought donut holes. I thought maybe you could catch me up? But if you don't want to . . ."

Oh, how Posey loved donut holes. There was a donut shop on the block of her old apartment and when she opened her bedroom window, she could smell the sugar and grease. The fact Sal thought of her, had brought donut holes for her, was touching. But no, she couldn't. There was no way she would be able to hold in the secret Athena had told her.

"I'm feeling tired," she said, which wasn't a lie. "Do you think I could send you notes instead?"

"Yeah," he said with the shrug of a single shoulder. "Sure."

"Sorry, it's—it's been a hectic day."

"I can't wait to hear about it," he said, studying her so intently she was sure he could see right through her, see everything she held inside her.

"But feel free to stay here," she said. "In the driveway."

He let out something like a laugh, though there was no smile, no humor in it.

"Thanks." He handed her the paper bag. "Maybe you'll want them later."

"Perhaps I will," she said.

Posey wanted to kick herself. She sounded so snobby and

strange and couldn't help herself. She forced a smile onto her face. "Have a good night and I'll get those notes to you soon."

"Hope you have a restful evening," he said in a tone that could have been sarcastic, who knew.

Posey shut the door and shook her head. She caught a glimpse of her reflection in the foyer mirror and demanded, "Why are you like this?" and then responded, pleadingly, "I'm just *like* this."

The donut holes were delicious—fluffy, soft, the glaze melting in her mouth. She ate them while typing up her notes for Sal about the day and with every bite, Posey felt more guilty. By the time Posey hit send on her write-up, she had a stomachache. She walked around her house and shut the curtains, lingering to squint and see if Sal's van was still there in her driveway. When she saw it wasn't, her hand flew to her mouth. He left. He sensed something off about her and he left. Now she felt really bad. All this weirdness, for what? Something Athena *thought* she saw when she was intoxicated, in a moving vehicle? How could Sal do that, how could Ms. Moses do that? It was so wrong. Imagining their lips touching, their faces smooshed together, it was unbearable.

This couldn't go on. She would have to talk to Sal about it.

Which meant she had to tell Athena.

Posey stalked upstairs with her laptop and phone, irritated to the bone. This drama was getting in the way of the story now. It was sucking up her energy, her time, and it was threatening her relationship with her partner in the case. This had to end. She plopped onto her bed and texted Athena.

> Athena, I'm sorry, but I have to talk to Sal about what you saw on prom night. I won't mention your name. But I have to figure out the truth about what was going on with them in order for us to report on this properly.

Posey held her breath as she watched the three dots appear and dance on the screen for what felt like a miniature eternity. During that miniature eternity, Posey began to expect that Athena was outraged at her, that she was writing a rant at her for the ages. But instead, when the message finally came through, this is what she got back:

> okiedokie. guess who I'm talkin to rn? tiff the psychic!! she got in my dms! she says she could offer us more help for just 100 bux??

Rolling her eyes, Posey texted back the word NO. Even after a sacred pinkie swear, Athena didn't even seem to care that Posey wanted to talk to Sal. Capricious girl.

Posey got a text from her dad saying he was stopping by the diner, breakfast for dinner. She imagined him there flirting with what's-her-face and grew annoyed. It was so late now, they were like ships in the night. But Posey knew how it was. She was a workaholic in training. After getting into her pajamas with kangaroos all over them, Posey got into bed and opened her email. She sent a DM to deadinside1234.

msposeyspade: Are you there?

deadinside1234: yeah

A little smile perked up Posey's lips.

deadinside1234: i just watched the episode. can't believe i missed everything. we need to interview doug again, that just makes him look bad, it's not fair

msposeyspade: It looks bad for him because it is bad for him, Sal.

deadinside1234: i'm just glad the search party didn't find anything

msposeyspade: Same.

Sal didn't respond. Posey's hands floated above her laptop for a second before she typed again.

msposeyspade: Where are you?

deadinside1234: parked at the end of a dead end st near the library. i can log onto the internet here.

msposeyspade: You can log onto it here too . . .

deadinside1234: seemed like you needed space

msposeyspade: But I like having you here.

Posey saw the words she had typed without thinking about them. There, on the screen, they looked like too much. Immediately, she added:

msposeyspade: It makes me less scared of bears.

Now, looking at those words, she felt even sillier. She looked at herself in the mirror and shook her head.

deadinside1234: you're weird, posey.

There it was, that word, that one harsh syllable: *weird*. It had haunted her since grade school. It had been hurled at her by bullies and uttered with disdain by people who failed to understand her. And now Sal was one of those people. Or so she thought—because then he added.

deadinside1234: good thing I like weird so much.

Posey became aware of how loud her heartbeat was in her ears. She tried to read the tone into his words, but it was hard without a voice. Was he joking? Sarcastic? Was he flirting with her? She didn't know, but she had a strange, fluttery feeling in her belly that she didn't think had anything to do with the donut holes.

msposeyspade: Sal, I need to talk to you tomorrow.
deadinside1234: ok. i work early, off at noon. what's your plan?
msposeyspade: Not sure yet. Just come over when you're done.

deadinside1234: what do you want to talk to me about? am i in trouble?

It would be a relief to get this off her chest right now, but Posey was exhausted. She was all wound up and sick to her stomach and feeling like she needed to pause for self-care or else she was going to run herself ragged and be a mess tomorrow. She needed to be sharp so she could figure out next steps, because right now the case was overwhelming and she had no idea which way to go.

Posey made an evasive comment, said goodbye, and changed into her bathing suit for the second time since she moved to Wild Pines. She made her way downstairs through the quiet, dark house and crossed the living room, standing at the sliding glass door that faced the hot tub. She flipped the porch light on. Yes, it illuminated the deck just fine. But it was the trees behind the deck she worried about. She could imagine yellow eyes staring back at her. And tonight, she was alone. If a bear attacked her, no one would even hear her scream.

Defeated, muttering to herself, she stomped back upstairs and changed back into her pajamas. She glanced at her phone—how long did it take her dad to eat breakfast for dinner anyway? As she nestled into her bed, she checked the video one last time before hitting the lights for her eight hours of sleep, one last scouring of the comments for any scoops she could pursue in the morning. The *Buzz*'s account had a new DM. Thinking it was a response from Mel, Ms. Moses's childhood friend, Posey clicked on it. But instead of a reply from Mel, it was an account that had Ms. Moses's picture as the avatar. The message was just one sentence long.

I killed Ms Moses & Athena Dixon is next.

TWENTY-EIGHT

The group thread exploded rapid-fire when Posey sent them the message. Yash thought they should dial 911, Jeremiah thought Athena should go into hiding, Lexy thought they should hire private security, and Athena herself blew it off like it was nothing.

> yawn. i should show you my DMs. you boos get your booty rest, we got work to do, ms mos will have been gone FIVE DAYS tmw. plus my parents have the a primo alarm system, mostly to keep my ass in, lol

The thread quieted after that. No one seemed to agree with Athena that this wasn't a big deal, but Athena apparently had more experience with death threats. Plus, she was right: Ms. Moses would have been gone five whole days on Sunday. It was sickening to think what the possibilities were at this point and easy to start losing hope. And Posey could not and would not do such a heinous thing as lose hope.

Posey was in bed listening to a meditation app with one earbud in when she heard the front door shut and footsteps tread quietly up the stairs. She shot up in bed, heart pounding, somehow afraid that it was *her* life in danger. Ridiculous. The threat wasn't even for her. But her body, stiffening in anticipation, didn't seem to get the memo. Even when she recognized the shadowy figure in the hall, her pulse was still galloping.

"Daddy!" she said.

He poked his head in. "I thought you were asleep," he whispered.

"Come in here," she said, beckoning him and pulling her earbud out.

Her dad walked in and sat on the edge of her bed. He brought a little gust of the cold with him, as if the night air still clung to his clothes. She reached out and grabbed his hand.

"Daddy, one of the members of the AV Club got a death threat in a DM on YouTube," she said, widening her eyes.

"Which member?"

"Athena, you know, the anchor?"

Instead of widening his eyes as well, her dad just let out a knowing "Ah."

"A *death threat*," she emphasized. "And they said they killed Ms. Moses too."

"Who sent it?" he asked, raising an eyebrow.

"I don't know. They started an account on YouTube with Ms. Moses's avatar."

"Sounds like a troll." He patted her back. "It's an unfortunate part of the business. I've gotten plenty of them. We had to evacuate the *Chronicle* office a few times because of bomb threats; we even had an anthrax scare once."

"But nothing ever happened?"

"Nothing happened, Pose. I know it's scary, though. Is Athena okay?"

"She's fine. She doesn't care. She has this enormous following on Instagram and, I don't know, I guess she's used to all sorts of weird messages."

"Forward it to the police first thing, but I wouldn't lose sleep tonight." He stood up and stretched. "What a day."

"Yeah," she said softly, laying her head back on her pillow. "Night, Dad."

"Night."

Posey didn't wait until morning—she wrote an email and forwarded the threat to the police department right then and there. Then she put the earbud back in and tried to never mind her relentlessly pounding pulse.

TWENTY-NINE

Sunday, September 15

Oh, how Posey loved mornings—the freshness of them, the quiet-ness, the shy way the low sun peeked through the trees. But what she loved best about mornings was the same reason she adored tomorrows: the potential. The glimmering, limitless potential.

Posey woke up Sunday morning with a feeling that Ms. Moses was out there and that they would find her. Today they were going to have a breakthrough. Today was the day some of the pieces were going to fit together and, with a positive mindset and a healthy breakfast, she might be able to figure out the best road to follow for clues. She started her day off the way she often did, with oatmeal and her laptop open to peruse the news. Her dad scurried off to work and kissed her on the head—it was his eighth day in a row, but who was counting—and Posey was once again left alone. She tried to ignore the prickle on her neck as she remembered the threat and focused instead on her screen, on catching up with any new details in the media. But there were no fresh stories about Ms. Moses posted anywhere today, so Posey decided the next chapter would have to be written by her team.

As if the universe truly heard her, Posey's phone lit up with an unrecognizable area code her phone labeled as *San Diego area* while she was finishing her oatmeal. She clattered her spoon into the bowl and answered the phone in a split second's time.

"This is Posey Spade, *Wild Pines Buzz* Director," she said in her most professional, grown-up voice.

"Posey? Hi. This is Melanie McBeal, Molly's friend."

"Melanie, thank you so much for making time," Posey said, putting the phone on speaker and opening the app she still had for recording conversations from her school paper days.

"I've only got a couple of minutes, I'm sorry. I'm on shift right now, ER nurse."

"Goodness," Posey said. "I won't take too long then. Would you mind if I recorded this for quotes? For our reporting, I mean?"

"Oh . . . um. Sure. Sure, I guess that would be okay."

Posey pressed the red button.

Transcript

POSEY
Listen, in your comment, you mentioned Ms. Moses called you in the past month, sounding distraught. Do you know the date the call occurred?

MELANIE
Gosh, let me think. It was a Saturday, because it was

right after Artemis's oboe recital so . . . hold on,
let me look at my calendar in my phone. (pause)
Okay, it was Friday, August sixteenth. She called
me that afternoon around three or so.

POSEY

Can you describe the conversation to me?

(Pause)

Melanie, are you still there?

MELANIE

She was in crisis—that's the only way to
put it. She was in crisis. She was—she was
all over the place. Overwhelmed, working two
jobs, trouble with her jobs it sounded like,
trouble with her husband, Doug . . .

POSEY

Trouble with her husband. Could you elaborate?

MELANIE

Let's just say the two have been growing apart
for some time. But she called because, um . . .
(sounding choked up) she was saying she felt

like she didn't have anything to live for. She was
afraid she was going to lose her job, she was
working herself to death to save in case she did,
her marriage was rocky, she—she just kept saying,
"Mel, I don't see a future for me. I don't." (a sob)
I told her to hang on and that I'd be there for
her no matter what. I told her to come live with
me if she had to, start over in San Diego. She said
she'd think about it. (sniffling) And that was the
last I heard from her.

POSEY
Mel, as you probably saw—yesterday Doug Moses's
truck was towed by the Wild Pines Police Department.
Do you think it's possible Doug was somehow involved
in her disappearance?

MELANIE
Absolutely not. There's no way.

POSEY
You sound so sure.

MELANIE
Doug is literally the sweetest person. Whatever
was going on with them, he is not a violent man.

I hope that Molly just left on her own. Just—just
decided to go have herself a holiday. That's
what I hope. (whispers) But I've just got this
bad feeling about all this, like something
happened to her. I sure hope I'm wrong.
(beeping) Oh God, code blue. I've got to go.

POSEY
Thank you for your—

(Click)

—time.

Posey listened back to the short interview once, drumming
her fingers on the table. On her laptop, she opened her Jamboard
and updated it with new details, like Mel's interview, Doug's truck
being towed, and the fact that he deleted her texts. For a few minutes, Posey followed the line of thought that Doug *had* done this.
That Doug Moses murdered his wife. At this point, the people
closest to him who she had interviewed vehemently denied he was
capable of such a thing. Posey's own opinion of Doug in the few
times she'd spoken with him was that he was . . . how to say it
nicely? Laid-back. Not incredibly bright. But was he ever violent?

It was easy to look at police records online these days. All
Posey needed to do was to sign up for a service and spend about
twenty bucks and three minutes looking him up to determine that

no, Doug Moses had no criminal record at all. His social media pages showed a man who worked part-time screen printing and tie-dyeing T-shirts and who passionately, relentlessly promoted his subpar band Killer Liver. That was it.

Posey closed that tab and opened one to visit the *Wild Pines Buzz* YouTube page and check the comments on their newest episode. After scanning, she decided there wasn't anything worth following up on. But—gulp—there was a new message. And when she clicked on it, she couldn't help the oatmeal that started to rise up in her throat when she recognized that same avatar with Ms. Moses's face on it.

> I stabbed her with a knife 33 times & left her to die just like Erin Englin. Athena is next & then WATCH OUT I'm coming for all of you AV CLUB MEMBERS. Lexy Kennedy & Jeremiah Blum & Salvatore Zamora & Yash Berman WATCH YOURE BACK

Posey read it over again, clutching her chest. Last night was bad, but this was so much worse! All their names listed there, all of them with targets on their backs! Then it occurred to her that *her* name wasn't on the list.

Why wasn't it on the list?

She squinted at the message one more time to be sure she didn't miss it and then sat up straighter, a little offended. What, they didn't think she was in the AV Club? She was the director! She wasn't worthy of a death threat?

Posey took a screenshot and sent it to the group. A freak-out of epic proportions, mostly by Jeremiah (MOSTLY IN ALL CAPS), proceeded. The club agreed to all meet up in the Wild Pines Police Department parking lot in a half hour to see if the threat could be traced and to submit it as evidence.

THIRTY

The Wild Pines Police Department parking lot was nearly empty when they arrived the next morning.

"Where is everyone?" Posey asked as they headed toward the entrance. "I expected more people here today."

"Church maybe?" Yash asked hopefully.

"My dudes, I really don't want to do this." Athena stopped in her tracks. She was literally wearing a bathrobe and had makeup smudged under her eyes. It seemed Athena had two modes: polished as an Instagram influencer, or proud, disheveled mess. "I don't think this is that big a deal—"

"And what are you going to do, boo, if I end up, like, *beheaded* and *bleeding to death*?" Jeremiah said, stopping to answer her with his hands on his hips.

"Pretty sure if you were beheaded, you'd already be dead, so you wouldn't bleed to death at that point," murmured Athena so low it was almost to herself, hands in her robe pockets.

"You think I want to be here, talking to a bunch of cops on

Sunday morning? During *brunch time?*" Jeremiah's voice had reached a high, shrill pitch. "Stop being selfish and think of other people."

"Geez, and you say *I'm* the drama?" she said.

"You're both the drama!" Yash boomed. "Cool it."

Athena, Jeremiah, Lexy, and Posey turned their heads in unison with silent shared shock that such a voice had come out of Yash, of all people.

"Damn, dude," Athena muttered. "That was a freakin' *dad* voice right there."

They moved together up the stairs and Posey pushed the front door open. It was quiet as a library inside the portable building, fluorescent lights humming on the low ceiling, that cringeworthy Comic Sans sign still hanging. As soon as Posey stepped inside, she was greeted by the back of an orange splatter-painted sweater.

"Chili cheese dog!" the person in the sweater squealed, and she turned in her swivel chair to behold the five AV Club members clustered in the doorway. It was the very pregnant receptionist Sherry. Sherry's face fell as she saw them. She was clearly in the middle of painting her fingernails—the smell was enough to make Posey woozy. "Oh, I thought you were my lunch."

"We need to speak with the deputy," Posey said, then had an idea. "Or—what about the sheriff? Who's the sheriff here?"

"Sheriff Singer's on a ten-day meditation retreat," Sherry said. "The deputy is who's in charge right now."

The sheriff was out of town. That's right. This was currently an under-resourced department, which would explain the underwhelming response to Ms. Moses's disappearance.

"Can we speak with the deputy, then?" Posey asked.

Posey preferred to refer to him out loud that way: "the deputy." His last name was too difficult to say with a straight face.

"Oh," Sherry said. "Sure. What's this about? Molly Moses?"

"It's about a threat to our *lives*," Jeremiah said.

"My goodness. Oh wow. Okay. Yes." Sherry turned and screwed the top on her nail polish bottle. "Deputy," she shouted.

"Yep?"

"Group of kids here to see you," she yelled shrilly. "Sounds serious."

"Go ahead and send them on in then, babe."

"You got it, babe." Sherry turned to the group. "Go ahead there, the room with the open door."

As they made their way to the hall, Athena whispered, "Real professional operation ya got here, WPPD." Lexy *shhh*ed her.

They stepped into the office. Posey was able to steal a quick glance at Deputy Butts's computer and her jaw nearly dropped when she saw it was a virtual game of solitaire. As soon as the group came in, he clicked to another window and then turned his swivel chair to face them.

"How can I help you?" he asked them.

"Hi, Deputy. I'm sure you remember me from our interview, and you got the email I sent? I'm here today with the *Wild Pines*

263

Buzz team," Posey said, pulling her laptop from her bag. "As you know, we got a threat via our YouTube inbox that I think you might be interested in."

"Let me take a look," Deputy Butts said.

Posey sat on the chair and opened her computer, turning it to face the deputy.

"The commenter says that he killed Ms. Moses," Posey said, as evenly as she could. "And that we're next."

"It lists our names," Lexy added.

"Death. *Threats*," Jeremiah emphasized.

Yash started, "Sir, if there's a way the department could trace the comment . . ."

But the deputy just shook his head as he scanned the screen. "Ugly. Don't think this is something we can do much about, unfortunately. Online stuff? We don't have a way to trace it. You tried reporting it to YouTube?"

"I did," Posey said. "All I got was an automated message that their 'safety team' is looking into it."

"Sorry this happened to you all. Report it to the platform, that's about all you can do." He clicked around the page a little. "So you're the team behind this show, huh?"

"We are," Posey said.

"You all have caused quite the stir," he said, raising his eyebrows.

"We're just trying to report the news, sir," Yash said, a bit defensively.

"Mmmm," the deputy said, closing Posey's laptop and shifting his attention to the group again. "There are professionals for that. What you kids have been doing is just inciting panic in our community. I know you're trying to help, but you're interfering with a police investigation."

"May I ask what you're doing to investigate the disappearance of Ms. Moses today?" Posey asked, as sweetly as she could muster. "I mean, when you're not busy with other important business, like solitaire games?"

The collective shock resounded through the small room like a sonic boom, ending in complete, dead silence thick enough to slice with a knife. The deputy's expression darkened and he sat up straighter. His cheeks flushed.

"We led a search party yesterday—" he started.

"That was yesterday," Posey said. "And it spanned one area. What about today? Do you have any results for the truck you towed—"

"DNA testing takes up to a week. And young lady, it is not your business how the police department runs its investigation." He cleared his throat. "Listen. I don't like your tone. You hear me? I don't like you following our crew around while we're collecting evidence—"

"Excuse me?" Posey asked, genuinely confused.

"Showing up at the Moseses' house yesterday, and the search party and—look, you all need hobbies, okay? Go find some hobbies and join some clubs—"

"We are a club. We're the AV Club."

"I don't know," he said, throwing his hands up in the air. "Enjoy

265

the sunshine. Chase some butterflies. But get out of the way and let the police do our jobs."

Posey stood up and replied curtly, "Thank you for your time. We'll note in our next episode that the WPPD wasn't interested in following up on a death threat."

The look on the deputy's face as the team left his office was priceless. There might as well have been steam coming out of his ears. Posey marched out the front door, passing a woman in uniform holding a plastic bag with what appeared to be to-go containers . . . and what smelled, unmistakably, like chili cheese dogs.

Unbelievable. One police officer was in his office playing computer games, the other was fetching fast food, and the receptionist was giving herself a manicure. Was this what happened when the boss left town? Posey was so stunned she could hardly speak as the group made their way back to their cars.

"The *audacity*," Jeremiah finally said.

"Right?" Posey asked, turning around. "The unprofessionalism is staggering."

"I'm talking about you!" Jeremiah said.

His eyes were wide. *All* their eyes were wide, eight wide eyes blinking back at her. The group was watching her like her hair was on fire.

"What do you mean?" she asked.

Athena nodded once. "Dude, that was badass."

"I can't believe you had the guts to talk to him that way," Lexy said.

"I was scared he was going to arrest us," Yash said.

Posey scrunched her brow. She didn't know what was so amazing about what she did. Isn't that how communication was supposed to work, regardless of the uniform someone wore? "All I did was tell the truth."

As she said those words, her voice broke. She was beginning to sound like someone with laryngitis.

"I mean, how many square miles did that search party even go over?" Posey went on. "Maybe we need to go form our *own* search party. Or maybe we should follow up with Abby or El again, I don't know, figure out if anyone suspicious had been around Pickins? I'm not sure we've fully explored—"

"Boss, you're sounding a little run ragged," Athena said.

Her team nodded. They were eyeing her with concern.

"My voice is just a little tired," Posey said. "It's no big deal."

"Why don't we split up?" Lexy asked. "Like, some of us go talk to the Pickins people, some of us catch up with anything new that's been posted online, or go look at the areas searched and find out where else we might look for her?"

"I volunteer to go to the Gas Up," Athena said, raising her hand.

"I also volunteer to go to Clown Hell," Jeremiah said. "And actually, wait, I have a map in the car from the search party yesterday, hold up." He opened his car door and grabbed it, giving it to Posey. "You want it?"

"Sure, I'll take it." Posey glanced at her watch and sighed. "I have to go talk to Sal."

"Where *is* Sal?" Yash asked, as if realizing Sal wasn't there for the first time.

"Work. Well, he's meeting me at my house. Let me talk to him and then we'll figure out our next steps." Posey put a hand to her forehead, remembering. "I totally forgot to tell you all I talked to Ms. Moses's friend earlier. Let me send you the audio clip. It's all we have right now for episode three."

"Roger," Athena said with a salute. She turned to Jeremiah. "Your car or mine?"

"Oh, I'm not getting in that trash pile on wheels," Jeremiah said, beeping his fob to unlock his car. "I'll drive and take you back here when I'm done."

"Seriously," Lexy said to Athena. "Your car should be condemned."

"Buncha wimps," Athena said, climbing into Jeremiah's passenger seat. She beckoned Posey. "Come on, sunshine, we'll give you a ride back to your place."

THIRTY-ONE

Five days deep into the disappearance of Ms. Moses and Posey's mind was beginning to wander to some dark places.

She was trying with all her willpower to stave off the horrible possibilities of how this search would end, but it was growing hard for Posey to stay positive in the face of them: a flashing image of Ms. Moses's body in the woods, or dead by her own hand in a blood-splattered motel room, or her corpse slumped and gruesome in the passenger's seat of Doug's truck. She tried to hold on to the images of Ms. Moses somewhere in her black SUV with the wind in her hair, but Posey's gut was telling her that wasn't what they were dealing with. Ms. Moses had never up and left Wild Pines before. She was the kind of woman who took every misfit at school under her wing, who adopted animals no one wanted, who stayed with her husband despite their marital problems, who remained at Wild Pines High despite the mortifying rumors circling the school about her affair with Sal, and despite the investigation. Ms. Moses was both too stubborn and too caring to leave without explanation—unless, perhaps, depression had her so tightly in its clutches that she wasn't thinking clearly.

Here was the thing about the possibility of suicide: Posey herself had seen Ms. Moses the day of her disappearance. It was heartbreaking to imagine her kind teacher could have been struggling with suicidal thoughts, but there wasn't any way to know what anyone carried inside them by looking at them. She wished she knew more about Ms. Moses's mental state in the days before she vanished. And then it dawned on her that there *was* someone who might know more about the inner state of their teacher than she did, and that was the boy pulling his van into her driveway right now.

"Hello, Sal," she said as she opened the front door.

He must have come straight from the mechanic's shop. He looked different in his blue Dickies button-up with *Salvatore* stitched in cursive on the front patch. There was a little grease on his jawline.

She realized suddenly she was staring at him and so she said, in a formal voice, "Thank you for agreeing to meet and speak with me today."

He touched his throat. "Your voice . . ."

"It's just a little hoarse," she said. "Do come in."

Do come in. Why did she have to sound like that? As he stepped in, Posey gave a quick glance to the mirror to give herself a warning look.

"Sit at the table?" she asked, gesturing to the dining room.

Sal had his hands folded in front of him as he surveyed the

room. "I like your house. Kind of feels like you're . . . inside a tree or something."

Posey glanced up and around at the wood-paneled walls, the steep slope of the vaulted ceiling. Then the many windows surrounded by pines—yes, she could see what he meant. She'd never thought of it like that before.

"Shall we?" Posey asked, pointing to the table.

Sal plopped onto a seat across from her. Posey scooted in her chair, corrected her posture. She was aware that the air she was giving this conversation felt more like a performance review at a job than it did a conversation with a friend. She didn't know how to approach this. She was nauseated to think about Sal and Ms. Moses . . . kissing. The image had been lurking in her mind since Athena told her yesterday, and it required mental work to push it out. Strangest of all was the vague hurt it seemed to bring along with it.

"Look . . ." Posey locked eyes with him. "Someone I've spoken with in the course of this investigation claims they saw something and I need to know, Sal, if it's true. Are you or are you not having some kind of"—she swallowed—"romantic relationship with Ms. Moses?"

"I am not," he said, crossing his arms. "What is this, an interrogation?"

"You didn't have any kind of . . . *thing* with her?"

He paused. "No."

It was easy to spot the telltale signs of lying: fidgeting, eyes darting, rapid blinking, taking a long time to answer. Posey had a book about it written by a former FBI agent. Under the table, Sal was jiggling his leg, his keys jingling.

An invisible hand seemed to squeeze her heart.

He was lying.

"You're not telling the truth," she said. "There *is* something going on."

"Come on." He threw his hands up in the air. "Really?"

There it was, another sign of lying: grand gestures and denials. She shook her head.

"Sal, if you can't tell me the truth, then we can't continue working together," she said. "Someone saw you and Ms. Moses making out. They *saw* it."

"What?" he asked, baffled.

"Prom night," Posey said, her voice a rasp. She took a cough drop out of her pocket and popped it into her mouth. "In a car. They saw it, Sal."

"Who saw it?" he asked.

"I'm not going to reveal my source."

"Are they in the AV Club?"

Posey didn't say anything, but somehow, it was as if Sal was reading the answer on her face.

"They're in the AV Club," he said. "No one on our team went to prom except Athena. It was Athena, wasn't it?"

"What does it matter who it was?"

"Athena is full of shit, that's why it matters."

"So you weren't making out."

Sal took the world's largest breath, bent his head back, and stared at the ceiling. Finally, he let the breath out. Then he looked at Posey again. "She *hugged* me. I was a wreck. She was hugging me. It wasn't like that."

Hugging? Even a teacher hugging their student (in a parked car in front of a liquor store outside school hours!) seemed a huge line to cross. Posey was so bothered by this on so many levels. She was prickling with fire ants along her arms at the thought of Ms. Moses crossing such lines with a student. Maybe the school administration was right for going after her. Maybe Ms. Moses left town because she was ashamed.

"Look, I needed a hug," Sal said. "She had picked me up and I was a wreck and . . . it happened once. One time. And of course Athena just happened to see it."

Though the fire ants on Posey's arms seemed to be fading, the sting in her throat remained. "So you—do you have feelings for her?"

"No. Not like that. Look, I'd been drinking that night. She found me brown bagging it out behind Mile High Drive. I'd been sleeping in this hammock out near the Forever Tree—you probably don't know what I'm talking about. In spring and summer, it's a place where some people camp out. People who don't have anywhere else to go. Ms. Moses found me there because she hadn't seen me in a while. She was pissed to see me drinking again. She told me she was going to take me to a meeting and get my ass together. Told me she was tired of trying to save me if I didn't want to save myself."

Sal stopped to put his face in his hands. Posey folded her arms and waited for him to continue, her heart still loud enough she could hear it in her ears.

"So I got in the car with her," he said. "And then I broke down. Like a giant baby. I—I was so glad to see her and so sad and so—so everything. I don't know. I guess she felt sorry for me and we hugged and we probably shouldn't have, but it made me feel better."

Posey breathed in deeply.

Sal wiped his eyes with the edge of his shirt. "I'm just a messed-up person, you know, Posey?" He swatted an invisible fly away in the air. "Never mind, you *don't* know what that's like. Little Miss Perfect."

"There's no such thing as perfect," she said quietly, automatically. It was a mantra she'd had to repeat to herself her whole life.

"I just—Ms. Moses was the first person who was actually *kind* to me." The color of his eyes was even brighter now, like the world after a good rain. "You know? The first person who gave a shit if I lived or died. Who pulled me out of the gutter and made me get myself together and then even when I fucked up again, there she was to pull me out again. I love her for that."

Posey couldn't help but ask again, "Do you have feelings for her?"

Sal shook his head. "Not like that. I swear."

Posey cocked her chin. "Then why were you having that intimate conversation the day she disappeared? You were super close, Sal. Her hand was on your shoulder. You both thought it was appropriate for that kind of—closeness?"

274

He stared at her as if he had no idea what she was talking about, running a hand along the stubble that just barely shadowed his chin.

"In the basement? During AV Club? I walked in on you both?" she went on.

"Ohhh," Sal said. "That was just—I was freaking out because I'd finally gotten hold of my parents and they refused to sign my emancipation forms. That was the day Molly said she'd go to court with me and help me figure out how to get emancipated *without* my parents. She was calming me down."

Posey chewed her cheek and studied Sal's expression. His blink rate was normal, his focus steady. The jittering leg under the table had stilled. His tone was even and not exaggerated. She believed him. That invisible hand in her chest didn't leave, but it relaxed its hold.

"Even so, I find it inappropriate," Posey said, and then cleared her throat to try to get the judgment out of her hoarse voice. "If anyone else had seen that—"

"Okay. Whatever. Maybe it was. Fact is, she's still missing. And this shit right now is just a waste of time when we could be looking for her."

Drawing in a breath, Posey reviewed the details he had shared with her. Her mind flickered, imagining Sal and Ms. Moses embracing in a car. They weren't having an affair, but his teacher did seem to have, in addition to her savior complex, a boundary problem with her students. But she could set those issues aside because Sal was right. However messy the situation had been and however flawed a character she was, Ms. Moses was still missing and this wasn't bringing them any closer to understanding why.

"Okay," Posey said. "Thank you for clarifying this information for me."

"Sure," Sal said. "Are we—are we good? To keep working together, I mean."

"We are good," Posey said, though not warmly. "I suppose I have a lot to catch you up on. I didn't tell you about the death threat, did I?"

"Um, no."

"Oh," Posey said, getting up to make some tea. "Yes, you should probably be aware that someone threatened your life. . . ."

THIRTY-TWO

A mountain of clues, a robust roster of possible suspects, a dream team at her side, and the greatest Jamboard known to humankind, but Posey had to admit it: she was stumped. It wasn't the kind of stumped she was used to, a writer's block where she had a hard time sitting in her chair and pounding out a story. It was a step beyond that. She didn't know which story to tell. This mystery felt less like something that could fit in a news report in five-minute bite-sized pieces and more like something worthy of a novel.

And as she hashed it out over Lemon Zinger tea at the kitchen table with Sal, he was no help. Sal scoffed at the YouTube death threat the way Athena had, waving it off as a troll; he was sure Doug didn't have anything to do with Ms. Moses's disappearance because Doug wasn't capable of it; he didn't think Ms. Moses would have left on her own, because of her promises to Sal and other people; he said there was no way she would have killed herself because she would never leave all her animals and people behind like that; and Sal was certain the police and school were incompetent, but he didn't think they did anything deliberate to Ms. Moses.

So where did this leave them, then?

Right back where they started.

Episode three, Posey's notebook paper said, with nothing written below it. She drank the last of her tea and stared past Sal. In the windows of the living room, the afternoon light was blazing gold through the trees. She had never really explored that far in her own yard, had never been close enough to touch those trees. The embankment was a little sloped and rocky and treacherous. And then there was the possibility of bears—no thank you.

It was like a bell in Posey's mind: *ding ding ding!*

"Sal," Posey said, putting her purple pen down. "There's an idea we haven't fully explored."

"Which is?"

"Something entirely accidental. Something like—like if she got lost in the woods. Just a few weeks ago there was the story about that man from New York who was rescued after getting lost in the wilderness near Tahoe."

"Wasn't that what the search party was for?"

"It only covered the area around Pickins. Maybe she drove somewhere else." Posey got up and put her mug into the sink. "Was she the type of person to go on hikes? Alone?"

"No. And what, at night? At ten-whatever at night?"

"Were there any places in nature that were special to her? Like the Forever Tree?"

Snickering, Sal got up to put his mug into the sink, too. "She's not at the Forever Tree."

"Somewhere else?" Posey clasped her hands. "Somewhere she came back to?"

Sal shook his head. "She isn't, like, an outdoorsy person."

Posey paced the floor, lifted a little by this new possibility that was forming in her mind. Five days, six nights in the wilderness. That was okay, that was survivable. Right? There were plenty of creeks and berries to eat and . . .

. . . *and bears*, she whispered silently.

"Wait." Sal put a finger in the air. "Wait. There is a place. There's a lookout spot up Blue Mirror Vista. It's this turnout where you can see the whole valley and Blue Mirror Lake and after a rain you can sometimes see Phantom Falls. You know?"

"No, but this sounds promising, Sal," Posey said, getting excited.

"She goes there sometimes after work and takes pictures and—there's this big, flat rock you can sit on in a clearing."

"Did she ever go there at night?"

"Sometimes. At night it's different. You can see the houses lit up on the hillside like tiny candles."

Posey stood against the counter, studying his expression. "Sounds like she took you there."

"She did, a couple of times." Posey must have had a judgmental look on her face, because Sal added defensively, "When I was staying at her and Doug's, just to help me clear my head."

It was entirely unacceptable for a teacher and student to have such a relationship, but Posey had to put that aside for the time being. They had a lead. A new lead. Something to go check out on their own.

"I think we both know what we need to do next," Posey said.

Sal took his keys from his pocket and Posey went to fetch her coat, energized by possibility—that wonderful antidote to doom.

Blue Mirror Vista was a road that zigzagged up the hills east of Mile High Drive. The more they drove, the taller the trees seemed to get. The sun disappeared behind them and a chill traveled down Posey's spine as the shadows multiplied. As the road winded up and up, it also narrowed, becoming so thin that Sal had to slow down and sometimes pull to the side of the road for other vehicles coming in the opposite direction. There was no railing either, just a plummet downward into a deep green forever of trees. Posey got carsick and had to open the window to keep from vomiting. She'd never been on a drive so beautiful and harrowing and sickening at the same time.

At the crest of Blue Mirror Vista, it dead-ended into a private dirt road with a high fence and a colorful, hand-painted sign that said CHILDREN OF TAD. Posey could see all sorts of brightly colored jackets, shoes, and even jewelry glinting from tree branches back there. Sal parked to the left, at a turnout, and Posey hopped out of the car, walking to peer curiously through the iron fence.

"You going to be okay, Pose?" Sal asked. "I was worried back there. Your face looked a little green."

"I'm fine," Posey said, waving her hand, even though her stomach was still wrecked from the ride. "What *is* this place?"

"Oh, that's where the Tad freaks live." Sal was wearing his hoodie again, hands plunged in his front pocket. He stood and stared through the bars with her. "I'll bet some wacky shit goes on in there."

"A cult," Posey said, fascinated. "You think this has something to do with Ms. Moses?"

"No. It doesn't. I'm talking about this spot, over here," Sal said, pulling her sleeve to follow him.

Sal led the way past where the van was parked, to the left of the private road. There was a shady, hidden path along a perfect line of pine trees. The sunlight peeking between the trunks hit Posey's eyes in rhythmic flashes. There was only enough room on the path for them to walk single file.

"What's a 'Tad'?" Posey asked as she followed behind him.

"It's like their messiah or whatever. They're led by a guy named Tad and everything that happens is 'Tad's will.'"

"We should do a report on them someday," Posey said.

As soon as she said it, it struck her that this was the first time Posey had seen a future for the AV Club's work and the *Wild Pines Buzz*. Maybe working with Sal like this wasn't just a fluke because of an emergency; maybe they were building something greater. But she tried to not get too ahead of herself. Right now the only thing that mattered was finding Ms. Moses.

At the end of the path, the trees parted, and they stepped through a golden doorway into the sunshine. There was, as Sal promised, a flat rock like a low table. The grassy clearing surrounding it was abloom with wildflowers—blue, purple, yellow, orange, and pink. To the right and ahead of her, a rocky cliff led farther up the mountain. To the left, the most stunning view of nature that Posey had ever seen. The valley of pines was like a deep green ocean, and Blue Mirror Lake in the middle really did look like, well, a blue mirror. Its reflection held the sky, clouds, the forest in it. From here she couldn't spot any houses or any phone lines or anything to interrupt the eternity of trees.

For a moment, it was as if her voice was fully gone. The wind seemed to dry her mouth and throat. It was so beautiful it stole her words. Finally, she managed one.

"Goodness," she said. And she meant it in more ways than one.

"Here," Sal said, staring down at the valley. "This is her spot."

After a minute of breathing the sweet air and taking it in, Posey's mind refocused on the task at hand. She edged her Mary Janes closer to the edge, where the clearing dropped off suddenly by dozens of feet. Anything that slipped would plummet into a dark web of trees. Her breath hitched, stomach jumping, and she stepped carefully back. If someone fell down there, in a place this remote, how could they ever be found? On top of that, Ms. Moses didn't have her phone with her. There was no way to even reach out for help.

Posey walked the premises, stooping to peer into the wildflowers in search of evidence. She stood up and parted some tall grass with her shoe, studying the dirt for any clues.

"She can't be here," Sal said, sitting down on the flat rock. "I looked for it. Her car wasn't parked anywhere on Blue Mirror Vista. How would she have gotten here?"

"True." Posey should have realized that already too. "Though we could have missed it?"

"I'm sure," he said. "Had my eye out for it the whole time. There's no way I missed it."

Posey walked a full round through the small clearing. There was no evidence of human beings here. It was amazing, actually, how untouched this was. In San Francisco, even the prettiest lookout spots were littered with crushed cans, broken glass, candy wrappers. But here there was nothing, nothing but the natural world.

Sal was right; this wasn't it. The facts at hand said Ms. Moses wasn't here. It was a bit of a relief to check this off the list of possibilities because it was highly unlikely anyone could survive a fall off that ledge. What a horror that would be if that was her fate, and how awful if they were the ones to find her.

She came and sat next to Sal on the rock. He must have known she wasn't here the second he pulled to the end of the road and saw that there were no cars parked anywhere in sight. If she had to guess, Posey thought he came here for something more than following a lead. This spot meant something special to Ms. Moses and, by extension, to Sal. She studied his profile as Sal faced the valley. The idea of Sal's teacher bringing him here to share it with him was bothersome. To bring someone to a place like this was for friends, for lovers, not teachers and their students.

"This place," he said, breaking the silence. "It was special to her. Holy, almost. It's where she came when she was lost, when she wanted answers. She said it was quiet enough here she could hear the universe talking to her." He turned to Posey. "I thought maybe if I came here, I don't know, I would figure something out too."

"Are you figuring anything out?" she asked.

"No. Not really."

A new staring contest started, but this one felt different. His gaze was soft. Vulnerable. Mesmerizing. Posey couldn't quite name what it was that was happening or why exactly it was happening right now, but there was a current humming between them, a magnetic electricity. It made her forget all about why they were there for a moment. But the buzzing of her phone in her pocket brought her back and she cleared her throat, breaking her gaze and losing the staring contest so she could answer it. It was Lexy.

"So Yash and I ran into Athena and Jeremiah downtown outside the sandwich place. Where are you? Are you still with Sal? Are you done with your . . . chat or whatever?"

"Yeah, we're done."

"What was that all about, by the way?" Lexy asked in a quieter tone.

"Nothing," Posey said, glancing at Sal and wondering if he could hear.

"Is there something . . . going on with him? Is he still part of the *Buzz* or no?"

Posey stood up and walked a few paces away. "He is. Everything's fine."

"Where are you? We should convene."

"We got footage!" Jeremiah yelled.

"Want a sando?" Athena yelled.

"Can you not, like, scream in my ear?" Lexy asked them. "Where are you?" she repeated to Posey.

"We're up at the end of Blue Mirror Vista. There's a lookout point."

"Okay . . . are you talking about where the Children of Tad place is?"

"Near it. To the left."

"We'll come find you," Lexy said.

"Ask if she wants a sando!" Athena yelled.

"Do you want a sandwich?" Lexy repeated.

"Sure. Something without meat. Sal? Sandwich?"

Sal shrugged.

"Yeah, get him a sandwich too," Posey answered. "Preference?" she asked Sal.

Another shrug.

"Get two of whatever you get me," Posey said. "See you soon." She hung up and said to Sal, "They're coming here."

"Who?"

"AV Club."

"*All* of them?"

"Yes."

"Great. Just who I want to see. Athena thinks I'm screwing Ms. Moses."

"Sal, can we concentrate on what's important right now?"

Posey said, drumming her fingers on the rock. "We have a little bit of day left. What direction do we go?"

"I don't know, Posey," he muttered.

Sal got up from his spot on the rock and went to the edge, admiring the view. Posey stayed seated and watched him. She lay back on the rock, which was warm from the sun, and closed her eyes. Posey wasn't one to ask the universe for favors, but she gave it a shot. If this was a place that was holy to Ms. Moses, a place she went for answers, maybe there was something there. *Universe*, Posey asked. *Give me a sign. Tell me what to do next.* But she heard nothing in response except for the far-off *caw* of a raven.

"The wilderness angle," Posey said, sitting up. "I don't know. Have there been any . . . bears spotted around her residence or place of work?"

Sal turned around. "Why is it always bears with you?"

"Bear attacks are a real thing, Sal."

"She wasn't attacked by a bear."

"How do you know?"

He closed his eyes, like she was too much to *bear* looking at. Posey didn't share the pun with Sal. She didn't even smile at her own pun either because the mood was too heavy for it.

"Over forty people are attacked by bears every year," she said. "Just last year, right outside Tahoe—"

"Can you just . . . stop talking?" Sal asked.

"Okay. Fine. If you don't want me to talk about bears, let's—let's keep exploring this idea of being lost in the woods, other places—"

"No, I mean, can you just stop talking? Completely? You talk so much I can't hear myself think sometimes. You talk so much you're losing your voice."

It was as if he'd slugged her in the stomach. She swallowed a lump of pain and nodded.

They sat listening to the wind whispering through the leaves. Posey knew he was right. She talked more than he did, more than most people. She just had so much to say. And there was this desperate foreboding growing inside her with each passing hour. Time was so precious, life or death on the line, and it felt like nothing had been learned today. No progress made. She didn't even know what they would be able to do for episode three, if there was any point—maybe they'd have to scrap it. It must have been the wind, how dry it was up here, because Posey's eyes were stinging and she had to close them so she didn't get teary.

She was wondering how long she would have to wait to speak again when she heard voices, and then the AV Club came through the trees one by one, Lexy leading the way with a white paper bag in hand. As soon as they got to the clearing, they stopped to take in the view, whipping their cameras out to capture it.

"What a *view*," Jeremiah said.

"This is ludicrous," Athena said. "How the *fuck* do we live here? Like, this is better than Yosemite right here."

"It was her spot," Sal said quietly, walking away from the group and returning to the rock again for a seat.

"Whose spot?" Athena asked.

"Ms. Moses."

"You were looking for her here?" Yash asked.

Posey nodded. "There's nothing, though."

The group turned to Posey and Sal, who were on the rock.

"You look sad, sunshine," said Athena.

Posey hadn't realized it. A hand fluttered to her face, as if it would be able to read her emotion there like braille. "I don't know what to do next," she admitted. "I just don't know." She laughed, but even the laugh felt wrong coming out, as if it had hard edges and not soft ones. "I feel like giving up."

"Posey!" Jeremiah said. "No!"

"Nothing we're doing has made any difference," Sal said.

"I agree," Posey said, not looking at Sal, still not wanting to meet his eyes after he basically told her to shut up. "We need to own up to the very real possibility that this is beyond us. Hopefully someone will find her. But it won't be us. Let's face it—we don't have the means. We're a bunch of high school students with cell phones."

"We've figured out more than the police have at this point! Give us some credit," Yash said.

"Who kidnapped our rosy Posey and left this girl-shaped *sadness* in her place?" demanded Jeremiah.

Yash was wearing a hunting cap and windbreaker and had a canteen with him as if he expected to go hiking. He was studying Posey's face and shaking his head in what looked like disbelief.

Lexy walked over to the rock, her long, flower-printed skirt billowing in the wind. "Here," Lexy said, dropping the bag on the rock. "Sandwiches first. Despair later."

288

Posey couldn't help but let out a chuckle at the choice of words. She looked up at Lexy, who was nodding at her. As Posey and Sal unwrapped their sandwiches, the rest of the group sat down in the grass, facing them.

Sal looked straight at Athena as he held his sandwich in his hand, not eating yet. "I want to clear up any bullshit rumors right now, okay? There was nothing going on with me and Ms. Moses. Despite what some people *thought* they might have seen. And the investigation at school. And me sleeping on her couch. I know how it looks. I know maybe it wasn't . . . appropriate or whatever in some people's eyes." Here, he glanced quickly at Posey. "But there was nothing romantic or anything like that. She was just someone who cared about me. And when you're me, people like that are hard to come by."

"Sal," Posey said softly.

"No, no, I just want to explain. I just want you all to know that you can trust me. Ms. Moses means"—his voice disappeared for a second—"so much to me. I don't think you know."

"Oh, we know," Jeremiah said, sitting with his legs in front of him, red Doc Martens crossed. At first Posey thought Jeremiah was being salty, but he wasn't. His face remained uncharacteristically solemn. "I think she means a lot to everyone here. Like, I literally would not be applying to colleges, especially art schools out of state, if it wasn't for Ms. Moses."

"I wouldn't have led that protest last year if it weren't for her," Lexy chimed in, picking grass off her skirt. "I made the graphic in her class about the situation in the cafeteria and how there were no

289

vegan options. She was like, 'Why don't you do something about it? Why don't you organize a protest?'"

"She's such a badass," Athena said. "That's one thing I love about Ms. Moses. She's got this big ol' heart and she's also got this *fire* in her. She's willing to burn it all down for the sake of doing what's right."

"She gave me pepper spray," Yash blurted.

Everyone turned to look at him there in his hunting cap, hugging his knees.

"She probably could have gotten fired for it, right?" he said. "But . . . there were these guys who kept coming after me. In the bathroom, at lunch, after school."

"Yash," Athena said sadly.

"Who?" Jeremiah demanded. "I will hunt them down."

"Godfrey, Porter, that crew," Yash said, rolling his eyes.

"I fucking hate those goons," Athena said.

"She noticed a bruise on my arm one day and pulled me in after class and I broke down. It was super embarrassing," Yash said, not looking up. "She told me to come join the AV Club and hang out there at lunch if I wanted a safe place to eat. Then she pulled pepper spray off her keychain and told me the next time they tried anything with me to spray them in the face."

Jeremiah gasped. "Did you?"

"I threatened them with it," Yash said. "They backed off after that."

"Hell yeah," Lexy said.

Posey, still chewing her sandwich, was taken aback that a

teacher would basically arm a student with a weapon and tell them to threaten another student. She wasn't sure how she felt about it— on the one hand, it was alarming and certainly against the rules. Not only would Ms. Moses have faced consequences if the school administration had found out, but if Yash had been caught with pepper spray, he might have been suspended or even expelled.

"Well, you all know that Ms. Moses is basically the reason I didn't drop out of ye ol' high school after the nervous breakdown of the century," Athena said. There was no smile on her face as she said it. She stared wistfully in the air. "Theater was my life. All my friends were in it. I was like this with Mr. Butts." Athena crossed her fingers. "Drama actress of the year, cast in every play, the lead in three of them. Yada yada yada. Then I took my leave of absence and when I came back, I tried out for the play and I got nothing. And when I talked to Butts about it, he told me that he needs to be able to 'cast actors he can trust' and that my 'behavior' had broken his trust." Athena mocked him as she quoted him.

"That is some ableist shit right there," Lexy broke in, her lip curled in disgust.

"Yeah." Athena's voice tightened. "I was like, I have an actual mental illness. Whatever. He didn't give a shit. All he gives a shit about is having a theater that wins awards and keeps raking in the donors, right? He doesn't care about his students." Athena's eyes were shining. "Ms. Moses, though, she was so fucking kind to me. She was like, 'You don't need those assholes in the theater department.' And yes, she said 'assholes.' Gotta love a teacher who swears."

Also probably against the rules, thought Posey. But that was beside the point.

Jeremiah put an arm around Athena. "Come here, boo."

"We love you, Athena," Lexy said, coming over and hugging Athena from the other side.

"Stupid leaky eyes," Athena grumbled.

"She never gave up on us," Yash said, slapping the ground for emphasis. "Every single one of us. She didn't give up on any of us, and we can't give up on her. If one of us was missing? And police were sucking at their jobs, and people were barely looking for us? You know it would be Ms. Moses leading a search for us."

"So true," Lexy said.

In the silence, Posey could feel the wind in her ears. This conversation was touching her deeply. They were right. This teacher of theirs had gone to such extraordinary lengths to stand up for misfits like them. She deserved their hope. If she were here, she would do the same for them. Posey closed her eyes, listening to the wind. And she wondered if this place was special, if the universe was answering her after all.

"We've got to keep going," Posey said, wrapping up the second half of her sandwich.

The group nodded and murmured affirmatively. Everyone except Sal, who had wolfed down his sandwich and balled up the paper in his hand. He was punching the hand on the other palm, seemingly in another world. Posey wondered if he'd even heard them or if his mind had been elsewhere.

"Sal," Posey said. "Right? We've got to keep going."

Sal looked up at the group, snapping to, and snickered. "Keep going," he repeated. "She has a tattoo that says that. Right here on her wrist."

"Oh yeah! She does!" Athena laughed.

"Cute," Jeremiah said. "It's a sign, for real."

"So yeah," Sal said. "We gotta keep going. No question. No doubt."

"Can I just tell you all how much I appreciate you all?" Posey said to her teammates, who had completely renewed her spirits. They were better than espresso. She felt energized again. "How do we feel about group hugs?"

Groans. Groans all around.

"I was kidding," Posey said.

Jeremiah gasped. "Does she have a sense of humor?"

"She does," Posey said evenly.

"Remember when you came into AV Club and wanted to do icebreakers?" Lexy asked, covering her mouth with her hand.

"I like icebreakers," Yash said defensively.

"Vomit," Lexy said.

"I'm just not sure which direction to go now, though," Posey said, thinking hard. "What do we do next?"

Lexy took her glasses off and cleaned them with her skirt. She put them back on and exchanged looks with Athena, Jeremiah, and Yash. "Well, boss, I think once you hear some of what we've been up to this afternoon . . . you might get some ideas."

THIRTY-THREE

First, there was the footage that Jeremiah shot a few hours ago of Athena interviewing Abby. Jeremiah passed his phone to Sal and Posey to watch it, saying, "She's sketch."

Sal pressed play. It was outside the Gas Up, where Abby leaned against a streetlight post in the parking lot.

On the screen, Athena stepped into the shot wearing her anchor costume.

Athena looked at the camera as it zoomed in. In her exaggerated newscaster voice, she said, "Abby, the *Wild Pines Buzz* is back to interview you once more about Ms. Moses's disappearance."

The shot zoomed dizzily to a close-up of Abby's face. "Look, I told you, I only got a minute before my shift starts."

Transcript

ATHENA
We saw you were part of the search party.

As someone who had a, shall we say,
unfriendly relationship with Ms. Moses, it
was interesting to see you there.

ABBY
I didn't want to. My mama was going and she said I
had to go with her. Maybe don't put that part in. Let
me start over. I went to the search party, even though,
yes, I'm no fan of Molly Moses. Tad's will is for us to
simply roll silently with the wind.

(Awkward silence)

ATHENA
Sure. Yeah. Okay. Hadn't heard that one before.
Can you tell us a little about the search party?

ABBY
It was just as Tad needed it to be. It was—
everything as he intended.

ATHENA
Okay. Sure. Abby, one of our commenters—
they said they thought they might have seen
Ms. Moses at the Gas Up the night she went
missing, Tuesday, September tenth.

The video ended there.

"That's it?" Sal asked.

"My phone ran out of juice," Jeremiah said sadly.

Sal asked, quietly, just to Posey, "Anything there?"

"I don't know," she murmured back. "I mean, I would have liked to have heard more about Ms. Moses being at the gas station."

"It's strange," Sal said, handing the phone back to Jeremiah. "But seems like Abby's just like that."

"Didn't she seem different this time?" Posey asked Sal.

"Yeah. Quieter."

After a pause, Posey said to the group, "I'll have to think about it. I'm not sure about how this would fit into episode three."

"Those Tad people are, like, brainwashed," Lexy said. "It's so creepy."

"Did Ms. Moses ever have any affiliation with them?" Posey asked.

Sal shook his head. "No, not at all."

"Let's table that for now," Posey said. "What else did you all find?"

Yash cleared his throat. "Well, this might interest you."

"This is amazing," Lexy smiled, covering her smile with her hand.

"That death threat we received?" Yash said.

Posey and Sal nodded.

"I, um, I figured out who it is. It's this junior high school student who lives in Arkansas."

"What?" Posey and Sal asked at the same time.

"Just listen to how he figured this shit out," Athena said. "Yash may look five years old, but he's a genius."

"I don't look five years old," Yash said, offended.

"Okay, fine. Eleven years old. Continue," Athena said.

Yash paused as if he was going to respond, but then went on. "Anyway. His avatar was Ms. Moses's picture from the Wild Pines High website. His *public* name was Ms. Moses's name. But if you looked at the URL it was @djwerewolverine. So I went and searched @djwerewolverine and I found it being used on a Reddit account. All that account posted about was shooter video games. But if you looked at the replies, you could see he was replying on all sorts of national news stories, ugly stuff about how he knew where bodies were buried."

"Yikes," Posey said.

"I decided to do a reverse image search on that avatar pic on his Reddit profile, though," Yash went on, his voice picking up speed. "It was of a hand with a middle finger sticking up. And there was only one other place that exact picture had been posted, and it was on an Instagram post from a kid named DJ Wolff who

297

lives in Springville, Arkansas. His account history is full of posts about the same video games as the Reddit account. He *also* has a history of leaving, like, weird, threatening comments on news stories. So I did a general search for DJ Wolff and found a picture of him in the video games club at a junior high school in Springville." Yash was breathless now. "When I went back and studied the original comment, I realized that there was a reason our names were listed in the order they were and why that was the picture he used—they're all from the AV Club page on the Wild Pines website. He just ripped them from there."

"Which was why my name wasn't on it!" Posey said.

"Exactly!" Yash said.

"Yash, I'm so impressed." Posey flashed him a big smile and a nod. "Seriously."

"It was super easy," he said. "I should have done it first thing."

"And can I just take this opportunity to tell you all I told you so?" Athena asked.

"No, you may not," Jeremiah said.

"Yeah, sorry we all aren't influencers who've dealt with death threats before." Lexy opened her backpack and pulled out her notebook, which had a printed piece of paper in the divider that she slipped out and handed to Posey. "Okay, last thing and then I have to go and do my actual homework. This is a list of donors for the theater department I found online. Remember how in Doug's interview he said Ms. Moses was trying to have an investigation into the theater department's funding? I thought it might be worth it for us to dig a little and see if something is there. But I can't do it because I have, like, a lot I've been procrastinating on."

"Yeah, I actually have to go work a shift at the store and I'm supposed to have band practice," Jeremiah said, standing up. "Is that okay?"

"It's okay," Posey said. "I understand."

"I have homework," Yash said, getting to his feet. "But I'm sure I could put an edit together if you need it. What are you thinking about for episode three, Posey?" As if Yash remembered Sal was supposed to be in charge too, he added, "Sal?"

"I don't think we have enough right now," Posey said. "The Abby thing . . . I don't know. I feel like it might be better for us to hold off for now until we have something more solid to build a story around."

"Man, if only we recorded that interaction with Deputy Butts this morning." Athena got up and reached down to help Lexy up, too. "Expose how little those fuckers are doing to help the case. Sitting around eating chili cheese dogs, come *on*."

"I wonder if it would be different if the sheriff weren't on vacation," Posey said.

"Bet it would," Sal said.

Posey and Sal stood up. Everyone zipped jackets, slung on purses and backpacks, and took one last look at the place that meant so much to Ms. Moses. This secret, gorgeous meadow on the mountainside with the stunning view. The six of them lingered, side by side, and Posey felt their smallness in the face of the endless skies above, the endless greenery below.

At least they were small there together.

THIRTY-FOUR

Posey, too, had homework she needed to do. She never missed deadlines or assignments, but she couldn't imagine abandoning this search for Ms. Moses now, not on day five. She was going to ask her dad for a note to excuse her late work—he would back her on this 100 percent. As Posey peered at her reflection in the side mirror of Sal's van during the twisty ride down Blue Mirror Vista, she noticed the circles under her eyes and looked away.

"Maybe we should get some coffee or something and dive into the donor list," she said, her voice a rasp.

"Sounds good," Sal replied.

Posey beamed a smile at him. As if he could feel the light of it, he glanced at her quickly and a smile flickered to his lips before he looked back at the road.

"What?" he asked.

"Sometimes you're easy to work with, Sal," she said.

"Sometimes so are you, Pose."

The Cat Café was bustling when they arrived, but Posey was able to grab a corner table near the cat apartment. Eight cats slept in the miniature building, fluffy tails twitching.

"Awww," Posey said, watching a calico give itself a bath. "I love cats."

"Yeah, me too. When I slept over at Molly's house, Cyclops used to curl up with me on the couch every night."

"Cute," she said, studying Sal as he took out his laptop and opened it on the table. Once upon a time, Ms. Moses had given him a warm place to sleep. Now the boy lived in his van. She felt bad for him, but she knew he didn't want her pity. Pity never helped anyone. She leaned in, lowered her voice. "Do you have a plan for where you're going to live, Sal? You can't keep sleeping in your van in the fall. It gets too cold at night."

Sal peered over the top of his screen at her. "Well, the plan was for me to get emancipated so I can get my own place. I'm seventeen. I can't legally rent a place."

"What if you stayed with . . . with one of us in the AV Club in the meantime?" she asked. "A lot of us have guest rooms. I mean, I do."

"That's nice of you," he said. "I don't really feel like sponging off my classmates."

"It's not sponging. I'm sure they want to help."

"They don't know I'm totally homeless, all right? They think I have places to crash. I don't usually go around telling people. You're the only one who knows I'm living out of my van."

In the silence, Posey's heart broke a little—all this time, he'd been keeping his situation a secret. And she was the only one who knew.

"Listen." He pointed at his computer. "How about we focus on saving Ms. Moses right now instead of saving me?"

"Okay," Posey said.

The two conferred briefly about next steps and then fell into a long, productive silence, the café's background noise a sweet lull: hushed conversations, the sound of milk steaming, and occasional mews. Posey spent time studying the map of Wild Pines. There were still so many unexplored areas—she didn't even know where to begin. But what a joke it was that the Wild Pines Police Department did one search near Pickins and called it a day.

"Posey," Sal said, tapping the table to get her attention. "Holy shit. I've found something."

She moved her chair to his side of the table. They were so close their arms were touching. He turned to her and she could smell the chai tea on his breath as he whispered.

"Okay," he said. "This is wild. This is—this is, like, next level."

"What is it?" she said, squirming with excitement in her seat.

"So the top donor for the theater department is this guy, Anthony Prima." Sal clicked to a tab with a web page open, showing a picture of a gray-haired, smiling man in a suit. He looked like a million men Posey had seen before. "Which is interesting. Because I was thinking about it and I was like, 'Prima, Prima. Where have I seen that name?' Then I realized I was staring at it last week through the window of my class—it was on all the trucks that were repaving the theater parking lot last week. He owns that company Prima Construction. I've seen them doing other work around campus, too—they repaved the quad last year."

"Interesting," Posey said.

"Here's where it gets weirder." Sal clicked to another tab. It was an archived news article from decades ago, announcing an engagement. "Check out the last name of the woman he's married to."

Posey peered closer at the screen.

Meredith Butts and Derek Butts of Wild Pines, California, announce the engagement of their daughter, Amy Fredericka Butts, to Anthony Prima. . . .

"Amy Fredericka is the deputy and Mr. Butts's sister," he said.

"Oh wow," Posey said, sitting back in her chair. She put a hand on her mouth as she processed what this meant. "So if I'm understanding this—the theater received big donations from Prima; in return, possibly, the school's using Prima's company. Prima himself is married into the Butts family. Which means that if Ms. Moses was looking for an investigation into the funding of the theater department . . ."

Sal finished, ". . . she was basically a threat to the Butts family."

Posey closed her eyes and tried to visualize this strange, nepotistic web that connected the deputy of the police department to the head of their high school theater department to a construction company. If only she had time to make a Jamboard! But this was bigger than a Jamboard. She opened her eyes again. A fat tabby had moved to the cat tree right next to their table and was staring at her with the same intensity that Sal was—as if they were both expecting something. She got up and walked a single step to pet the kitty.

"Was she uncovering something *illegal*?" Posey asked Sal.

"Maybe," Sal said. "Or maybe it was just, you know, quid pro quo."

Posey raised an eyebrow. For some reason, it made her heart skip a beat that Sal knew what "quid pro quo" meant—a favor given in return for something. It was something her dad had explained to her once.

"I saw a documentary about the New York mob and how they ended up controlling construction companies all over the city in the 1980s," Sal said, standing up to join her at the cat tree, where he scratched a calico's head and made it purr. "Not just construction companies, but everything. They even got politicians and judges elected. The FBI had to have this enormous task force to take them down."

"Are you comparing the Buttses to the mob?"

"I'm just saying that sometimes these things are super complex," he said. "They can run deep within a city."

Another staring contest ensued, this one pensive. She could see her own unblinking face in the pupils of his eyes. It occurred to Posey that a week ago, she didn't know this boy. And somehow, in just seven days' time, he had become her Watson. At best, it seemed like the police department had a good reason to drag their feet when it came to Ms. Moses's disappearance. At worst— it seemed bonkers to think it, but—they could have had a reason to get rid of her, whether that meant running her out of town or . . .

"Sal," Posey finally said. She wasn't trying to whisper, but her hoarse voice caught in her throat. "I think we need to bring this to my dad."

"Your dad?"

Posey nodded.

"Why your dad?" he asked, shoving his hands back into his hoodie pocket.

"Because he's not just a reporter, he's an editor in chief. He's worked on major stories. He'll know what to do with this."

"Okay," Sal said.

Posey studied Sal's expression, the subtle way his eyes dimmed.

"What?" she asked.

"Nothing," he muttered, breaking their gaze and losing another staring contest. "Parents are just not usually a big fan of me." He snickered as he turned to the table and clapped his laptop shut. "Even my own."

It was a heartbreaking statement. Part of Posey wanted to hug him and tell him it was going to be okay. But she knew that wasn't appropriate and it also wasn't what he needed right now.

"Sal, don't pout," she said instead. "It's unbecoming."

"*You're* unbecoming," he said, shooting her a dirty look.

But it was fine. A dirty look was better than self-pity. She beamed a smile at him as they headed out the door.

"I think I'm very becoming," she said, pushing the glass door open and stepping into the chilly sunshine.

"You're becoming a pain in my ass is what you're becoming," he said.

But he said it with a smirk. It was undeniable, Sal liked her. Not just as a work partner—as a human being. He trusted her. He cared about her.

And now he was going to meet her dad.

THIRTY-FIVE

The *Sierra Tribune* office was tucked on a back road that inter-
sected with the end of Mile High Drive, a single, nondescript,
two-story office building made of concrete. The wooden sign in
the parking lot that said *Sierra Tribune* in a Courier font looked
so old it was possibly put there when the paper was established in
1926. There were only two cars in the parking lot and one was her
dad's Prius, littered with pine needles. Which showed how long
her dad had been here already today. According to Posey's watch,
it was five p.m. Her stomach was beginning to grumble and the
sun was receding behind the line of trees. The somber thought of
Ms. Moses being gone yet another night crossed Posey's mind,
but she didn't share it with Sal. She was sure he was already
aware and probably working to push the same thought out of his
own head.

"I didn't even know people still read newspapers," Sal said as
they walked toward the building.

"They do, but print media is definitely on the decline," Posey said. "I've been trying to tell my dad that the *Sierra Tribune* needs to do more in the digital space, but it's hard. They have a staff of, like, five people."

"Your dad works Sundays?" Sal asked as they walked up a path toward the stairs.

"My dad works seven days a week."

"Huh. Now I know where you get it from."

Posey ignored the comment and put her hand on the rail to begin up the stairs. She spotted her father through a window, talking to a man in a work shirt who wore earmuffs and goggles.

"Daddy!" she yelled, waving her arms.

As soon as Peter recognized his daughter, his eyes widened in surprise. He patted the back of the man he was talking to and hurried to greet Posey. She still had the same feeling she did as a child, visiting her dad in the office—a deep respect for him, a wonder at how the news was made, and flattery that no matter how busy he was, her dad always seemed to drop everything and come to her when she needed him.

Outside, her dad shut the door behind him and turned to Posey with a worried expression. He gave her a side hug. "Everything okay?"

"It's fine," Posey said. "I came for advice."

"Jesus, are you getting sick? Your throat—"

"I'm not getting sick," Posey insisted. "I'm just a touch hoarse from all the talking."

He looked at her skeptically. Posey had, since a young age,

refused to acknowledge when she was sick. She would ignore it, pretend it wasn't happening, push through it. He knew better than to argue with her.

"Can we go upstairs?" Posey asked. "Oh, and this is Salvatore Zamora, by the way—codirector of the *Wild Pines Buzz*."

Her dad turned to Sal, who he hadn't even acknowledged until now. He nodded at him and put out his hand for a shake. "That's some fine work you all have been doing."

Sal shook Peter's hand and met his eyes, straightening his posture. "Thank you, sir."

Her dad squinted past him, seemingly noticing the van in the parking lot. "Are you also the gentleman who's been parking his van in our driveway?"

"Um," Sal said. "Yes, sir. I hope that's okay."

"It's fine. But stop with the 'sir,' I'm not a drill sergeant." He looked at his phone. "Let's go upstairs, I have about ten minutes."

They followed her dad up the steps to the office at the top of the landing and went inside. The newsroom was silent, the lights off, computers dark, the two cubicles empty. A vase of withered flowers sat on a coffee table. There was a Mexican blanket folded on the beige couch—Posey knew her dad used it when he took naps here. Sal and Posey sat on the couches as her dad rolled an office chair to join them.

"Water?" her dad asked, pointing to the water cooler.

"We're okay," Posey said. "Daddy, I think Sal and I have stumbled upon something so big I don't know what to do with it.

I don't know how to frame it or how it fits into Ms. Moses's disappearance."

"Your voice sounds terrible," he said. "You want a cough drop or something?"

"I'm fine," Posey said, annoyed. "We don't have time for that. I need you to hear me right now."

Her dad turned his attention to Sal. "Why don't *you* tell me so Pose can save her voice, how about that?"

"Oh. Um, sure."

Sal took his hood down and finger-combed his hair. He looked to Posey, who nodded for him to proceed, even though she was irritated because she was certain she could sum it up better than Sal, no offense to Sal.

Sal started, "So Mr., um—"

"Peter."

"Mr. Peter—"

Her dad put his hand up. "No Mr.; just Peter."

"So, Peter, we think Molly Moses's disappearance could be related to a quid pro quo deal between Wild Pines High's theater department and Prima Construction, and here's why. . . ."

Sal laid out the story right now with a polish that was new to her. The way he summarized their findings, the relationships between the Butts family and city connections "rife with nepotism," the investigation that Ms. Moses was pressing Wild Pines High administration to pursue on the matter . . . it was so articulate that when he got to the end, Posey had to begrudgingly admit to herself that he said it better than she could. All this time that they worked together, her brooding partner had sunk into silence and let Posey take the lead. And she realized that's what had happened—he *let* her take the lead. Because he could be leading it himself. And it was easy for her to forget, but before she joined the AV Club, he did.

"Okay," her dad said, sitting back in his chair. "Interesting. I know about the Butts family. I didn't know about the link to Prima Construction. There could be something there. You think Molly Moses was pushing for an investigation into that, you said?"

Sal nodded.

Peter slipped a pack of cinnamon gum from his pocket and held it out in offering. Sal took a piece, thanking Peter, and Posey shook her head.

"Who did she report it to?" her dad asked.

"Probably . . ." Sal looked to Posey. "Ms. Vance, you think?"

"Yeah, the principal," Posey said. "And Daddy, did I tell you? I was putting up flyers about Ms. Moses's disappearance in the hallways of school, and Ms. Vance made me stop! She pulled me into her office like I was some kind of delinquent or something and then acted completely dismissive—"

Her dad winced. "God, your voice hurts my soul. Posey, you need tea and soup and rest. You don't sound good. You really don't."

"It's just the dry air—" she began.

Putting a hand up, her dad gave her a grave look. "Don't. Look, I know the two of you have a lot of interesting leads here. The link to Prima, the investigation—it's interesting. Could be something dodgy going on there. Or it could be completely legitimate.

It would take more digging to know. The link to Molly Moses? Also interesting, but not sure where you're thinking that leads."

"We need to know what to do for episode three," Posey said.

"I'll tell you what you need to do for episode three," her dad said, standing up. As if he were mirroring him, Sal stood up, too. "Give it a rest."

"Daddy," Posey said, her tone darkening.

"I mean it. Give it a rest." His face was stern. He made eye contact with Posey first, and then Sal. Her dad had a relentless gaze, dark blue as a twilit sky. And those staring contests Posey was so skilled at? She learned them from the master. "You. Come on, listen to her voice. You hear how run-down she is? She needs to give it a break and so do you. You'll have a fresh head in the morning."

Sal stared back at her dad without blinking. There was something stirring in him—Posey couldn't tell what it was. He nodded. "You're right. Okay."

"Sal," Posey protested, but though she pushed for it, her voice was barely there. "What about Ms. Moses?"

"You've done all you can today."

"What if someone has information out there? We need to air episode three!"

"Episode three can wait," her dad said, reaching a hand down to help Posey up. It was a kind and helpful gesture, but Posey also recognized it for what it was: an invitation to get out of there. "Who said you had to put it out tonight? Who put the deadline there? You did. So move it. If you work yourself too hard, you're not living. Give yourself a break, Pose."

The irony of her dad saying that to her! Posey stewed in a hot feeling for a moment on the couch, perfectly still and staring at her Mary Janes. She waited for the unpleasantness of it to pass like a snake in the grass. It didn't really, but she stood up on her own, not taking her dad's hand. She nodded. "Thanks, Daddy. Sal, let's go."

"Nice meeting you, Sal," her dad told them. "I need you to make sure she takes care of herself, okay? Promise me."

"I promise," Sal said, waving.

THIRTY-SIX

Posey didn't say a word as she tiptoed back down the stairs and along the pebbled path that led to the parking lot. When she and Sal were back in the van buckling in, Posey let out a sigh that had been stuck in her lungs since they were upstairs.

"Obviously we won't be listening to him," she said, her voice breaking like a pubescent boy's.

Sal looked at her like he pitied her. He shook his head as he put his keys in the ignition.

"Maybe we could go interview Doug again." She tried clearing her throat, but it was no use. "Or the deputy."

"Your dad's right," Sal said, starting the van. "You need rest."

"As if my dad's one to talk—he practically lives at the office!"

They pulled around the corner and back onto Mile High Drive, passing shops with windows glowing and lit-up fairy lights strung between the pines. Jeremiah's car was parked outside The Vinyl Word. She thought she caught a glimpse of him inside the store.

"I need rest too," Sal said. "I've barely been sleeping. I feel like a zombie."

"But we can't stop now, she's been gone five days," Posey said.

"You think I don't know that?" he said sharply. "Pose, taking a rest doesn't mean you're stopping, you're just hitting pause. Like, go watch a movie."

"There's nothing I want to watch."

"Read a book."

"I'm too distracted."

"Hit up that hot tub, I don't know! Do whatever you do to have fun. Or do you even know what fun is?"

"I know what fun is."

"What is it?"

"It's not this, I'll tell you that much."

"Do you hear your voice? You sound like a broken trumpet."

"I do not!" Posey said, her voice breaking again.

Sal turned up her street. She didn't want him to. She wasn't ready to go home—there was a tiny sliver of daylight left and they shouldn't be wasting it.

"Look, I just promised your dad I'd take care of you," Sal said as he pulled in front of her house. He sounded deflated, his own voice a little ragged. "That means go home and just chill tonight, okay? We can meet up with the club tomorrow at school and we'll figure out what's next. Who knows, maybe in the meantime Molly will come back."

"Where are you going?" she asked.

"To that spot I was at last night. I'll see you tomorrow, okay?"

Posey didn't say anything. She unclipped her seat belt and gave him one last, slit-eyed look. "I hope you have a good evening," she muttered.

"You too. *Relax.*"

Those two syllables were like nails on a chalkboard. Posey so disliked when people told her to relax, as if it were something under her control. She hopped out of his van and headed up the stairs and back into her cold, dark house.

It didn't matter what her dad said or what Sal said. Posey wasn't done yet—though she admitted to herself that yes, it was too late to probably get episode three finished tonight. She made an avocado sandwich and ate it at the counter like a chore, brewed a cup of chamomile tea, and headed upstairs with her laptop. She went back through their shared group drive where Yash had organized the raw files and rewatched some of the earlier interviews, starting with Abby's first. Was that only a couple of days ago that she and Sal had gone to that clown-filled hellscape? It felt like so long ago now. Posey watched the interview twice with her pen poised, but took no notes, because nothing seemed to stand out except that Abby was a quasi-unhinged woman who was so angry at Ms. Moses she was yelling at the camera. She must have been a morning person, because in the second video Jeremiah shot, she was way calmer.

You know who they didn't follow up with? Who they didn't see at the search party? El. Posey wrote that name down on her paper. Tomorrow if there was no new information, they would go back and do second interviews with everyone.

Posey shut her laptop and lay on her bed. A tension head-ache was starting. She would never say this *aloud* of course, but Sal was right and her dad was right, too. She needed to give it a break, even though the case weighed on her heavy as a cement block. Changing into her bathing suit, she trudged downstairs and opened the sliding glass door. Behind the floodlights on the patio, the night was black as outer space. Crickets chirped and the icy night air cloaked her, exploding shivers all over her skin. The hot tub awaited her.

"There are no bears," Posey said aloud, tiptoeing to it. "There are no bears. I mean, there *are* bears. Bears exist. But there are no bears *here*."

She slid the cover off and it landed on the deck with a *thump.* Even though she was expecting it, she jumped a little. The water was warm and smelled of chlorine. She put a hand in—so inviting. If only Sal were close by, she would feel less wary of getting in. But that was silly. She didn't need him. A week ago, she hadn't even known him. Oh! Posey turned and realized she needed a towel. She went back inside and headed upstairs.

Once she was up there with a towel in hand, she checked her phone. Ugh, the AV Club thread was asking her about episode three. She didn't have the energy to explain she had nothing, she felt as lost in this case as she did the day they found out Ms. Moses disappeared. She just texted eight words:

Nothing tonight. See you in AV Club tomorrow.

Immediately, she got a text from Lexy.

> you ok?

> Fine, why?

> i've never seen a text with you that didn't include exclamation points

Posey smiled at how well Lexy seemed to know her, even in this short period of time.

> I'm just tired. 😊 See you tomorrow?

> see ya

Posey headed downstairs with the towel draped over her arm. It lifted her spirits like a small wind to know she wasn't in this alone. In San Francisco, she worked with folks at the newspaper, but they weren't friends. She had Hannah, but Hannah was just one person. Posey had never been great at group projects—unless you counted doing all the work for them herself. She—

Stopping at the foot of the stairs, Posey froze as still as Lady Liberty.

No. No way. This couldn't be real.

Her throat constricted.

Her skin crawled.

Her ears rang.

Terror held her in one place and stole the breath from her lungs as her eyes stayed glued on the sight in front of her: there was a bear in her hot tub.

A *bear*! In her *hot tub*!

Lounging in it! Like a person!

This was not a joke. This was not a visual hallucination brought on by days of exhaustion. It was a B-E-A-R with black fur, a snout, curled little ears, and it was in her hot tub on the back porch of her house, right in the place she was supposed to be relaxing. Posey turned and leapt up the stairs with a sudden burst of adrenaline. See where relaxing got you? See where it got you? It got you hot tubbing with predators! Posey didn't usually swear, but sometimes she let loose in her head and right now was one of those times. Shit! Fuck! A bear! She could have *died*.

Posey ran into her room and locked the door. She collapsed on her bed, shivering in her bathing suit. She didn't know what to do. What do you do when you see a bear in your hot tub? Were there . . . bear people you called? She picked up her laptop and opened it to search. The ping of an instant message sounded. It was from Sal.

deadinside1234: please tell me you're not working on the buzz rn

msposeyspade: SAL THERE IS A BEAR IN MY HOT TUB!!!

deadinside1234: shut up

deadinside1234: pose i'm gettin a lil worried about you

msposeyspade: I'M NOT LYING!!! Who do I call? Animal control?

deadinside1234: did you take a pic? vid?

msposeyspade: Did I . . . why would I do that?

deadinside1234: i think you need to get some rest

deadinside1234: do you have a fever?

msposeyspade: Ugh good night and thanks for nothing!

A *picture*. What, he wanted her to prove it? Posey looked up the number for animal control and emerged from her room with her phone, tiptoed to the top of the stairs, and peeked her head down. There was no bear in the hot tub anymore. She walked a few steps more, cautiously, her hand on the railing. Still no bear. Hand to her chest, holding her breath, she walked to the sliding glass door.

There was just a hot tub. Just a bubbling, normal hot tub under the patio lights. Nothing in the scene that would indicate danger. The bear, what—went for a short dip and went on its merry way, leaving her to look like she'd lost her marbles?

Gaslighting bear.

Posey held a hand up to her forehead. She did feel a little bit hot. Was it possible she was a touch delirious? Her throat hurt when she swallowed. Maybe she was . . . no, she couldn't afford to be sick. She *couldn't*. Posey took a deep breath and headed upstairs for vitamins, cold medicine, and—*fine*—the thing everyone had been bothering her about all evening.

Rest.

THIRTY-SEVEN

Monday, September 16

Posey was barely settled in her seat in first period when her biology teacher—Mr. Wu, known for his bad jokes and whimsical bow ties—announced, "Posey Spade, Principal Vance would like to see you."

A hush blew through the room as students exchanged wide-eyed glances. A visit to Ms. Vance's office generally meant bad news. A wave of guilt for absolutely no reason at all washed over Posey as she stood up and slipped her textbook back into her bag. As if a spotlight were on her, and her fellow students had suddenly become her audience, she exited the quiet classroom. In the hall, her shoes clicked on the linoleum as she slowly made her way to the administration office at the end. What on earth would Ms. Vance want to talk to her about? Was this about their meeting last week, about the flyers?

The woman at the front desk pointed to Ms. Vance's glass office and Posey saw how full the room was. As she approached, she recognized the people in there: Sal in his hoodie; Lexy in a flowered dress that reached her ankles; Jeremiah looking incredibly annoyed with headphones hanging around his neck; Athena, who appeared to have shaved off her eyebrows; and Yash with an ashen face, hugging his backpack on his lap. Ms. Vance was pointing a red fingernail in the air and speaking very animatedly. Posey was in for it. She took a deep breath and opened the door.

". . . without *any* permission whatsoever," she was saying. Ms. Vance turned her beady gaze at Posey and gestured to an unoccupied folding chair that was, unfortunately, the closest to Ms. Vance. "Posey Spade. Close the door behind you. Sit down, please."

Posey smiled at her fellow club members. No one looked her in the eyes or smiled back. The temperature in the room was at least ten degrees hotter. Maybe it was all the bodies packed in here or maybe it was the mood. Posey wiped a bead of sweat from her brow as she settled into her chair.

Ms. Vance inhaled deeply through her flared nostrils. "As I was just telling the rest of the AV Club, the Wild Pines High administration is extremely disappointed in the"—here Ms. Vance used finger quotes—"'news reports' your team has been putting out. Not only are we disappointed, we are *embarrassed.* We are embarrassed to have Wild Pines High affiliated with the program that was *never* approved by anyone in administration. Additionally, I was informed this weekend that three of you approached a teacher on their private property Friday afternoon for an 'interview' *and* you were openly hostile and threatening."

"*Threatening?*" Posey couldn't help repeating in her talked-tired voice.

"Threatening," Ms. Vance replied, her gaze searing. She shifted it to Sal. "I heard you said the f-word."

"Give me a—" muttered Sal.

"Ms. Vance, with all due respect, we didn't threaten anyone," Posey broke in, wanting to be the one to lead the conversation, not Sal. They couldn't afford to mess this up. She could feel the crosshairs on her club, on this club she worked so hard to shape into something productive and promising and important. She couldn't lose it. Not now, not after they'd put out two engaging episodes that created a community. "All we're after is the truth. You would think the Wild Pines administration would support a student-led search for a missing teacher. Why aren't you in support?"

Posey asked it innocently, at least she thought she did. But she could feel Ms. Vance's rage rising. She could see it in her pinking face.

"As of today, the AV Club is disbanded," Ms. Vance said sharply. "Since you no longer have a teacher to lead you, the club is no longer viable. You were never given permission to put out any media affiliated with Wild Pines High. This ends *today*."

"But Ms. Moses is still missing!" Posey said, her voice breaking.

"She is, and that is a shame. But you are high school students, not private detectives, and certainly not journalists. This. Ends. *Today*."

"This is ridiculous," Posey said, looking around at her fellow club members, who all stared at the floor with faraway looks on their faces. "Right? This is ridiculous." She tried to meet Lexy's eyes, especially—Lexy, the activist! The one with a backpack jingling with pins that had slogans like SPEAK TRUTH TO POWER and GOOD TROUBLE. But no. Even Lexy wouldn't meet her eyes. "We're not going to stop looking for our teacher and telling the truth. We didn't do anything wrong."

Ms. Vance said, "If you continue to push back on this, there will be consequences, up to and including suspension and/or expulsion. Do you understand?"

"We didn't do anything wrong," Posey said, softer.

"Do you under*stand*?" Ms. Vance nearly shrieked.

Posey took one last disbelieving look at her team. They continued to avoid her eyes.

"Yes," Posey said, the word hurting as it left her throat.

Ms. Vance flicked her fingers in the air as if she were throwing invisible confetti. "You are dismissed."

As they stood up and filed out of the room, Posey burned from the inside out. Her face was hot, her lungs were stinging, and her eyes prickled with tears she blinked back. All they had done to build this show, all their success, the explosion of engagement, the leads they had chased—it was gone with the snap of some fake red fingernails. Ms. Moses was still missing. And now their club was over, too. Worst of all, they took it without a fight, without a single word. She followed Sal out of the administration office, glaring at the skull on the back of his sweatshirt. As soon as they were all out in the empty hall, Sal stalked away and threw his hands up in the air, saying, "Fuck this place! I'm done!"

The other five students exchanged worried glances.

"Sal!" whisper-shouted Posey, hurrying after him.

"Fuck this school, fuck this town, fuck it all!" he yelled, spinning a three-sixty turn to deliver this last remark before storming out the front school doors. A couple of teachers popped their heads out of doorways with quizzical expressions.

Posey glanced behind her shoulder as she pushed the front doors open. The rest of the AV Club was following her, too. She was surprised by the sight of them, still a group even after they didn't defend the club, still moving like one thing. They stepped into the sunshine together, sweet morning mist clinging to the air as they went down the stairs.

"Fuck this place!" Sal was yelling as he bounded toward the parking lot.

"I think our pal here's lost his mind," Athena said as they followed Sal.

"Plot twist: I think he might be the drama after all," Jeremiah said.

"Sal, don't do anything stupid," Lexy called ahead.

"Um, where are we going?" Yash asked, power walking.

"Sal!" Posey yelled, jogging to try to catch up with him.

Soon the whole club was jogging too, down the steps and into the full parking lot, startling a group of ravens—an *unkindness* of ravens was the technical term—and sending them cawing into the sky. Posey caught up with Sal just as he got to the corner where Gramps was parked and the four others arrived behind her seconds later.

"It's so fucked!" Sal turned around to scream at them.

"It is!" Posey yelled back. "It's . . . fucked!"

Hearing this word come from Posey's mouth appeared to shock Sal so much that he didn't respond, panting to catch his breath and squinting at her as if he didn't recognize her. Judging by Jeremiah's unhinged jaw, Yash's wide eyes, Athena's raised eyebrows (or rather, the place she once had eyebrows), and Lexy's little O of a mouth, he wasn't the only one shocked to hear the f-word leave Posey's mouth. But the f-word, to Posey, was like the hot sauce of words: to be used sparingly and occasionally, but used nonetheless.

"I can't believe that Ms. Vance just pulled the plug on everything we've worked so hard for and you all just sat there and took it," Posey said, raising her voice as much as she could. "Ms. Moses is still missing and there's so much we're uncovering and what? We give up? Ms. Vance says stop and you just listen to her? I can't believe no one spoke up in there. Am I the only person who cares about this club?"

"Look, *sunshine*, you've never been in the crosshairs of that administration before, but I have," Athena said, pulling her beanie off and running her fingers through her yellowy bleached-blond hair. "You do realize I had to basically beg to not be expelled last year? I can't be getting my ass in trouble."

"I'm graduating this year!" Jeremiah said. "And right now, I'm scrambling to find a letter of recommendation for my college application with Ms. Moses *poof*, gone. I can't be getting into some fight with Ms. Vance!"

"I'm sorry I didn't speak up, Posey," Yash said. "Honestly, Ms. Vance scares me."

"I was just stunned in the moment," Lexy said. "I—I didn't know what to say."

"I'm done," Sal said softly. Right now he looked inches shorter than his usual self, and it was all in his hunched posture—the incredible shrinking boy. He looked Posey in the eyes. "I'm not coming back. I don't want to be here anymore."

"Okay, we're not . . . we're not talking about doing anything *stupid* here, are we, Sal?" Athena asked.

"I'm going to do what I should have done a long time ago and get the hell out of Wild Pines. And you know what? Maybe that's what Molly did. Maybe *this* is the truth." He looked up at the trees. "Maybe this town just drove her out of it."

"You know that's not what happened," Posey said, shaking her head. "It doesn't add up."

"Then what happened? What? What *happened*?" he demanded.

"That's what I've been working tirelessly to try to find out!" Posey shot back. "And now we're not going to know because Ms. Vance shut us down and none of you said word about it!"

"*You've* been working tirelessly? I haven't *slept* in a *week!*" Sal shouted.

Jeremiah leaned over to whisper to Athena, Lexy, and Yash, "Mom and Dad are fighting and I don't like it."

"Look, both of you shut up, okay?" Athena said to Sal and Posey. "Sal, you don't need to leave town like a Pouty McPoutface, for shit's sake. Posey, life ain't over because AV Club doesn't have WPH's blessing. We can keep doing our thang and looking for Ms. Moses, we just have to be careful about it and rethink the show. I'm not about to give up. I know if Ms. Moses were here, she'd be working to figure out some loophole way to make it work. That's how she rolled, you know? And that's how we'll keep rolling."

"I can't believe she's been gone six days," Lexy said. "Six days, and what? One half-assed search party around Pickins?"

"Excuse me, I used my *whole* ass and risked my *life* wading through snake-infested grasses," Jeremiah said.

"Yes, we've heard about the snakes, boo," Athena said. "About six thousand times."

"The search party only searched one side of the highway, too," Yash said. "The side she would have driven home on."

"No, that's not true," Jeremiah said. "There was another search going on the other side. It was just a smaller group." He nodded at Posey. "You got the map, right?"

Posey nodded, realizing it was still in her peacoat pocket. She reached in and opened it. "Right here." She peered at it and Yash came to stand next to her and look at it, too. She pointed to the shaded areas marked with numbers for the search parties. "Yeah, both sides were searched."

"See, though, if it had been me, I would have had the bigger search party on the other side," Yash said, pointing to the gray area that had only one search party number on it, number six, as opposed to the other side of the highway, which had one through five. "Because last night I was thinking just of, like, you know, retracing her steps? And yeah, she would have driven home on that side where one through five were. We know she got off work, right? And left in her car?"

Posey had no idea where Yash was going with this, but she was curious to hear it. "Yes."

"Well . . . but what about her phone?" Yash asked.

"What about it?"

"You leave your phone at work, you realize it pretty soon, right? Wouldn't you, like, go back for it?" He pointed to the other side of the highway, his finger tracing the gray area with the lone search party number, six. "But they concentrated on the other side, the side where she would have driven home from work."

Posey's mouth dropped. Yash was right—that stretch that had the smallest number of people looking was also where Ms. Moses would have been driving had she decided to head back to Pickins. Sal peeked over their shoulder and then so did Lexy, Athena, and Jeremiah. Yash showed them the map.

"So they had, what—how many people were in the search parties, Jeremiah?" Athena asked.

"There were eight in mine," he said.

"Eight people," Athena said. "Eight people searching a full square mile plus of highway. And not even, like, cops—untrained people." Athena clapped Yash on the back so loud it startled him. "You're right, Yash. There should be another search of that side of the highway."

"Great," Sal said, walking away from the map to go lean against his van. "We'll just call the cops up and tell them. I'm sure Deputy Butts is dying to hear suggestions from us."

"No," Posey said, folding the map back up and putting it in her pocket. "We don't need the cops. We can do it."

"*We* we?" Yash repeated, pointing to himself. "I mean, us?"

"Yeah. Come on, let's pack it in Gramps and go."

Everyone remained frozen, staring back at Posey as she stood next to the passenger door of Sal's van.

"Like . . . ditch class?" Yash asked.

"After what happened in there with Ms. Vance, you really think this is a good idea?" Athena asked. "I will be put under house arrest if my parents get a call from the Truancy Bot."

"Just explain you were doing it for justice," Posey said.

"Oh, Dad'll *love* that one," Athena said.

"I've never ditched class before," Yash said.

"You're ditching it right now, friend," Jeremiah said.

Yash gasped, as if he only just realized this, and craned his neck to look longingly back up at the school they had rushed away from.

"Fine," Sal said. "Sure. Whatever. Why not."

Posey felt the smile spreading on her face. Not all was lost. They were still in this together. They hadn't given up, not yet.

Sal turned around and opened the sliding door, revealing a mattress with a sleeping bag on it, some fairy lights strung up on top, and a long row of bookshelves that ran along the top. "You're all going to have to pile in here."

There was a long, thick silence as they beheld the interior of Sal's van.

"Sal, are you—do you *live* in here?" Athena asked.

Lexy had a hand over her mouth. "I thought that was a rumor."

Jeremiah crossed his arms and shot Sal a stunned look.

"Excuse me, you told me *explicitly* when I asked that you had a place to crash."

"I do," Sal said. "This is the place I crash."

"You totally could have stayed at my house," Lexy said.

"Can we not have an intervention right now?" Sal said. "We're looking for Ms. Moses. Everyone get in the van."

"Without a seat belt?" Yash said.

Athena crawled in first, saying, "Do it for justice, Yash."

"Shotgun!" Jeremiah said, raising his hand in the air.

"Posey gets shotgun," muttered Sal as he rounded to the driver's seat. Posey stood, utterly touched, for some reason, that she automatically got to sit shotgun. It felt like a privilege. She climbed into the seat, stealing a long look at Sal's profile and thanking the universe that he hadn't run away from Wild Pines. Regardless of his outburst, he still thought there was hope, too.

"Ew, Sal, is that a piss jar?" Athena asked, eyeing the jar on his floor.

Lexy screwed up her face. "Vomit."

"That's soap," Sal said as he started up the car. "Everyone settled?"

"Um, as settled as we can be sitting on a mattress in the back of a van," Jeremiah said.

"Drive carefully, please," Yash said.

"Sal's a very good driver," Posey assured them.

It was true. Posey had perhaps never felt safer in a car than she did when she was riding shotgun with Sal.

THIRTY-EIGHT

The drive from Wild Pines High took about ten minutes and it was a quiet one. Posey leaned her elbow on the window, chin in hand, as she watched the forest whip by in shades of green and brown. She didn't know why her heart was beating so quickly, why she had a sick-nervous feeling in her gut. They were still chasing Ms. Moses but with this many days behind them, with this much wilderness spread around them, Posey was a little bit afraid of what they might find now if they found her.

As they pulled over to the shoulder of the highway, Posey saying, "Here, Sal, here," Posey finally realized what was happening, why she felt so tied up.

This was the same stretch of highway where Peter and Posey almost veered off the road, dodging a deer.

"This is how we do it, team," Jeremiah said, clapping his hands. "I know, because I'm the only one who has *been* to an actual search party." He let that statement breathe for a moment, looking smug. "We split up into teams. Posey, map?" He snapped his fingers, a bit rudely in Posey's opinion, but she gave him the map anyway. "So we're here right now, right in the middle. That way, between Needles Drive and Ridge Road, will be Yash and Lexy. This middle spot between Needles and Sparrow, that's Sal and Pose, and then from Sparrow to Garden Pass is me and Athena."

"I should have brought bug spray," Yash said.

"We'll be walking eight feet apart in pairs, from the highway to where it drops off." Jeremiah pointed his index fingers toward the meadow that stretched about fifty feet until it ended in a shadowy thicket of pines. "If you see something, take a pic and text it to the team. Don't touch it."

"I can kind of understand why they sent less people to this side of the highway now," Athena said, pulling a ludicrously oversized pair of rhinestoned sunglasses over her eyes. "This area is way narrower than the other side of the highway."

Posey nodded, scanning the horizon—but there was nothing but long, knee-high grass bending in the wind. "Well, let's get started," she said.

While Athena and Jeremiah went walking up toward where, distantly, the Pickins sign glowed red, Yash and Lexy walked the opposite direction toward Mile High Drive. Sal and Posey started straight back from the road toward the thicket of trees, eight feet apart, walking in unison and studying the ground as they took it step by step. There were stones, weeds, beetles, lizards, and a bottle cap, but nothing unexpected.

"I don't know that you're wearing the best outfit for this," he said to her after walking in silence for five minutes.

Posey looked down at her tights, Mary Janes, and peacoat over her striped shift dress. "Excuse me?"

"I mean, I guess you didn't get dressed today thinking you were going to be forming an impromptu search party."

"I'm always dressed for both professionalism and practicality."

"Same."

She gave him a look, eyeing his outfit. "You dress like a cartoon character."

"How's that?"

"Wearing the same thing every day."

"I'm nothing if not dependable."

She made a *pfft* sound.

"What?" he asked.

Posey shook her head and tried to ignore him, keeping her eyes peeled as they made their way toward the thicket of trees.

A full minute must have lapsed before Sal tried again, asking, "What, Posey?"

"Dependable?" she snapped, her own tone a surprise even to herself. "Less than an hour ago you were about ready to not only drop out of school, but leave Wild Pines forever."

"I was in my feelings, okay?"

"You're always in your feelings."

"Yeah, well, I'm sure you don't know anything about that, being a robot and everything."

Posey stopped in her tracks. This insult was so outrageous it required a full-on glare from her. "I am not a robot."

"I am not a robot," Sal said in a robot voice.

"Sometimes, Sal, I actually think you might be my nemesis," she finally answered.

She could have won this staring contest, easy. But they had work to do, so she broke her slit-eyed gaze and continued toward the trees. She decided, to hell with Salvatore Zamora. She was at the end of her rope. Her throat was sore. She was falling behind in school. She was ditching class to follow his theatrics out the door. And now, after convincing him to stick with them, here he was, *insulting* her. Next time he threatened to leave, she was going to wave an arm toward the exit and sing goodbye. Working with him was an exhausting emotional roller coaster. Even when he was here with her in a field, in silence, eight feet away, his presence took up so much space. She felt it, even when he said nothing at all. It was hard to understand, but even after everything she disliked about him, something about him compelled her toward him like a magnet. It was hard not to look up and meet his gaze. And that made her incredibly annoyed.

"I don't think you're my nemesis," he said as they reached the shade, the part of the field that met the trees. Pine needles crunched underfoot and a steep drop-off sloped downhill. Here, in the tree-shadowed gloom, everything suddenly smelled like rich soil. She shivered as they stopped near the edge.

"What am I, then?" she asked.

He shoved his hands into his hoodie pocket. They were supposed to be eight feet apart, but he stepped nearer to her, his eyes glassy and bright and reminding her of water. "I thought you were my Holmes."

335

"Yeah, that's what I thought too, but how can I trust you when you're willing to just throw a tantrum and threaten to leave when things don't go your way?" Her voice caught in her throat. "Watson would never."

"Posey," he said, coming closer. He reached out a hand, tentatively, and touched a lock of her hair that had pulled loose from her low ponytail. "I'm sorry, okay?"

"If you were truly my partner, you wouldn't do such a thing."

"Are we partners?" he asked. "Is that what we are?"

His hand floated, gently, to her shoulder and Posey shivered. It was a good shiver, one that made her a little scared. She had no idea what was happening, but *something* was happening. He was looking at her lips instead of her eyes and the force of his gaze was so intense she had to look past him. Yes—she, Posey Spade, lost a staring contest.

"Posey?" he asked softly.

But Posey's eyes were now squinting at something, something strange and glimmering in the trees ahead. It looked like a light shining, a tiny beacon in the pines. She walked past Sal to get a closer look.

"Um . . . Posey?" Sal said.

Leaves crackled beneath her shoes as she hurried through the brush. A light? A flashlight in a tree? No. It was square-shaped, the size of her hand, and about ten feet forward now in an unreachable tree. Carefully, she inched her shoes as close as she could to the edge. She took out her phone and framed it, zoomed in on it. She snapped a picture.

"It's a mirror," she said in disbelief, showing it to Sal as he joined her.

He pulled her back a step from the edge, gently. "Posey, you're making me nervous."

"It's the side mirror of a car," she said, louder, her heart picking up speed. She pointed.

Sal put the phone close to his face, really taking it in. "Holy shit," he whispered.

"Sal," she said. "What if—what if she's—" Posey gestured wildly to the drop-off. She edged closer, looked down. All she saw was a steep drop thirty feet or so into a darkness of trees. You wouldn't want to fall there. But maybe, if they were careful, they could reach that place by scaling and holding on to rocks and roots along the dirt. It wasn't a ninety-degree slope, it was more like seventy. She looked at his pale face, still processing the image, and held her hand out for her phone. "We have to go down there."

"Are you kidding? Pose—"

But Posey had already found a tree whose roots reached down the hillside and was turned around and climbing down the embankment and deeper into the forest.

"What if you slip and fall?" he demanded from above. "Look at your shoes!"

"I won't," she said. "These shoes have amazing traction."

Sal blew out a sigh and went after her, carefully climbing down the tree's roots like a ladder.

"It's actually not bad," she said as she held on to a bush and carefully took another step onto the rocky hillside. Her foot slipped and a few pebbles went tumbling into the darkness below. She held tight to the bush for a moment.

Gulp. Okay. This was like writing, right? Like driving in the fog. Like anything, really. She couldn't look too far ahead or she would get overwhelmed. She had to focus on the next thing and the next thing only, and that was a great, jagged stone a little farther down the hillside. She let herself slide in her shoes for a couple of feet and then grabbed the stone and caught her breath. Looking up, she saw that Sal was right behind her, holding on to the bush she held before.

"You good?" she asked.

"I wouldn't describe myself as 'good,' no," he said, his tone more high-pitched than usual.

"You're fine," Posey said, looking down not at the yawn of the void below but at the next thing: some smaller rocks embedded in the dirt. She made her way down, step by delicate step, holding on to whatever she could grab hold of, leaning her weight into the cliffside. Sal was right behind her. It got steeper the farther they got, to the point where all conversation ended and Posey had to aim every bit of attention she had left on hanging on for dear life.

Then, with a snap and a shuffle and a cloud of dust, Sal began to slide.

Posey looked up just in time to see the terror flashing in his eyes as he fell onto her and the two of them plunged downward, with no hands on the mountain anymore, both thrust into the nothingness of trees below.

They landed side by side in a thick cluster of ferns. It was a much softer landing than she had expected. The cold of the forest shadows was a shock to the skin. Breathlessly, she said, "Are you okay?"

"Are you?"

"I'm fine."

"Holy *shit*, Posey." He got up, brushing off fern leaves, dirt, pebbles, and everything else that clung to him from the treacherous path down the embankment. "We could have *died*."

"But we didn't," she said, her voice so hoarse it was a croak. It was as if the shock had finally done it: it finally took the last sad wisp that was left of her voice. She stood up and brushed herself off. "We're fine. It's fine."

Really, though, Posey's hands were trembling and the adrenaline flooding her system was making her weak in the knees. She didn't want him to see it, though. Clearing her throat, she looked around her at the deep forest floor that they had reached. And that's when she saw something that stole the air from her lungs.

It was an upside-down black SUV.

THIRTY-NINE

Unable to speak, Posey grabbed Sal's arm and shook it and pointed. As he turned his head, he said, "Oh my God" and went completely still.

Posey clamped a hand on her mouth.

"Oh no," he moaned. He grabbed Posey's hand and looked at her with anguish. "Posey, what do we do?"

Her mouth opened, but no sound came out. She shook her head.

"Is she dead?" he said, beginning to cry. "Oh my God. Oh my God, she's dead—"

"Stay here," Posey said, handing him her phone. "Call for help. I'll go look, okay?"

He nodded, but the pained look on his face seemed wrenched permanently into place. Posey turned around and hugged herself, shivering, her ears ringing as she approached the overturned vehicle. She couldn't believe this was happening. She couldn't believe this was real. All this time, all the theories that they had come up with, they had never entertained the idea that Ms. Moses had driven her car off the highway. She must have rolled a long way before falling through the trees and ending up here. The search party must have not even come down this far.

Posey's stomach might as well have been filled with shrapnel as she stepped through the broken glass, around the back of the car, and then to the front. She could see a figure there, dangling, a fire of red hair. Trembling like a girl-shaped earthquake, Posey tiptoed over and squatted to get a closer look.

It was Ms. Moses all right.

And Ms. Moses was dead.

She was still and pale, her arms limp and hanging, her forehead purple with bruising. Her eyes were closed.

"Oh no," Posey said, her eyes filling with tears. She put her fingers to her lips and pressed hard. "Oh, Ms. Moses."

How was she going to tell Sal? How was she going to stand up and tell him that after all this, Ms. Moses was dead? How could it end this way? It wasn't just heartbreaking, it made her so angry she wanted to scream. This wasn't fair. This wasn't how this was supposed to end.

She stood up to go when a gust of wind blew, moving Ms. Moses's hair, really giving it the illusion that it was made of flames. It seemed to breathe. It seemed to move. Which was odd, actually, because the air felt quite still. Posey stooped again and saw that Ms. Moses's eyes were partway open. Were they open before? Posey got nearer, crawling on her hands and knees to put her face right up to where the window should have been.

"Ms. Moses?" she said. "If you can hear this, can you let us know? Ms. Moses?"

She reached in and brushed her fingertip on Ms. Moses's cheek. Ms. Moses's eyes shifted to her and, with chapped and dry lips, mouthed the word, "Happy."

Posey swallowed. "Ms. Moses!" she whispered. "You're alive! Hang on, okay? Hang on, we're calling for help right now—" Getting up and stumbling over her feet as she ran back toward him, Posey yelled, "Sal, she's alive! Tell them to send paramedics! Now! Quick! Before it's too late!"

They waited for emergency services to arrive, every minute an eternity. Posey texted the group to let them know the incredible news but was too focused on Ms. Moses to answer any of the responses that lit up her phone. The whole time, Sal reached his hand in and rested his fingers on Ms. Moses's shoulder, crying and begging her to hang on.

"Just stay with us," he said. "Please, Molly. Stay with us, don't go."

Posey stood back and paced, feeling like she was witnessing a private moment between the two of them that should be theirs and theirs only. She remembered the day last week when she'd seen them during that familiar moment in her office. She remembered how Sal spoke about his teacher, how he thought she was the only person who ever cared if he lived or died. Posey knew this person meant everything to him. And she was terrified Ms. Moses wouldn't hang on long enough for this story to have a happy ending.

"Happy," Sal said, wiping his eyes and looking back at Posey. "She keeps saying 'happy.'"

"She's probably happy to see you," Posey said.

"You have no idea, Molly," he said, turning to her.

Soon, Molly Moses slipped into unconsciousness, despite Sal pleading with her to keep with them. He was beginning to hyperventilate when the paramedics came around the corner, apparently having come down a much less treacherous and more walkable path about fifty feet away from them. Sal and Posey stood back, huddled together and watching as the firefighters and paramedics stooped and removed Ms. Moses from the vehicle and put her on a gurney that they hurried back up the hill at rapid-fire speed. Sal and Posey lingered a few minutes to give their account to a firefighter, whose walkie-talkie was blaring with a flurry of activity.

"How old are you two, if you don't mind me asking?" the firefighter asked as he led the way back up the hill on the path.

"Seventeen," Posey and Sal answered in unison.

"Aren't you supposed to be in school?" the firefighter asked, hoofing one rubber boot in front of the other.

"We . . ." Sal said, trailing off, looking at Posey.

"We played hooky," Posey said. "To search for our teacher."

"Who knew playing hooky could save lives?" the firefighter joked. "Just kidding—don't tell my boss I said that."

Back up at the top of the hill, the ambulance was driving away with its siren wailing. The police car had apparently just arrived and now, joining the three fire trucks and two California Highway Patrol cars on the side of the highway, Deputy Butts and his partner were rushing out of their cruiser to join the crowd.

"Deputy Butts," Posey said with disgust.

"A man who truly lives up to his name," the firefighter said. "Don't tell my boss I said that, either."

Posey snickered. "Not a fan?"

"Well, let's just say if the sheriff had been in town, I'll bet your teacher would have been found a lot sooner than this. I mean—I shouldn't speculate." He held his hands up. "But the deputy's only been on the force three years."

Posey wanted to ask more questions, but the firefighter, understandably, was busy. He jogged away from them, back to the truck. Posey and Sal could see the AV Club huddled near the police car talking to Deputy Butts. They were waving their arms in the air excitedly. Running through the grass, Posey and Sal hurried to join their crew.

Up close, Deputy Butts was sweating and red in the face, running a hand along his bald head. He let out a guffaw as he saw Sal and Posey, as if they were long-lost friends. "Well, look at this, the junior crime squad. This is a job well done, kids." He held his hand up in the air, waiting for Posey to high-five him. Instead, she crossed her arms and served him the world's most withering glare. His smile melted and he slipped his hand back onto his holster. "I'll need to, uh, get your statement when you have a moment."

"We need to get to the hospital," Sal said, taking out his van key.

Posey looked at the deputy. "Please meet us in the ER waiting room. We'll speak there." She walked over to Yash, Athena, Jeremiah, and Lexy and reached her arms out, hugging all of them at the same time. "We did it."

"We sure fucking did," Athena whispered.

Jeremiah said, "This is the *only* acceptable time and place for a group hug. Hell yes, team."

"I can't believe it!" said Yash. "You know?"

Posey pulled away and nodded. "She just kept mouthing the word 'happy.'"

"Happy. I'll bet. Oh my God, how is she even *alive*?" Athena clapped a hand over her mouth. "I'm sorry, Sal, I shouldn't—"

"It's okay," he said. "Let's just—let's just all get to the hospital."

The fifteen-minute drive in Sal's van was without any conversation whatsoever. In the silence, the memory of what just happened washed over her again and again, and the disbelief began to fade into acceptance. This was reality. In the side mirror, she could see Deputy Butts driving behind them in his patrol car with a morose expression. Posey had so many questions on her mind, but the big, glaring one was simple: Was Ms. Moses going to make it? But she had a feeling that, if Ms. Moses had clung to life this long, she wasn't about to give up now. If there was one thing she had learned about the character of their beloved teacher since this mystery had started, it was that Ms. Moses was stubborn. And guess what? Stubborn people survive.

"How are you?" Posey asked Sal softly as they pulled into the hospital parking lot at last.

Sal looked over at Posey and offered a tentative smile and said a word she'd never heard him use to describe himself before. "Happy."

FORTY

Turns out, Ms. Moses wasn't saying the word *happy*.

After emergency treatment for a dislocated shoulder, three broken ribs, and beginning dialysis treatment for kidney failure due to dehydration, Ms. Moses was able to give police her account of what she remembered—leaving her job at Pickins Tuesday night, gassing up, and then driving back to work to grab her phone. There was no memory of the accident. But she did remember when, days into the horror of hanging upside down and waiting for rescue, a familiar face had appeared through her broken window. That face belonged to Abby Frost. And then that face disappeared from sight.

Ms. Moses wasn't saying the word *happy*. She was saying "Abby." Because she had waited and waited for Abby to go get help and help never arrived.

"Why the fuck would she—what the fuck?" Sal asked.

The AV Club was in their seventh hour occupying the emergency room waiting room, all standing up and getting the story from Doug. Doug's face was as swollen as a puffer fish from all the crying he'd been doing all day since his wife's rescue and, since they had last seen him, his beard had grown in and made him look far older than he had looked before.

"I don't know, man, I don't get it, either," Doug said. "She was in the search party, and, like, I don't know, the deputy's off interviewing her again to figure it out. But Molly says she's sure she saw her. And you know, Abby was in the search party that looked at that side of the highway."

"That is bananasville. Why would someone sign up for a search party and then find the person and not tell anyone?" Athena asked, leaning against an aquarium in the waiting room that took up an entire wall but had only one sad goldfish in it.

"Yeah, makes zero sense," Lexy agreed from a corner where she appeared to be napping under a sweatshirt but apparently was listening to every word said.

"She did seem really different in that second interview," Posey said, putting down a *National Geographic* that had been open on her lap unread for the past hour. "I noticed that when I rewatched the interviews back-to-back. In the first she was so angry. In the second, she was way more peaceful. I just thought maybe she was a morning person."

"Are morning people for real?" Jeremiah asked. He was lying across five chairs in a pose worthy of a *Vogue* photo shoot. "I always thought they were legend. Like, you know, fairies. Or Bigfoot."

"Hey, Bigfoot *exists*," Athena said.

Posey, herself the very definition of a morning person, was

not about to get derailed into a conversation about morning people or Bigfoot.

"Also, she said she only joined the search party because her 'mama' told her to," Yash reminded everyone. He was doing his calculus homework at a coffee table, sitting on the floor. "So obviously she wasn't really invested in finding her."

"If this is true, I hope she dies," Sal said, staring out the window through the blinds.

The room erupted in disapproval. While no one was a fan of Abby Frost and all were disgusted by her actions, Sal was going too far.

"Fine, I hope she goes to jail," Sal corrected himself.

"I consider myself an abolitionist but even I'm tempted to agree with you," Lexy said.

Doug crossed his arms. "Apparently, the cops can't actually do anything. I mean, they're going to take her statement. But, like, Butts said he doesn't think they could press charges."

"What?" Sal said, whipping around.

"You're kidding," said Posey.

Doug shook his head. "No, it's apparently totally legal to not help someone."

"In a *search* party, though?" Athena nearly shrieked. "Jesus."

Posey verified this information with a quick Google search on her phone. Doug was right; one could literally walk by someone dying and asking for help and there was no penalty for not helping them. She slipped her phone back into her pocket and watched as Doug went over to Sal and talked to him quietly. Poor Doug. All this time, everyone had suspected him of the worst act possible—of killing the woman he loved most. And he was innocent. She would remember this outcome forever. Sometimes Occam's razor was just plain wrong. Doug patted Sal on the back and Sal nodded, turning around.

"I'm going to go see Molly," he said to everyone.

"Send her our love," Athena said.

"Is there any way you could get a quote for the next episode?" Posey asked. "I mean . . . sorry, don't mean to be tactless. But I'm sure our subscribers will want to hear from her."

"Um, remember, boo? The show is history," Jeremiah said.

"Actually, Yash and I were talking about that when we were out searching today," Lexy said, nodding at Yash, who looked up from his homework.

Yash put his pencil down. "Um, yeah. About that? Ms. Vance can't actually pull the plug on the show, technically speaking."

"Because . . ." Athena said, rolling her arm in the air, impatient for the answer.

"Because, like, the way I set the account up? It's a personal email address I made in Gmail, you know. Not affiliated with the school. And, like, *Wild Pines Buzz* . . . it's not 'Wild Pines *High* Buzz.' We don't actually mention in the episodes being affiliated with the school. We just say we're the AV Club."

"And, like, the episodes were almost totally filmed and produced outside school hours," Lexy said. "So Ms. Vance doesn't have the authority to tell us to stop. We could just say we do this outside school time. It's a hobby, like Jeremiah's band. Ms. Vance can't tell Jeremiah to stop playing with his band."

"She should, though," Athena teased. "Cuz they suuuuuuck."

"If I weren't so lazy, I would kick you," Jeremiah said.

Posey was still processing what Yash said, chewing her cheek. A little burst of excitement swept through her and she smiled. "He's right," she said. "There's no branding for the school anywhere on our channel or in the episodes. Vance can't do anything about it."

"So . . . yeah, get a statement, if you can," Lexy said. "Sal? For our viewers?"

"Sure, I'll try," said Sal as he crossed the room, hands in pockets. "Posey, want to come with?"

Posey was so shocked she pointed at herself. "Oh, I'm not sure—"

"I mean, you saved her life," Sal said.

From across the room, Doug collapsed in a chair. "You should go with Sal, Posey."

"Okay," she said uncertainly. She stood up, joining Sal at the doorway. She had expected to wait here all day for news—she hadn't expected to see Ms. Moses herself. "Be back soon."

Even though Ms. Moses had only just been moved to her own hospital room, there was already an entire table bursting with flower arrangements.

Posey smiled and stood near the doorway, marveling at the sight of their teacher. Yes, she was hooked up to an alarming array of machines. There were oxygen tubes in her nose, IVs running into her arm, and she looked frail and her skin colorless—a contrast to her shock of red hair. But she was *alive*.

"Hi," Posey said shyly. "Um, you might not remember me. I'm—"

"Posey Spade," Ms. Moses croaked, her lids half shut. She looked either exhausted or maybe sedated, probably for her pain. "Yes, how could I forget? Salvatore."

Ms. Moses reached her arms out and Sal came to her bedside and leaned down, giving her a long hug. He murmured something in her ear and she murmured something back. And unlike the other time Posey saw them exchange a moment of affection, Posey saw something in this moment she didn't see before. Maybe it was context making all the difference. But it reminded her very much of seeing a mother embracing a child and it made her hurt a little bit, in a sweet way.

Sal pulled back and wiped his eyes. He put a hand on Ms. Moses's shoulder. "I brought her in here because seriously, Posey is the person who made all this happen. She fought for you when no one else would. She wouldn't let any of us give up on you. She led an entire investigation and got everyone in town to take notice. Without her, you . . ." Sal shook his head, unable to finish his sentence.

"I'm just so glad they found you," Posey said, squirming under the shine of the compliments. "I don't deserve the credit, though. The entire AV Club has been working nonstop."

"We made two episodes about it and they went viral," Sal said proudly.

"You made *episodes*?" Ms. Moses asked, speaking slowly, as

if every word took immense effort. "I don't know what amazes me more, Posey Spade—the fact that you found me knocking on death's door or the fact you got that group of goofs to actually do something for a change. Maybe you should be a teacher someday."

"I'd rather be a journalist," she said, and then wondered if she sounded ungrateful and added, "But thank you for saying so."

"Can I get you anything?" Sal asked.

"Doug's going to get my clothes and phone and everything," Ms. Moses said. "I'm okay." A beat passed and Ms. Moses shuddered with a sob, the façade breaking for just a second. "I can't believe it."

"We can't either," Sal said, squeezing her hand.

"Just . . . hanging there upside down for days, unable to really move, nothing to eat or drink, wondering if anyone was going to find me, wondering if I was going to die first. I couldn't move, couldn't call anyone, couldn't scream for help." She wiped her face with a shaking hand. "I'm scared to go back to sleep, scared that this is a dream and I'll wake up there stuck in the car again."

Posey nodded, uncertain how to respond. "You're awake now," she answered. "It's over. This is real life and the nightmare is over."

Ms. Moses nodded and took a tissue from Sal, who held a box. "Thank you. It's going to take a while." She looked to them again, first Sal, then Posey. "Thank you," she repeated.

As Lexy requested, they did get a statement. It was short and sweet.

The waiting room was a far different place than they had left it.
None of the AV Club members were there anymore. Now, as if
word had spread, it was full of reporters. One yapped into a cell
phone near the fish tank, an anchorwoman was interviewing Doug
with a cameraman in tow in a corner, and then there was Posey's
dad sitting at a chair staring at his phone. She was sure he was
there to cover the story, but as soon as he spotted his daughter,
Peter stood up and engulfed her in a tight, lasting hug.

"Pose," he said. "My God."

"Hi, Daddy," she said.

Through the bustle, the action, the wild turn the day had taken,
she had completely forgotten to call her dad. He must have heard
the story break before she got to tell him. There in her dad's arms,

Posey felt her smallness suddenly, her delicacy, and she closed her burning eyes. There was nothing in the world that brought her back to herself the way her dad did. She pulled back and wiped her eyes.

"Are you here to cover the story?" she asked.

"Am I . . . no, no." He shook his head. "Of course not. Someone else has been covering the story. I'm here for you. I'm here to take you home."

Posey nodded. Though maybe she shouldn't have been, a part of her was surprised. This was the biggest story Wild Pines had seen for a long time. As if on cue, the anchorwoman who had been in the corner popped out just then to say, "Hi! Gloria Tran with KWPL News. Are you Posey Spade, part of the rescue team?"

"No comment," barked her dad.

"I'm sorry, are you part of the rescue team?" Gloria said, shifting her attention to Sal, who had been awkwardly standing a few feet away during Peter and Posey's reunion.

"No comment from either of them," her dad said. "Come on, Pose, come on, Sal."

He led them outside while a swarm of reporters who apparently smelled a story began following them toward the elevator.

"Those are some of the AV Club kids!" she heard someone yell.

They got into the elevator just in the nick of time, facing the lobby where a dozen desperate people were shouting and asking for a moment of their time. The silver doors closed.

"Good Lord," Posey said in the quiet of the elevator. "I wonder what happened to the rest of the club?" She checked her phone and noticed a text on the group thread from Athena.

> MAYDAY . . . LOBBY IS FILLING UP WITH WEIRD NEWSY DOUCHEBAGS. ONE OF THEM TRIED TO CORNER YASH IN THE MEN'S ROOM. WE LEFT BUT GIVE MS. M OUR LOVE

"Oh," Posey said, showing Sal the text. He nodded, a faraway look in his eyes. "You okay, Sal?"

"Yeah, fine," he said.

"Let me buy you both dinner," her dad said.

"That's okay," Sal said. "I'll leave you two to catch up. It's been a day."

"I want to take you *both* to dinner," her dad said, exchanging a look with Sal. "I'd like to hear about the day from you, too. Plus, it would be nice to learn a little bit about this mysterious boyfriend Posey's been spending all her time with."

Utterly mortified, Posey turned to her dad and corrected him. "He is *not* my boyfriend." She cocked her chin and smiled at Sal. "He's my Watson."

"Your what?" her dad asked. The elevator doors opened. "Never mind, I don't want to know." And he pulled Sal and Posey behind him, clearing a path through another crowd of media people and shouting, "No comment, no comment, no comment . . ."

FORTY-ONE

Saturday, September 28

Posey could feel it: autumn, crisp and promising and sweet as an apple. It was in the bite of the air, it was in the ice that clung to pine trees in the mornings only to melt by lunchtime, it was in the pumpkin spice that had invaded every product, from lattes to air fresheners to potato chips. Yes, not even potato chips were safe anymore. Seven days into the new season, Posey stood with the rest of the AV Club in a crowd at the pumpkin patch where, two weeks ago, they had watched a search party depart to look for their missing teacher. And now here they were waiting to get an official "Medal of Bravery" from the Wild Pines Police Department. Sheriff Singer was at the microphone right now, giving a long-winded allegory about brave mice versus a lion. Posey had tried to pay attention, but Sheriff Singer was such a soft-spoken man he should have done ASMR instead of crime-fighting for a living. Behind him, Ms. Moses sat in a chair on the stage, the medal around her neck blaring in the sun. Molly Moses. She had to remember to call her Molly now that she had decided to take a leave of absence from Wild Pines High and her future career plans were indefinite.

"Medal of Bravery," Athena muttered, shoving another pumpkin spice potato chip into her mouth. "Did they just make this shit up?"

"Yes," whispered Jeremiah. "Yes they did."

"Shhhh," Posey said, nudging Jeremiah. "It's a nice gesture."

Posey had met Sheriff Singer only briefly this morning, when he had shaken her hand and told her what a "fan" he was of her "work." This man was a stark contrast to Deputy Butts, who was currently enjoying a long bout of unpaid leave. Local media coverage had decimated his team's investigation and the *Sierra Tribune* had written an entire spread on it the previous week connecting Deputy Butts's bungled work to his brother Mr. Butts's ongoing fight with Ms. Moses. The edition also included an editorial calling for Deputy Butts's firing titled "It's Time to Kick Local Deputy's Butt to the Curb."

"Trail mix?" Yash asked Lexy, who was filming the sheriff's speech on her phone.

Lexy shook her head. Posey couldn't help but notice how Athena kept slinging her arm around Lexy. Meanwhile, Sal stood next to Posey but with six inches between them. She smiled at him and he smiled back, then they both went back to watching the speech.

There had been so many emotions over the past few weeks that Posey felt a little wrecked. In the confusion of the investigation, the elation of Ms. Moses's return, the sweet apologies from school administration as fake as Ms. Vance's manicure, episodes three and four featuring Ms. Moses herself . . . it had been easy to get caught up in these moments and to not know what was down and what was up. And what was up was, she had no idea how she felt about Sal. She knew she liked him. She knew he liked her. She knew this without needing words to explain it, and Posey was *never* a person who didn't need words. Yes, he slept in his van in her driveway. Yes, her dad invited him inside for dinner most nights. But the idea of crossing that line with him—touching him, kissing him, opening her heart to him—it was too much.

A year and some change ago, Posey had done the same thing with Hannah. She had crossed a line with her best friend in the entire world and at the time, it hadn't only felt like the best idea, it had felt inevitable. Who were you supposed to fall in love with if not your best friend, if not the person you wanted to spend every waking minute with anyway? But it had ended with Posey giving Hannah everything and Hannah then deciding that she didn't want to be with Posey "like that" and then Posey didn't just lose the girl she had a crush on—she lost her best friend. She lost *everything*. And if she were being honest, Posey would say this: she loved Sal too much to let herself fall in love with him.

No, nothing was going to happen between them. But she did like the way he stole glances at her when he thought she wasn't looking, how he said good night to her online every night before falling asleep, and how once, when he thought she wasn't watching him, he leaned over and petted her scarf as it hung on a chair and smiled as if just the feel of it made him happy.

"Chip?" Athena asked, offering Posey the bag crinkling in her hand.

She shook her head.

"Hey, you know what I was thinking about?" Athena asked, whispering in Posey's ear. "Remember Tiffany the Psychic and how she said something about Ms. Moses doing a cartwheel and holding a baby deer?"

Posey didn't answer, trying hard to listen to the sheriff onstage.

"Get this," Athena whispered. "So, like, Ms. Moses *tumbled* down the ravine, right? As in . . . cartwheel?" She whispered louder, "Right in the spot your pops almost hit a *deer* with his car?"

It was sunny, and Posey was warm in her peacoat, but she still got a little shiver. She turned to Athena and raised an eyebrow.

"See?" Athena said, nodding. "Maybe if we'd listened to Tiff and shelled out a few buckaroos, we could have found her even earlier."

Posey wasn't sure what to think about this, but it was okay, because at that moment Sheriff Singer let out a "Let's hear it for the *Wild Pines Buzz* crew for their bravery!" and the crowd erupted in applause.

It was easy to be brave. It was harder for Posey to be the center of attention. As she and the rest of the AV Club climbed onstage, she smiled shyly at the hundreds of people who had gathered. The news crews, her beaming father, the Wild Pines students cawing in the air, Principal Vance clapping for them as if she hadn't tried to destroy their work, Doug, and strangers, so many strangers.

Posey and the AV Club stood together and received their medals and grinned at one another and she wondered—was this her peak? Was it all downhill from here? Then she dismissed the thought. No way. It was only September. They had so many more episodes to produce, a whole school year ahead. This wasn't their peak, no way.

This was only the beginning.